The Eloquent Parrot

A Novel By

Robin Knowles

Waterhole Press
3402 G Seven Ranch Road
Ruskin, FL 33570

ISBN-13: 978-1519362261
ISBN-10: 1519362269

This story is completely a work of fiction.
None of the characters in this book exist today.
The author suggests the best audience for this book is responsible adults who are of an age to separate reality from fantasy and fiction.
The story is intended to entertain – nothing more.
Happy reading.

The soul of a pirate
Sleeps deep inside many a salty sailor

This book
Is for the woman who waited patiently
Then woke one such man with a kiss.
My Lady Peg

Mix the following:
A Voodoo Priestess
A Pirate of sorts
A Golden-hearted Whore - or three
A Drug Dealer and his friends
A Bad-Ass Irish thug
A few Lawyers – Some good, some bad,
and a short fat Judge to make life difficult.
Airboats, drunks and drum circles at sunset.
Sex? Just enough.
Violence? Only when necessary.
And a parrot who has timely,
witty offerings at odd moments.
And of course, it's all in Florida,
where crazy is normal.

A story has to follow. Turn the page.

Table of Contents

Prologue

In a bar, a parrot sits on perch. A brass plaque is
directly in front of him.

A few feet to the side hangs a brass bell
with a braided lanyard attached.
The parrot, Blackbeard, typically dances
for – or talks to – attractive women only.

When a likely conquest gets Blackbeard to say
something – she's allowed to ring the bell.

That's when the Captain comes out.

CHAPTER ONE
CHAMELEON AND SOCIOPATH

It was an unlikely friendship. Intelligence aside, they had little in common. They growled, snapped and sparred incessantly with selected quips. Yet the barbs and spot-on exchanges were never mean-spirited. As true friends will, if one asked a favor of the other, it was granted without question. So when Chip the lawyer called, Edward the pirate responded.

In the middle of downtown Sarasota where parking was tight, Edward shoehorned his full-sized pickup truck next to Chip's BMW in two moves. He'd done this before and been there before, but usually at times of his choosing, not Chip's.

He exited his truck at the professional building, then strode in long no-nonsense strides, passing doors bearing signs of mortgage brokers, high-end realtors, a title company, and a handful of aspiring artistic providers of financial chicanery. When he came to suite 104, the law offices of Chip Hardy and John Danker, attorneys at law, he stopped, checked his watch, and prepared for Rosemary.

Rosemary, Chip's paralegal, would flirt with him as soon as he opened the door. She always did, sometimes with a simple flutter of eyelashes, sometimes with a light touch on the arm, sometimes more blatantly.

"Sir," she said as he filled the doorway, "if you're here to pillage, plunder, rape and do terrible things, be merciful. Spare the young and innocent. Take me instead! Do your worst! "

Indeed, Edward looked like the sort of man who could and would do terrible things. So tall, he barely fit through the door, his blue eyes fixed on hers and maintained contact. Square-framed, muscular, flowing black hair with just a trace of grey, a beard to match and dressed in black, he could easily pass for a man capable of ravishing an entire convent in short order. Alternately, he could pass for an evangelist preacher who might vanquish Satan's thoughts from all the harpies in hell in a single sermon. Rosemary had suggested many such possibilities in the past.

"Perhaps, dear Rosemary, one day I will indeed take you up on one of your lewd suggestions," he said in his deep dry voice. "But not today, or any other day ending with the letter *Y,* so long as you work for Chip. Some flowers are meant to be smelled and not plucked. I smell fresh coffee, and unless I'm mistaken, you've started wearing a new perfume. Chip called. Said he needed me. I hope it's important. I was busy."

"Coffee it is," said Rosemary, shrugging her shoulders. She stood, smoothed her dress and walked to a sideboard where she'd just finished brewing Edward's favorite coffee blend. "He's waiting. But you can flirt with me for a moment while I pour you a cup. It's been a long day, and even an old widow lady like me needs to enjoy a moment of wicked thoughts before she goes home to toss and turn alone in an oversized bed all night. Say something dirty in your deep-deep voice. It'll give me something to dream about tonight."

"A widow, perhaps, but not too old," retorted Edward. He dropped his voice to a lower growl, just for her benefit. It was an ongoing game they'd been at for years. "Obviously, everyone else has gone home except for you and Chip, or you wouldn't be playing the part of a brazen hussy. You should be spanked for your impudence."

"See there? It's working already. Now I can end the day a happy woman. Here's your coffee, go on in. Are you sure I'm too old? Because if. . . ."

Edward took the cup of coffee to join his best friend and left Rosemary.

Chip started in as soon as the door closed. "Edward, as your unofficial psychiatrist-headshrinker, I've concluded you're part chameleon, and part sociopath, but in a good way." He smiled big, exposing clean white teeth. He reclined comfortably in his executive chair and made no effort to get up to greet Edward.

Edward took a moment to settle into his favorite seat, a sofa to Chip's right, took a sip of his coffee, raised an eyebrow, then patiently waited. Chip didn't amplify.

"You ask me to come at this hour while I'm otherwise productively disposed, to say *that?*" Edward said.

Chip's smile didn't change.

"Then I must deduce from the aforementioned allegation, that you need something that has a modicum of antisocial behavior as a requisite ingredient," Edward said. "Perhaps the reference to chameleon means I need to appear to be something other than my normal jolly self."

Chip snorted an involuntary laugh and nodded.

"And, the sociopath you refer to, which I neither admit to being, nor resent the characterization of, will require the use of my powers of persuasion and charm," said Edward. "Perhaps the addendum of *in a good way*, implies that the intended outcome is a noble one. Hopefully, murder isn't required this time. "

"Damn, you're astute," said Chip. "I need a small favor. A one-day assignment. I need you to take my place in a wrongful death negotiation. Niceties aren't required, because if they were, I'd opt elsewhere. Other guy is a major power to reckon with. He never loses. I need a ringer. That would be you."

"An unusual request, considering some of the past sleuthing assignments you've cast my way in the past. So there's a challenging twist upcoming, huh? Could be fun under the right circumstances." said Edward. "This a paying job?"

"Why not?" said Chip. "My tab at *The Eloquent Parrot* grows and grows. One day, I suppose you'll bring me a bill, and I'll have to pay it. Add it to my tab."

"Fair enough. So I take it there's an urgency?"

6

"Sure is. The difference between justice now and justice served at a later time is substantial."

"Fill me in later, after the early evening crowd leaves *The Eloquent Parrot* so I can put myself into the proper frame of mind. You called me here while I was otherwise disposed, doing what I'm paid to do, playing the part of a barkeep living in an illogical time warp. Unless there's something else you need, I'll return to the here-and-now ho-hum. I presume you'll be there shortly thereafter – to add to your tab and elucidate me."

"Damn, not only are you good, you're *very* good," said Chip. "Against you, Sherlock wouldn't stand a chance. I'll be there shortly."

"Against James Cowles Prichard, you make an excellent modern-day lawyer," said Edward. He rose and grabbed the handle to the door leading out of Chip's office.

"Huh? You got me with that one. What's that supposed to mean?"

"You lightly suggested I'm a sociopath. A scurrilous characterization at best. I suspect you've been reading up, trying to codify my peculiarities as they relate to society. The syndrome was described by James Cowles Prichard, in 1835, when he coined the term Moral Insanity. Nowadays, shrinks use the term sociopath. You're a great lawyer, but need a touch of polishing in the shrink capacity."

"Touché," said Chip. "See you in about an hour."

CHAPTER TWO
NEGOTIATIONS PRECEDE PIRACY

In Fort Myers, just past the Edison and Ford winter estate-museums, on a well-tended road lined with coconut palms, a car sat with its engine running. The car, positioned so the driver had a frontal view of a prestigious law firm a half-block away, remained there for a full ninety minutes. A passer-by with an active imagination might have mistaken the occupant for an undercover cop on stake-out if they could have seen through the dark-tinted windows, for the driver clearly had an interest in the comings and goings at the law firm. But undercover cops don't typically drive an expensive Mercedes Benz.

Edward sat parked across the street from his target from seven-thirty on a sultry Friday autumn morning until just before nine. As new interests came into view, he used field glasses, noted the license numbers of cars, studied postures and mannerisms, and made notes about the drivers and occupants coming to work. Simultaneously, he toggled among several websites to retrieve information on his laptop so he could supplement his notes. Minutes before the appointed hour he drove into the lot and parked on the front row at a spot designated for visitors.

He got out of the car and stretched. He closed the front door, opened the rear door, removed a tailored silk and wool black sports coat from a hanger, put it on, flexed his shoulders then shook his arms until the jacket fit to his liking. Looking around casually, he then bent over, retrieved his briefcase from the back seat, and a tracking device attached to a magnetic donut from a box on the floor before closing the door and locking the car.

Turning to his right along the row of parked cars, he located a Mercedes almost exactly like his, circled it once, bent over, faked a shoe tie, then pushed the tracking device to snap with a resounding thunk under the wheel well of the passenger's side.

With a full-on business stride he walked into the front entrance of the law firm and approached the receptionist there.

"I have a nine o'clock appointment with George Abernathy," he announced, then picked up the visitors' register and scrawl illegibly on the next available line without being asked to do so.

The girl behind the counter seemed startled. Her eyes widened momentarily. Trying to regain her composure she took a moment to confirm George Abernathy, senior partner, had an appointment with Attorney Chip Hardy.

Edward located a comfortable chair in the waiting area, took up a newspaper and sat down to read it before the girl dialed Abernathy's office extension. "Mister Abernathy, your nine o'clock appointment with Attorney Hardy seems to be here. Shall I send him in?"

"Let him cool his heels for a minute, Megan. I'll buzz you when I'm ready to see him," replied Abernathy curtly.

Thirty minutes later, Edward rose from his seat, returned the newspaper he'd been reading to the coffee table, walked across the polished wood floor and approached Megan's desk to say, "Miss, I had an appointment with attorney Abernathy for a pretrial negotiation at oh-nine hundred hours this morning. I announced my presence and signed in at five minutes prior to the hour. It is now half past the hour."

"Yes sir," she said. "He's aware you're here."

"Kindly advise him I'm dis-inclined to suffer additional time delays. I'll be leaving now. Accordingly, we will advise the Fourth Judicial Court that Publix through its representatives has demonstrated clearly it has no intention of negotiating a settlement with the estate of David Cooley. Additional contact prior to the trial will be meaningless. Good day."

The girl blinked, then stammered, "It's just been thirty minutes. . . ."

Edward smiled for the first and only time, turned on his heel and exited through the door he'd entered earlier.

He made it halfway to his Mercedes before a slim, fit man just shy of thirty years of age came tearing out of the six story law firm at a dead run yelling for him to please wait.

Edward smiled, paused, forced the smile to disappear, then turned slowly, invading the personal space of the young man and frowned, "Yes, what can I do for you?"

"Wait please," said the younger man. "I'm Tommy White, we were in a meeting and I got detained. Megan said you became angry and left. Really, there's no reason to leave in a huff."

"Not in a huff," said Edward. "And I didn't have an appointment with you. I had an appointment with Mr. Abernathy. For a pretrial negotiation. He didn't see fit to attend. Simple as that. I don't take it personally. Good day."

"Can you come back inside please?" said Tommy. "He was just detained for a moment. I promise you, we'll be with you right away."

"And exactly who is *we?*" said Edward. "I didn't have an appointment with anybody named *we.* I had an appointment with Attorney Abernathy. Either I meet and make my demands to him, or I don't. He either meets my demands or he doesn't. Simple as that."

"Please, come back inside, he's ready to meet with you now. I'm sure we can get this taken care of," said Tommy.

Edward noted the time conspicuously by looking at his Rolex, then accompanied the young man, stride for stride, neither ahead of, nor behind him.

"Follow me to Mr. Abernathy's office," said the young man as they passed Megan.

Edward stopped walking.

11

When the young man turned back, Edward smiled and said, "I'd be far more comfortable in your conference room. Kindly show me where it is."

"Um, but we usually. . . ." started Tommy. Edward let his smile disappear and tilted his head, suggesting it wasn't negotiable.

Inside the mahogany clad conference room there were five identical chairs along the right and left sides and two slightly larger chairs at the ends, Edward pulled out the chair at the head out of the table, put his briefcase down, and sat. The young man named Tommy scurried out, presumably to fetch Mr. Abernathy.

Two minutes later, a pretty girl with long flowing auburn hair and blue eyes poked her head inside the room and said, "Mr. Abernathy will be with you immediately. Can I bring you a cup of coffee or a soda or a glass of orange juice or anything?"

She seemed surprised at the seat Edward had taken.

"No thank you," said Edward. "Something wrong?"

"Umm, oh. No, not really," she said. "Mr. Abernathy usually sits there. Clients and opposing council sit over there," she pointed at the middle of the table. "So that they can, um, lay out their evidence and records."

"I'm quite comfortable here," said Edward. He looked at his watch.

He didn't have to look at his watch again. George Abernathy himself, with a clenched jaw, and fiery eyes hurried into the conference room. Nearly seventy, fifty pounds overweight, once an intimidating man, bald with a comb-over, and a reddish nose, he came into the room in a hurry, then stopped abruptly when he saw where Edward sat. He didn't introduce himself.

"I normally sit there," he said and moved in Edward's direction.

"So your pretty errand girl said," said Edward. "I'm on time. You're not. Sit anywhere you like except on my lap. I'm prepared to agree to a reasonable settlement on the behalf of the estate of David Cooley, recently deceased. I'm not here to drink coffee, make chit-chat about golf scores or be treated rudely by your underlings or by you either. Now we've come to be in the same place, would you like to hear our requirements?"

Abernathy slowly took the seat at the other end of the table, then said, "Look, let's not get off on the wrong foot here, Mr. Hardy. I know you typically represent defendants in medical malpractice suits, and occasionally corporate clients in wrongful actions and wrongful deaths. It's a different circumstance being on the plaintiff's side of the table, believe me, I know. Been on both sides, you see. Maybe we could talk for a few minutes, see what we need to do to make your client happy and get the ball rolling. This doesn't have to be a federal case, you know."

"I'm not Chip Hardy," said Edward. He sailed a plain white unsealed envelope across the table like a bartender sliding a beer mug down a long bar. "The contents of this envelope might help. I'm a specialist he uses on occasion to get specific results. A fixer of sorts, if you don't mind the term. You can call me Mr. Teach. As you can see by the documents enclosed in the envelope, I have full power of attorney in this matter for one day – that would be today."

"Seriously?" said Abernathy after he opened the envelope and tried to digest the contents. "One day? What happens at the end of one day?"

"Negotiations end after today. We're ready to set a speedy trial date. No mediation, no phone calls, just a trial. Simple as that," said Edward. "Not to go crazy with the chit-chat, but I'm a very special purpose associate. I don't work by the hour. I fix things that are amiss – quickly. I do things the way I want to do them – without oversight."

"So you're not Chip Hardy. Who are you then? Can't say as why, but I have a funny feeling we might have met or done business before, Mr. Teach," said Abernathy. "Give me a moment or two, and I'll recall it. Big tough guy like you, hard to forget. I just can't place the event."

"Maybe, maybe not," said Edward. "I'm certainly not a fan of rude, but can we get to the matter at hand?"

"Of course," said Abernathy, "but in all fairness, you understand we're still doing our own investigation into the incident. The degree of culpability on the part of my client, or the deceased is not clear at all. By all normal metrics, this might take a while to sort out."

"We have until midnight," said Edward. "Afterwards, there will be no negotiations. Mr. Hardy and I agreed on that prior to his engagement of my services. I'm aware circumstances like this typically stretch out for more than two years in courtroom pleadings, discovery, depositions, negotiations, and of course the attendant legal fees charged by respective attorneys.

"It may very well go that route, sans the back and forth negotiations of course. Failing an equitable outcome today, Mr. Hardy will certainly press for swift certain court dates and will not agree to delays.

"After all, Mr. Abernathy, it's been sixty-seven days since John Burnett, a four-year employee of Publix Super Markets, a man who does *not* have a superior record of driving, does *not* have a record of courtesies or patience to other drivers or pedestrians while driving, does *not* have a record of domestic tranquility, or even-temperament, sped through a no-truck access road in a Publix truck laden with forty thousand pounds of frozen produce, ran a stop sign and ran over my client's only living relative – a brother with whom he was very close.

"Crushed the man so badly there was no option of an open casket funeral.

"Certainly you have all the data you need to know this will not look good for Publix's image or Publix's bank account when this goes to trial. As you might guess, we'll insist on a jury trial. Juries love to give away money.

"I'm aware of the extent of liability insurance coverage your client has, and I'm aware of your ability to negotiate on behalf of the insurance carrier to the limit of their coverage. At trial, the insurance coverage will be insufficient. I'm sure the stockholders won't be happy with having to fork over the excess of the insurance coverage."

"I didn't say we couldn't talk," said Abernathy. "It's just these things aren't black and white. There's a lot to understand here before we can make a decision."

"It's not even close to midnight yet," said Edward. "Would you like to collect and examine or reexamine your informational resources before you hear my settlement demands?"

"Um, yes, perhaps that would be a good idea," said Abernathy. "Give me two hours. In the meantime, can I have Miranda get anything for you?"

"Miranda is quite fetching," said Edward, "but I think I'll decline for the moment. It's just barely after ten now, say we meet at exactly one o'clock?"

CHAPTER THREE
MARTINI,
IT'S WHAT'S FOR LUNCH

Back inside his car, Edward sent a brief text to Chip, drove around the corner, parked, opened his laptop computer, brought up a program that tracked the GPS tracking device he planted in Abernathy's Mercedez, watched the screen, and waited.

Just after one o'clock, Edward resumed his position at the head of the conference table. This time, he didn't have to wait.

George Abernathy came into the room; breathing heavily, his tie loosened, his nose redder than before. The scent of gin followed him. Miranda came in seconds later. She brought in two file folders and a cardboard box with a fitted top. *Cooley v Publix* had been written with magic marker on the side. The box didn't look heavy. Two younger attorneys, one of them the man who chased Edward down earlier that morning and another, a clone of the first, came through the door with eager determined faces and took seats on either side of Abernathy who sat down heavily at the other end of the conference table. Abernathy closed his eyes for a long five seconds before opening them again.

"So, we've gone over. . . ." started Abernathy.

"Again with the *we*," interrupted Edward. "This is you and me. Your boys aren't necessary – no disrespect intended. They can go. I'm sure you

17

know law, statutes, and case history better than anyone else in the building. By now, you know enough of the basic facts to make a decision without any hand-holding. Miranda can stay, just in case one of us needs a cup of coffee or if you need to retrieve a citation of law or something. We're here to negotiate a settlement. Once they go, we can start."

"Look," said Abernathy. "This is my law firm. I'll negotiate with whatever team I choose."

Edward smiled, looked at his watch and said, "Tick tock. Time is running out. Your law firm, our law suit. Your client wronged my client, not the other way around. We're the privileged vessel in this channel of justice, you're the burdened vessel. Today and only today, we have a chance to decide on a number – or not. If you're the decision maker, then make decisions. Be the man the letterhead says you are. Just you and me, pal."

"Dunno what the *hell* you're talking about," mumbled Abernathy. *"Privileged, burdened, or channel either* for that matter. Oh, what the hell. Not rocket science, we're not going to get anywhere today anyway." He set his jaw and gestured at the two subordinates. They left.

"It seems like you and your Mister Hardy are hell bent to go to trial," he said when the door closed behind them. "I'm not accustomed to being spoken to like this. For the sake of formality, tell me your demands, I'll listen, make a counter offer, you'll refuse and you can end your day. I didn't really have high hopes for a settlement today to begin with."

"Sounds reasonable," said Edward. "Miranda you can take notes if you like, but at this point in time, I'm going to formally ask Mr. Abernathy – George Abernathy for the record, and under penalty of perjury, are you recording any part of this or prior conversations with me? You *are* aware it's a felony to do so without express permission, which I haven't given and won't give."

"Um, well, we like to keep accurate records."

"Turn them off. Then swear out loud what is said or revealed here by both parties is off the record, and no video or audio recordings are being made of today's negotiations. Then have Miranda type it up, so you can sign it in front of a witness. If, in the final event we *do* come to an accord or settlement, Miranda will type up a summary of our agreement. It will be witnessed and each of us will part with a signed copy. Today. Agreed?"

Abernathy turned bright red beginning with his neck, and didn't stop turning red until the top of his balding head was as red as his nose.

"Whatever," he said. "I'm ready to be done for the day. Give me a moment to catch a breath of air and insure we're off the air, err not being recorded. Miranda would you do whatever is necessary to insure Mr. Teach isn't using any kind of recording device. I wouldn't put it past him."

Abernathy stood, swayed slightly and then tilted full steam toward the conference room door, bursting through it noisily as he left the room. Edward stood and stretched. Then, spreading his legs and opening his arms to his sides he said, "Take as much time as you like Miranda. Search me". He smiled.

She giggled. "It's all right. I'm sure you aren't wearing a recorder. You're pushing your luck with him, you know."

"Make a small bet?" He smiled, then winked. "You'll lose if you do, but the stakes won't be unbearable."

"Mr. Teach, I really don't know how to take you," she said.

"Take me seriously for the moment," he said in a very low, hushed voice. "If Abernathy is watching and listening on video camera, you need to do your job. If you happen to find a small recorder tucked into a holster at the small of my back, you'll be a heroine. The bet is, I get him to agree to a settlement on my terms. All I want if I win, is the presence of your charming company for dinner tonight."

Miranda blushed furiously, yet approached him awkwardly, trying to figure out how to search for the alleged recorder.

When she was two feet from him, he whispered, "Slide your hands inside my jacket, pat a little bit, then slide your right hand around me to the center of my back. You'll find it without committing a felonious search."

She did as he suggested, and just as she found the recorder and the wire leading to his lapel, he said, "I like your perfume."

She backed away as if she'd been touched intimately.

CHAPTER FOUR
ZAT ALL? SERIOUSLY?

When Abernathy returned, he carried a cup of black coffee unsteadily in his right hand. "Okay," he said. "No recording devices. Off the record, except of course if we come to an agreement." He had to concentrate to put the coffee on the table without spilling it.

"Then we can begin," said Edward. "Typically, in negotiating a monetary settlement, the first party to declare a settlement number in negotiation becomes the loser. One tips one's hand, so to speak. But, as I said, I'm a specialist. I have complete knowledge of all pertinent facts here, so if you like, I'll share them. Once I've done that, you can accept my demand, or refuse it as you deem appropriate."

"I think I remember now," said Abernathy, "who you are. "You're the guy who's hell-bent on the perfect deal. The do-the-right-thing guy. That guy who only makes one offer."

"Who I am," said Edward, "is irrelevant. The only relevant thing you need to remember is the clock is ticking. Do you want to hear my demand, or not?"

"Sure," said Abernathy too loudly. "What's fair today?"

"Publix will lose at trial. The most reasonable estimate, taking all the facts into consideration, is the trial will take three weeks to prosecute.

It won't get to the courtroom for a year and a half plus. Publix will bear your half-million legal fees and will hope Mr. Hardy's firm will run out of money before you do, in discovery, depositions and the like. You're counting on wearing him down. You have two partners besides yourself, eight associates, and a staff of fourteen including Miranda here, who, by the way, you've probably underestimated. Mr. Hardy has a partner and a cracker-jack paralegal. You haven't done enough research on Mr. Hardy to know his style or probably even his success rate. You don't even know what he looks like, hence the mistake in identity earlier." Edward paused to let what he'd said soak it. It took a full minute before Abernathy replied.

"Got some of your facts right. No big deal. Not an unlikely scenario, either," conceded Abernathy. "Publix could lose, there's fault there, that's pretty clear. But a quick win isn't likely, and there's appeals and so forth. By the time the plaintiff sees any money, he'll be an old man collecting social security and in a wheelchair, I can promise you that."

"Worst case for you," said Edward, "would be a three and a half to four million judgment, plus fees."

"Not likely, but whatever you say, I'm listening," said Abernathy one slow carefully thought out word at a time.

"Facts are simple enough. I recited some of them earlier. Your driver was at fault. He isn't exactly a sweetheart. Marginal at best. But then, neither was the victim. Victim was toxicologically clean on the day he got run over. There are three solidly unimpeachable, and two marginally reliable witnesses to the incident. There's the truck's computer log showing his route, his speed, and his transgressions of the laws during the delivery route. No blood tests, but I've got witnesses who will *not* paint him pretty for the forty-eight hours previous to the accident. The absence of a negative blood test is a bad thing, and nobody on your side secured one. You dig all this so far?"

"More or less," said Abernathy sleepily. "Keep going."

"Now, if the victim was a banker, a lawyer, or god forbid – a preacher, then he'd be worth at least five million in a coffin. But he wasn't. He didn't have any kids or a wife. He was a construction laborer with a net worth of less than the balance on your American Express card. Truth is, he had only one living relative – a brother—and that's going to cost you some money. He and his brother were tight, evidenced by his unfailing payments of premiums on life insurance in favor of the brother."

"So, what's all this boil down to?" asked Abernathy. His eyelids were half down and he was beginning to slouch in his chair.

"Boils down to two-hundred-fifty thousand dollars, net," said Edward. "Plus the estate's fees, my fees and all associated costs. Publix's insurance company cuts a check to the estate for the net amount, and pays the costs. Not a penny less. That's fair. Hell to pay if you refuse."

Abernathy blinked. "So, whaz the catch? Zat all? Ssshit, you taking all the fun outta thiss."

"Payment to be in full, no games. Three weeks from today – or less. Expenses first, then the settlement check," said Edward.

"Lemme think," said Abernathy.

Edward sat and waited without replying.

Abernathy shrugged his shoulders. "Sounds reasonable enough. It's all your boy Hardy would get anyway at trial. Publix doesn't need the notoriety. Tell me we can get the records sealed, no public statements – stuff like that, and I think we can do business. But I want this Hardy to sign on, err off, this."

"Not a problem. Draw it up in memorandum form. Sign it, and have Miranda witness it. I like her. Fax it to Mr. Hardy before I leave," said Edward. "I'll wait around to take the original."

"Done," said Abernathy. "I'll get one of the boys to draw it up and we can go have a nice steak and a martini or something. I'm still trying to remember where I know you from."

"A joint memorandum will do," said Edward. "Binding on both parties. Payment to be full as I said, and effected in no less than three weeks, I'll sign it and you can sign it and fax it to Chip for signature, then we're done."

"Okey dokey," slurred Abernathy. "How about that dinner?"

"Actually, that's a great idea," said Edward. "now business is concluded, I'd enjoy a quiet dinner, and a sip of something intoxicating. My good fortune is that, I have a prior engagement with an attractive young woman. You'll forgive me, I'm sure."

"Whatever," slurred Abernathy. "Manda, get Tommy to do what Eddie here wants. Then we can call it a day."

CHAPTER FIVE
SCRUPLES ? – NO, NOT REALLY

It took a few hours to fine-tune the wording, but by seven o'clock it was a done-deal.

Miranda begged for and got an hour to dress for dinner before Edward picked her up. As they left her apartment and set out for the restaurant Edward chose, Miranda was in full girly-girl mode, chatting constantly, asking questions.

"Married? Ever been married? How long have you been in Florida? Where did you go to law school? No law school? Well college then, you're clearly quite well educated. Are you a partner, because if?" She got no answers. Regardless of his continued parries into his personal life, the questions continued.

Then she began asking about the case at hand. Still Edward evaded.

"Slow down," he said finally. "Take a breath. We're both professionals, from opposing camps, I might add. The day's negotiations should be over."

"I'm the one being compromised," she replied. "Dinner was your idea, remember?"

"It was. I was under the illusion it was I who was about to seduce you. Perhaps I was the prey, not the predator."

A giggle confirmed his suspicion.

"There's something else going on," he said. "You've got an agenda. Let's have it."

Another giggle, not quite so sincere. "You're really quite sexy," she said. "Don't tell me girls don't come on to you. Maybe I like older guys. Why should I have any agenda other than to be seduced after a nice dinner?"

Edward checked his rearview mirror, then pulled off the road into a half deserted parking lot, put the car in park, left the engine running, and swiveled towards Miranda.

"I've had a lot of one-night stands," he said. "Illicit steamy seductions are something I have a great fondness for. I like younger women. But most often the girl in question is out for the thrill and gets caught in my web, not the other way around. Let's be honest for a minute. You're not the kind of girl who typically ends up doing unspeakably intimate things in bed – not even with a confirmed sinner like me. You've been busting your ass working full time, and going to law school, an incredibly difficult feat, for over three years. You just passed the bar exam. I'm guessing Abernathy doesn't know about the law school. Or the bar exam either. So maybe you think this could be a job interview? Or is it something else, maybe?"

Miranda had been leaning towards Edward, but jumped back, making a thump as she hit the passenger's door. "Shit, how'd you know? About the law school, and all."

"Student parking permit on your car. Simple query at the law school after."

"Well, that's one for you," she said nervously. "But I wasn't exactly looking for a job. I wanted something else too."

"So, what then?"

"Tell me how you maneuvered him so perfectly. You did it all day. I've sat in on dozens of pretrial negotiations. He never folds. Ever. You had him on the ropes all day. How?"

"Are we negotiating?" he asked, "for that meaningless steamy moment when you give it all up?"

"I want to know. Yes, we're negotiating, I suppose. I'm compromise-able. At least right now I am."

"Yet you aren't the kind of girl who sleeps with her professors, or even sleeps around." It wasn't a question.

"I really want to know," she said. She was shaking as she unbuckled her seat belt and turned in her seat, her legs tucked under her, exposing thighs, her knees pointed at him. "A lot," she added.

"We're enemies, so to speak. Soldiers from opposing sides. Abernathy would likely fire you if he knew what we're up to. We're a generation apart. I'm a man with no scruples. You're a girl with high moral intentions. And yet – here we are."

She nodded her head.

"You still want to know how I did it?"

Another nod. Lips parted. Her breathing got heavier.

"Research," he said. "Your law firm has a very detailed profile of partners associates and employees on the internet. The young puppies he has are eighty-hour-a-week billers and keep up on case law. They're fresh. They're tireless. I researched the insurance carrier. If the facts are there and the award is less than half a mil., they settle cases like this just short of a hundred percent of the time. They roll over easy. They've taken him to task several times in the last two years for stretching out the inevitable.

"My game plan was research, keep him off balance, know his weaknesses, tire him out, then hit him with an offer he couldn't refuse. Abernathy works four and a half days –half the hours the puppies work. Friday is his half day. He drinks his lunch at the yacht club on Fridays, gets smashed, and calls it a day. He followed the drinking routine today – I tracked him there and back. He presumed we'd be done by noon, then meet again, and again, and again at other times. I threw him off stride with the schedule I dictated. Sat in his seat. Insulted him. Refused to let his mongrels join the fight. The thing with the recorder was a time-stretcher. I wanted him to be ready for a nap. I had all the facts. He wanted to delay. When I showed him he had a loser, he had no choice. If he'd failed to negotiate, then the insurance company would have fired him anyway. My client wanted fast. I got fast."

"So the insistence on Friday as a day to meet, was because he drinks on Fridays," she said softly.

"I spent almost a week researching. I know everything about the case and everything about everybody who works at the firm. I even talked at length with the bartender at the yacht club. I know what he drinks and how many. Over-preparation, but I had to do this in a day."

"Well don't overlook there's the fact that physically you're a very imposing man," she added with a laugh. "A hard man to say no to, under any circumstances. So, shall we have dinner now, or should we go back to my place?"

He smiled, put the car in gear, and did a u-turn in the direction of her apartment.

"Can I ask one more question?" she said.

"I think I'm done," he said.

"What's your moral compass? Where do you draw the line?" she persisted.

Edward barked a loud guffaw reverberating through the car. "My moral compass? Har har har. Okay, okay. I'm very nearly pissed off with the questions, and you ask me that silly question. It's simple – I have no problem with breaking any or all of the commandments. But I rather like to remember a line or two from an oath I once took - *With regard to healing the sick or those in need, I will devise and order for them the best diet, according to my judgment and means; and I will take care that they suffer no hurt or damage. Nor shall any man's entreaty prevail upon me to administer poison or pain to anyone; neither will I counsel any man to do so.* There's more, but I'm about done with the silly questions."

"One more question, please. Just one."

He frowned. "You said *one more* a minute ago. This inquisition is over and done with. We're here, at your apartment. And my phone is vibrating for the fifth time. A friend is calling, and it seems to be urgent. It's starting to break my mood."

"Sorry," she said. "What's your life-goal? Before you die, what do you want to do or get done, or get remembered for?"

He frowned, and then let his voice get deep and angry, "Don't be disappointed. I don't believe in God. No heaven and no hell. No kids, now or ever. No permanent fixtures. No epitaphs, nothing like that. When it's time, I want to die quickly, attempting to fix something, but it would be nice to not fail at my last attempt. End of interview – period. I have to take this call."

Miranda scooted as close to him as she could, reached over and kissed him lightly on the mouth, then unbuckled his seatbelt.

"Take your call," she said. "The door will be unlocked." She opened her door and walked to her front door without looking back over her shoulder.

Edward's phone vibrated again. He answered it.

"Chip, I've been reliably informed the memorandum of settlement you required has been received by you, signed and it's now a done deal," said Edward when he answered the phone. "Why the call?"

"It's been received," said Chip. "Thanks. Got a moment or two to talk about it?"

"Not really," said Edward. "I'm at the end of a second and completely separate negotiation, and I'm suddenly quite tired. I got what you asked for. Not much else to talk about. See you on Monday?"

"I guess so," said Chip slowly.

"You sound down," said Edward. "I did get what you wanted, right?"

"I suppose you did. Another problem came up. Same case. Nasty little wrinkle nobody saw coming. I'll tell you about it on Monday. Good night."

"Good night," said Edward.

He put the Mercedes in gear, backed out of Miranda's driveway, and then drove to his home in Siesta Key at five miles an hour less than the speed limit, thinking all the while, but he never looked back. Neither did he think of Miranda again.

CHAPTER SIX
A PAINTER MEETS A PIRATE

Three weeks later, two streets away from the sandy white beach of Siesta Key, not far from Sarasota, a pickup truck pulled into a parking lot. The truck was red once. Now it had the color and texture of a faded old brick.

The gravel parking lot at the end of a cul-de-sac serviced an inconspicuous two-story wood building. A sign out front suggested a bar and grill inside. The driver stopped abruptly in a handicapped space. The tires crunched in the fresh gravel as the truck slid the last six inches.

A four-foot by four-foot hand-carved wood sign on the front of the bar announced *The Eloquent Parrot.* Underneath, in smaller letters, it proclaimed - *Warm Beer - Lousy Food - Surly Waitresses.* The small number of vehicles baking in the relentless sun at two in the afternoon on a lazy hot autumn day indicated slow business inside.

An ox of a man with a scowl on his face sat behind the steering wheel. A pert young woman sat with him. "Should I wait in the truck?" she asked.

"Probably not," he answered. "You'll sweat your pretty dress up and melt out here. So, what you do is this. We go inside. Assuming the place is open, you get a booth or a table in the back. If somebody asks you what you want, ask for a Coke. I'm gonna see a man about what the judge did – that just about got me a month in jail."

"Okay," she said.

"Might be a short visit," he said. "Hope not. I've been run out of enough bars and courtrooms lately to last me a while."

Roger Cooley opened the driver's side door and dropped solidly out of the truck. He circled around the truck at a careful pace and walked to the passenger's side. He opened the door, let the woman out, and escorted her to the massive oak and iron entrance door.

A rush of cool, flower-scented air greeted them as they entered, and the duo stopped for a moment to let their eyes adjust to the dim inner sanctum of the bar. Unlike the sun-bleached bland unimpressive exterior of the building, the inside mixed the ambiance of tropical islands with just a hint of a time gone by – when sailing schooners and pirates roamed freely in the Caribbean.

A long glossy mahogany bar with a shiny brass foot rail ran down the length of the room. Two dozen empty bar stools sat silently in unison along the length of the bar. He didn't notice why at first, but something about the stools caught Roger's interest. He watched his woman walk to a booth at the far side of the room. She sat down primly when she got there.

Roger looked to see if the man he wanted was in sight. He wasn't.

Instead, Roger spied a parrot, an African Grey, untethered and perched on a carved piece of twisted driftwood behind the bar. The perch was set in a horseshoe-shaped turnout halfway down the bar. There, the bird was a full three feet from anyone sitting at the customers' side, yet bartenders could move back and forth swiftly behind it, never in range of the bird's beak. There was a brass plaque tacked to the bar in front of the parrot.

Roger could see an inscription but couldn't make it out. He had come to see the man who owned the place, not a parrot.

He walked to the far side of the turnout and stood between two driftwood stools. All the stools along the bar front were similar – gnarly and stout – but each was different because of the natural twisted weathered shapes of the wood. In their own unique way each had a comfortable appeal.

He leveraged himself up onto the closest stool, flexed his shoulders and tried to ease the tension from his arms. His perpetual smile grew more intense.

A tall, strikingly attractive girl with short curly hair, shiny black skin, and intensely radiant eyes seemed to float from the distant end of the bar. She wore a pirate's peasant blouse made of thin white linen, an ankle length flowered skirt slit up the side that flowed easily, a hibiscus behind her ear, and she smelled nice – very nice. She wasn't wearing a bra and Roger momentarily forgot why he was there. From the working side of the bar, she said in a soft Jamaican accent, "What can we get for ya', mon?"

"Beer. Whatever you have on tap," said Roger. "And I want to see the big guy. The pirate guy. The guy who owns this place."

The girl with the hibiscus behind her ear stood in front of a row of beer taps. She touched the handle of one that said *Miller* on it and looked at Roger. He nodded.

"Dis place belong to da parrot, mon," she said as she filled a tall glass. "Talk nice to 'im. Doan expect 'im to talk back. Most he only talk to pretty girls. Da man you want to see, he own de building. But de parrot own dis place. You 'ave an appointment mister?" Her voice was musical and soothing.

Not an easy target for practical jokes, he replied, "No ma'am. But I really do want to see him. I was referred. How old is the parrot? What's his name?"

She cocked her head, trying to decide whether or not to ask more about the nature of Roger's business. Ignoring his smile, she looked directly into his eyes which were now bright and smiling. "De parrot is Blackbeard. He over tree hudret years. Dat de truth. Lemme see if Cap'n Teach got time for you."

She didn't bring him the beer she'd drawn. Instead, she left it under the tap, and walked through a doorway behind the bar. Strings of dangling wooden beads served as the door. The beads clicked together loudly as she passed through.

She'd been gone for a long three minutes when a giant of a man came through them. Almost six-foot-six, Caucasian, sporting a full curly black beard and curly grey and black hair cut fashionably long combed straight back. A brief glint of light from a diamond stud in one ear contrasted with his otherwise black attire. His eyes were blue and inquisitive, not friendly at all. He didn't look like a man who spent hour after hour at the gym, but still he was clearly in shape and in charge. His lengthy arms ended with fingers long enough to fully circle a softball. With broad shoulders and narrow waist, Captain Teach easily weighed 245 pounds with little fat on his frame. Like Roger, he was not a man to mess with.

He took the beer from the spigot where the black girl had drawn it and put it in front of Roger. He didn't let go of the beer. His eyes met Roger's. Roger didn't reach for the beer.

In a voice was slightly deeper than Darth Vader, the tall man with the beard said, "I don't know you. We don't have an appointment. You said you were referred, but I didn't get a referral call. So, I reckon we don't have any business to do together. The beer is two dollars. You can pay me now. And when you've finished it, you can take your pretty wife and kindly leave."

"Damn," said Roger.

The man with the beard let the corners of his mouth rise to a hint of a smile, raised one eyebrow, and waited.

"That's a record. I've been run out of a lot of bars. But before now, there was a reason. You're

Mr. Chip's best friend. Rosemary told me. I said something un-appropriate in court a minute ago. Judge wanted to throw me in jail for it. Chip stopped him, but I think he's pissed at me for a minute or two. Rosemary told me about you in the parking lot after. She said you were scary but the kind of man who could help me. I'm trying real hard to be polite here, I swear. She said to remind you about a trip to Ft. Myers you made on account of me and you'd know who I am and what's going on."

In contrast to the tall-man's echoing boom, Roger's was a soft, laughing tenor. As he said it, Roger took out his billfold and took three one-dollar bills out. "The buck extra is for the girl. What'd I do to make you want to run me off?"

The man with the beard let go of the beer. Roger let it stay without touching it. The three bills rested.

"You look like trouble. Simple as that. Your hands have too much scar tissue across your knuckles. You've been in too many bar fights. I don't cater to trouble in this bar. Big guy like you, you could mess a place up before you kiss the gravel in the parking lot if I have to toss you out. Your nose has been broken once or twice. You got trouble written on you, and on your truck, and the way you walk. You parked in a handicapped spot, and you aren't handicapped. But you escorted your wife in here like a gentleman, I'll give you that. You're the brother of the Publix truck victim."

He nodded to the beads, put two spread fingers to his eyes indicating he'd been watching Roger. "Closed circuit TV. While I do the books. Gentleman or not, you got trouble written all over you. That's strike one. And like I said, I got no referral call from Chip, but if Rosemary said to ask, then I'll listen, but I'm not easily persuaded."

"No trouble for you," Roger said. "I swear. No trouble for you. Look, I need help – bad. Rosemary said maybe you would and maybe you wouldn't. Said you were the smartest and baddest man in the whole world. Mr. Chip was there in court today. Can't believe what happened. I spouted off, and almost got put in jail."

Edward raised an eyebrow inquisitively.

Roger smiled hard and held it. He gave the man with the beard his best smile ever.

Edward offered, "I'm Edward. Edward Teach. So Rosemary has been meddling again, has she?" He didn't extend his hand. "Or, does Chip think some follow-on negotiations are necessary? I thought a fast-pay on the settlement for your brother would fix things."

Roger broke into a long and spontaneous laugh. He laughed loud. He laughed the laugh of an Irish tenor.

"Sorry about laughing. It's the name. Dude, I'm not all that savvy. But I know parrots don't live longer than sixty, maybe seventy years, not three-hundred. I know Edward Teach was the baddest pirate ever. But probably not as big or as bad as you. They called him Blackbeard. They caught him, killed him and cut his head cut off, and then hung it on the bowsprit in 1718. I think it was 1718, maybe. But I know ain't no parrot owns a bar and I don't really care if you work for the bird or if the parrot works for crackers. But I'm grateful you did whatever you did for me in Ft Myers."

Edward relaxed and let the corners of his mouth lift as if he was amused. Then his face became passive again.

"So?" said Roger. "Oh, and my name is Roger Cooley. I don't know if Chip ever got around to telling you about me. It really is my name. David was my brother. Neither of us are related to any pirates. Just a poor, redneck, Irish, badass-sumbitch trying to make do, who has a brother that's dead. That's me. And I just said something about killing some people in open court. Which, when I think about it, wasn't really all that smart."

Edward said, "My name really is Edward Teach. Says so on my driver's license. The parrot really does own the bar, and I really do work for him. Nobody knows how old Blackbeard is. I got the job and the bird from a friend who died. He got the parrot from a friend who died before that. And so on. The list is long, so how old the parrot is, is debatable. He doesn't ask much of me, so we have an agreement. His vocabulary is extensive and colorful. He keeps the bar and I get to keep a paycheck and all the girls Blackbeard can seduce for me. We let Hibiscus think whatever she wants

41

to think about our ages. She believes in Voodoo - or Vodou if you're from Haiti – ghosts, and pirates too. So, tell me about your current problem, Roger Badass Cooley, besides having a nasty mouth in a courtroom. Oh, and sorry for the loss of your brother."

"Well, I heard you were an interesting man. Maybe you can help me." said Roger. "So here it is. My wife ran off with a nigger and…."

"Excuse me," said Edward, "Strike two. I'm an open minded guy. Not a Republican and sure as hell not a Democrat. Not socially, or politically correct or political-minded in any way. I don't march for any cause for anybody - ever. Live and let live. But don't disrespect my friends. Ever. Some of them are black. Some of the hardest working and most respectable deck hands I ever worked with are of African descent. Hibiscus and I sometimes sleep in the same bed."

"Guess you don't want me to say nigger – again then," said Roger. He tried to smile bigger.

"That would be correct. So please continue with your story. Three strikes and you're out."

CHAPTER SEVEN
She Ran Off With a Guy

"Okay, so I got three kids with my wife and..."

"So then, who's the lady that came in here with you who's sitting in the booth in the back? She looks like she'd prefer a cup of tea to a beer." said Edward.

"No, that's Dewey, which is her nickname on account of she's always excited to see me and, you know.... She ain't my wife. Would have been better off if I'd taken up with her instead of Linda. She takes care of the kids while I'm at work. Linda is my wife. The guy she ran off with, and her lawyer, and maybe even the judge, they ought to get hung and castrated, or run over for trying to steal what's mine, but I won't say it anymore, in a courtroom for sure. She ran off three years ago with...you know...."

"Sounds like the first page in a script for a soap opera," said Edward. He turned his head slightly, and said, "Hibiscus, please tend to Mr. Cooley's friend, Dewey." He didn't smile. Looking at Roger, he said, "Please continue."

"So my wife ran off...with this guy. Fine by me I guess. She's lazier than a two legged hunting dog. Left me with three kids, twins first, then Clarissa. I've been doing pretty good by them since she took off, and Dewey is a big help. They get good grades in school and I make sure they go to Sunday school too. Dewey takes 'em. I stay home and sleep late on Sundays. Together, we keep 'em clean and fed. They're happy."

"And?" said Edward. "

"So my wife runs off, does some prostituting and sells drugs with this guy. They do some bad shit. They beat on each other regular and I've been told they use some underage, wetback girls to prostitute when Linda ain't in the mood to bang half of Miami. Been gone three years now.

"So, you already know it, but grocery truck from Publix runs over my brother down in Ft. Myers and it's the Publix fault. You already know about that. Between what you and Chip got for me from the Publix people and a life insurance policy I never knew about, things are looking nice. Easy money, except...."

"Except, your wife hears about it and wants to be a wifey-mommy again," said Edward. "Chip filled me in. You got notice the same day we completed negotiations. Chip was pushing so you could get the money, move it around and fight about it later. I'm guessing his motion didn't fly."

"About right," said Roger. "Her lawyer got an emergency hearing which Chip tried to throw out, but the judge didn't even let us even get in a single word. Said maybe later. Wouldn't throw it out. Linda didn't even show for the hearing. Judge said it wasn't necessary. Some pock-faced, mealy-mouth, Jew lawyer from Miami was there and did all the talking.

"She wants custody and support and alimony and we never even got divorced yet. She's not entitled to a penny. I'm not sure about the law, but Chip said."

"So, why are you telling me all this?" said Edward. "I did my part. Chip does the legal stuff."

"Well, if I fix it my way, I do twenty to life and I'd druther spend the next twenty years with my kids. I been told you fix things that can't be fixed in a courtroom."

"And you want me to fix this man of color," said Edward. "Or should I fix Linda, or maybe the judge?"

"Be nice if you fixed all of them," said Roger. "And Linda should get run over by a Publix truck and I maybe get another settlement – seeing as how she thinks we're still married."

"Well, Rosemary was right. I do fix things in addition to negotiating deals on occasion. But it doesn't necessarily include killing people for money. They cut off your head and hang it from the bowsprit for that, or so I've been told.

"Let me be direct about this. I've been around the world once or twice. Maybe it was more than twice. Lost count, actually," said Edward. "Sometimes people die untimely deaths in places that are hard to find on a map or a chart. The reasons, causes or justifications vary as do methodologies employed. Best if there are no questions asked before or after. Wasn't fun. Wasn't avoidable either. Might be easier to do it sometimes, but I prefer teaching enduring lessons to bad people. And I'm not particularly economical. I'm expensive. Even to nice guys like you, who open up truck doors for pretty girls to get out of."

"Best quote I got from Chip is about twenty thousand," said Roger. "And he wouldn't promise me I'd be happy how it turned out. Said he'd have to bring his partner into it because he doesn't normally do domestic law. Before this bullshit hearing I just had to go to, Chip was gonna do all my legal stuff for a grand."

"So, it's twenty thousand minimum now," said Edward. "But it was a thousand dollars before Linda found out. Sizable difference."

"If I thought that's all that it would cost, okay," said Roger. "The deal you and Chip got was almost a hundred grand more than I expected. But having her get a piece of my brother and getting boned by this...guy... is too much for my head."

Edward took a damp towel and wiped the bar. The beer glass had begun to sweat. The tree one-dollar bills were puddled in some of the moisture. "You still got Chip lawyering for you, I hope. I'm sure he got a continuance after the judge ruled against you today. He won't charge you much for that. I could make a trip down to Miami someday soon if that's where all the terrible whoring and drug selling is going on.

"Give me the papers they served on you. I'll check into this and get back to you. Just one or two rules."

"Sure," said Roger. "What rules?"

"You pay me full boat, twenty grand, if I get a satisfactory outcome. No, come to think of it, twenty grand total. What Chip charges you counts toward the total. I'm going to have to talk to him. Rosemary, or no, he's the boss. If he doesn't approve, I'm not in. He's fair on his bills. You never, ever, ever tell Chip or anybody in his office what I do or don't do to get this problem solved. He keeps his nose clean. He won't have to lie about me if he doesn't know. But you give him permission to keep me in the loop on the legal stuff. Also, I get to know what I need from whomever I need to know it from, and you just need to hear about results. Got it?"

"Okay," said Roger.

"Also, you pay me full boat, twenty grand if you tell me even one tiny little lie. Tell me one lie, and I'm done and you pay me in full and you get nada in return. Everybody pays me when I make a deal. Everybody. Always. It's the only way I work. You do understand that, right? No exceptions. I'm particularly and peculiarly inflexible."

"Okay," said Roger. He said it slowly after he'd thought for a second.

"You got anything you want to tell me? Any inaccurate statements you made so far you want to clarify, or set right?"

"No. Well, my youngest girl Clarissa, she don't exactly make straight 'A's in school, but she's trying. Other than that, I been pretty straight with

47

you. And maybe Linda don't deserve a grocery truck. More like a bicycle should run over her from one end to another. Leave skid marks though, and squash her girl-parts shut, so nobody else would park their junk between her legs. Drives me crazy to think about her and that...guy. That would be fair. She was a lot of fun 'till we had kids. After that, it went all to hell. What else I gotta do to get you to sign on?"

Edward smiled a real smile for the first time. Roger looked for a snicker, but didn't get one. "If I don't get results, you owe me nothing," said Edward. "I'll get you your money, and the judge will sign off, and the wife will not bother you anymore. Shouldn't be too hard. About the man who sells women and drugs, I'll have to think. That kind of trading has been going on long before they cut off somebody's head and hung it on a bowsprit. Still going on, worldwide. Gotta think about that one."

"Fair enough," said Roger. "Tell me more about the parrot and the nice smelling girl with the flower in her ear. I'm intrigued. And where did these bar stools come from? They gotta be hand-made. No two are exactly alike. Never saw anything like them."

"I made them. Tell you about it another time," said Edward. "You seem to be well read. It was in fact, 1718 when they cut the head off a pirate up off the coast of South Carolina. Not too many guys who spray paint for a living on farm implements or

48

tractors read up on pirates and use words like *intrigued*."

"I didn't tell you where I work or what I do," said Roger. "Chip, or Rosemary fill you in?"

"You got overspray on your boots - John Deere Green. Hands and fingernails tell a lot too. So, be honest. The guys you work with. Do they think you're all baddass muscle and no brains?"

Roger's grin broadened to become a smile showing white teeth.

"Thought so," said Edward. "One last thing. Parking space you're in. It's for handicapped. You aren't. Your disdain for signs is noted. Next time you come to *The Parrot*, park someplace else besides a handicapped spot." He turned, and then disappeared through the bead curtain that made the same clicking ruckus as when he'd come in.

A moment later, the black girl with the hibiscus behind her ear came out of the clicking bead curtain and walked up to Roger. She said, "Cap'n Teach wan' you to sit wit de pretty girl you brought in, and finish your beer. He runnin' a tab on you now. He said you to gib me the court papers before you go." She left the money on the bar for Roger to retrieve.

Roger nodded, lifted his beer for the first time, took a sip, and then turned towards Dewey. As he turned, it seemed to him as if he'd caught the eye of the parrot Hibiscus called Blackbeard. Somehow he couldn't help himself. He said to the parrot, "So, bird. What do think about all this?"

Blackbeard ignored him. Then as Roger was halfway across the room, he heard a loud, raucous voice; *Every harlot was a virgin once.*

CHAPTER EIGHT
Divorce? Well, Maybe

Roger was uncommonly quiet as he and Dewey drove back to his trailer house. Dewey let him be. His face seemed to be painted with concentrated thought as he held the steering wheel of the truck lightly. He didn't appear to be as intense or unhappy as when they'd driven to Siesta Key. Now, he seemed almost content.

"I shoulda divorced Linda," he muttered. "Couldn't afford it. But I should have done it anyways."

"This guy Chip, who is helping you with your brother Dave's insurance and with the Publix thing. Can he do divorces?" she asked.

"Probably."

"How much would it cost?" she asked. "Maybe if we...."

Roger interrupted her with a laugh. "Hey, you just gave me an idea. This guy Edward told me a price. It includes his take and the lawyer's take. So, the total they get from me is gonna be the same irregardless. Maybe I can get the divorce thrown in for free. Kinda."

Dewey beamed her brightest smile.

"Say, what time do we have to pick the kids up from your sister's?" asked Roger.

"Anytime before bedtime. She said if we were late, she could feed them and get them ready for bed. Their TV is broke, but she could read them a pirate story from one of the books you loaned them. Maybe we could go to Steak and Shake or something?"

"I was thinking of something else," said Roger. His smile got a bit bigger.

"We could do that," she giggled. "I'm getting extra dewy right now. Just the way you like me."

Roger drove faster.

CHAPTER NINE
Post-Coital Cognition,
Second Thoughts

An hour later, post-coital cognition set in for Roger.

"You know, when my lawyer gets me divorced from Linda, it ain't gonna change anything between me and you," he said.

"You mean you're not going to marry me," Dewey responded flatly.

"Nope."

"It's okay. I wasn't planning anything. I'm happy with the way things are. Sort of," she said.

"So you ain't mad?"

"Course not. You can't make me pregnant. You told me about the operation you had. So why get married?"

"Right. Marriage messes things up. We got enough kids. We're doing good the way things are. Three kids is enough for anybody," he said.

"And if things ever turn bad between us, or if I want babies of my own or somebody else comes along, well, I'm free to do what I want. So, I'm not upset about us not getting married," she said.

"Whoa. I thought you were happy with me and the kids," he said. He said it slowly.

"Of course I am. I'm just saying...you know. So, I'm kind of hungry. You want to play some more, or should we do the Steak and Shake thing on the way to pick up the kids?"

"Well, I ain't saying I don't love you. I do. You know that. We're practically married now as it is. And once I get divorced from Linda, maybe...."

Dewey began touching him in a way that always brought him to attention.

"You keep doing that and the kids might have to spend the night at your sister's," he said.

She wetted her fingers and started to do the thing to him that ensured a happy ending.

"You got all turned on looking at the black girl that waited on us, didn't you?" she said. She said it in a way that told Roger it was all right to think of the girl.

"She smelled like flowers and sex. She knows Voodoo. And she and that pirate guy sleep together upstairs above the bar," said Roger. "I'll bet that would be something to watch." His erection improved.

"Oh my," said Dewey. "Well, I'm not jealous, if you aren't. I kind of liked looking at the guy you called Edward. The diamond stud stuck in his ear was kind of sexy. Fair is fair. Looks like she cast a spell on you. And until you get rid of the devil inside you, I'll have to...."

Further conversation became unnecessary. Roger had an exorcism of sorts to perform. Indeed, at some point in his sweaty coupling with Dewey, Hibiscus seemed to fill their bed with her personal flowered scents.

Whatever spell Hibiscus might have cast didn't bother either of them.

CHAPTER TEN
Unscheduled Appointments
and Who's on First?

"Rosemary likes it a lot when you schedule an appointment with me," said Chip the following morning. "In fact, Rosemary likes you a lot. Just don't take advantage of her more basic instincts."

There had been no appointment, in spite of Chip's sarcastic quip. He rose from behind his desk to greet Edward.

"Well, I could say I was sorry about that," said Edward. "but I'm not. Roger isn't normally the kind of guy I'd want hanging around *The Eloquent Parrot*. When he showed up yesterday, his body language spelled *attitude*. I was in the process of inviting him to leave when he dropped the big clue. He's the beneficiary of the estate of the late David Cooley."

"He is," said Chip. "Maybe you're right. Yesterday was a bad day. The judge we drew for Roger's hearing ruled in direct contradiction to Florida Law. An inheritance is not subject to property settlement. They're claiming it was an *award similar to a winning lottery ticket,* and would therefore *would be*. Judge wouldn't let me say a single word. Listened to stupid drivel the opposing attorney spouted for an entire half hour. Hearing was only scheduled for thirty minutes. Then to top it all off, Roger goes batshit crazy and says maybe he could arrange for a truck to run some people over and sort all this out. The judge sentenced him to thirty days, and it was all I could do to get the judge to let him off with an apology. In spite of wanting Roger to get his money, I wasn't fond of him for that moment in time. It was Rosemary who came to the rescue. She appropriately pointed out you often solve problems without a courtroom. I should have given you a heads up, my apologies. I would have called first, but Roger was already on his way. Besides, you've been treating me like your personal shrink too much lately, which I'm not. I decided that a small surprise wouldn't tax your powers of deduction too much."

"You're cheaper than a shrink," said Edward. "You don't require an appointment – most of the time. Rosemary is always glad to see me. And you're smarter than you think you are, except about me being a sociopath. Ten markers identify a sociopath, I only qualify for about seven. Makes me a saint, I'm thinking. So, about Roger, what's the story there? I didn't think you normally handle cases like his. Roger isn't the typical candy-ass, rich-as-hell, corporate defendant kind of guy you usually work for, for one thing. Where'd you find him?" asked Edward. "Sort of a colorful guy. In the right circumstances, he's likeable."

"Colorful? Colorful? Talk about the pot calling the kettle black!" Chip laughed. "Edward, you aren't colorful, you're a whole box full of Crayolas. The 64 color box. I've got the same name I was born with. You're on your third."

"I have my reasons," said Edward.

Chip smiled condescendingly, then continued. "You've married almost as many women as the original Blackbeard himself. You've run away from two of the most lucrative professions on earth, and now you work for a parrot. Tell me that's not colorful."

"Marriages performed by the captain of the ship are good only for the duration of the voyage," said Edward with a smile. "Same for defrocked village priests with no church standing. Meaningful relationships don't count at all. I've been married in the legal sense exactly once. Stella is dead and gone now, which you keep reminding me of. And don't go on about your theory that Hibiscus put spell a on her to make her choke to death. I'm not in the mood today," said Edward.

Chip continued in a softer voice. "Okay, so about Roger. Former client asked me as a favor. Client was before you got into the business of fixing people's problems. You were still captaining tall sailing ships full of naked divorcées around the coast of South America for grins when I first met the client. Roger still works for the former client. Roger played amateur detective in that case, so I had a vague acquaintance with him before this. Roger needed a lawyer in a hurry after his brother got run over. Somebody told him to go to Morgan. The client hears Morgan's name and goes nuts. The client calls me and asks me to help. Then he tells

Roger to call me. He did, so now he's mine. Except I'm sharing him with you."

"Thanks. The former client Roger works for. He a candy-ass rich corporate guy? He connected in any way to the problem at hand?"

"No. And no, he works for a living," said Chip. "I told Roger I very rarely do plaintiff work and almost never do domestic. The long way down this road if he wanted to use my partner, John, was kind of expensive. Muscle alone won't do it, although Roger would be willing to pitch in. He just doesn't need to get caught. He has a bit of a record with the law. He'd get in deep-shit trouble if he goes it alone."

"Yeah, that's consistent with what I dug out of the computer after he left *The Parrot*. It doesn't look like he has any internet accounts. In fact, I'm pretty sure he doesn't even own a computer. Neither does his girlfriend, Dewey. His legal-wife Linda, on the other hand is a bird of a different feather – altogether. She's got a smartphone, past due in payments. Several internet accounts, and spends lots and lots of time surfing the net.

"Roger's been busted for some really silly stuff. Mostly barfights with men who were rude to women. That, and he has a thing about collecting traffic violations, moving or otherwise. He's constantly in jeopardy of losing his license. Probably resents authority figures."

"You're a detail nit-picking researcher always" said Chip. "In addition to being licensed by half a dozen governmental permissions to sail boats full of LNG or naked women around the world – and then there's the surgeon in you."

"Listen Chip, medical school was a long, long time ago. Quit reminding me about it or I'm gonna tell Rosemary about you propositioning Hibiscus. She knows about the flirting, but not the proposition. And if Rosemary finds out, she'll tell your wife and there will be hell to pay. So, no more brain surgeon references, okay? It's bad for business, and it's not me anymore. Lighten up. I like my life now. No more MENSA jokes either."

"Do you miss it?" said Chip. "The other life. The life at sea."

"Naww. Not really. Twenty years was enough. Still got enough saltwater in my veins to last me a while. And I still have access to a few boats with masts and Dacron sails to use when I want. Ironic though, isn't it? Chief died and left me a bar and a parrot who thinks I work for him. Now Roger's brother gets killed by a truck full of food and you get to sort it out," said Edward. "Two crazies with tattoos galore, food, and an unsuspecting inheritor. This could be interesting. Better than the last two you clients you referred to me. I'm thinking crazy dudes like Roger, Chief, and I are your thing."

"You get to sort it out. I'm just the lawyer."

Edward sat patiently. "Give me the lowdown on Roger. All I got was his version, which was a bit tall to swallow in one gulp."

"Lowdown is this," Chip said, "His ex ran off with a man of color. Name's Valmay. Don't know his last name, or maybe it *is* his last name. Tall, good-looking guy about thirty, so Roger says. Ghetto look. Has an attitude. I don't know for sure, but it's a good guess Roger did some sleuthing on a trip to Miami to satisfy his curiosity. Anyway, we both know some women dig guys like Valmay. Sorry, I don't have a picture for you to give to Hibiscus so she can put a hex on him."

He laughed at his own joke. Edward didn't.

"So, he openly admits his wife ran off with a black guy," said Edward. "Strange. Most men would be embarrassed – to say the least. Man-pride thing."

"Roger isn't shy about much of anything," said Chip, laughing. "So this Valmay, he deals drugs. Used to work as a cook for a classy restaurant in Hyde Park, Tampa. Sold drugs on the side, but he's graduated to corporate clients now – again, according to Roger. Sells coke to rich guys, coke and anything else these executives want. Including Linda, who by the way is a very beautiful woman. Roger still keeps a picture of her in his billfold. He showed me.

"Sometimes this guy Valmay includes an underage girl fresh from Columbia or Costa Rica – according to Roger. Valmay has only one arrest for possession. It went away. He might be connected. Roger says he is, but the only way to tell for sure if

Roger knows something absolutely is when he says, *I swear.*

"I don't think Linda has a record except for a DUI a few years back. Valmay's pimping transitioned from hundred-dollar dudes to five-hundred dollar dudes. Your best bet is to catch them dirty. Maybe if you set them up, get them arrested on possession with intent to distribute and solicitation – that could end it all. It's public record if you get that. She can't ask the court to be a mommy after that. And The Judge gives us a divorce, and Roger gets to keep his winning lottery ticket, even if The Judge has a different agenda."

"Fast and easy appeals to me," said Edward. "What else you got?"

"Currently there isn't any public record I can use in court to tarnish Linda's mommy desires," said Chip. "So, at the moment, she and Valmay can lie and claim to be deacons from the Church of the Late Repenter and I can't impeach them until you do your thing. Her address is on the court papers Roger gave you. Don't know if the wife Linda, and the bad guy Valmay, are living together."

"What about The Judge?" said Edward.

"Careful bastard. Been around," said Chip. "Boring in the courtroom. No humor. Looks like Charlie Brown from the comics. But not funny at all. My partner normally does the family law work, and he says it's generally known The Judge is on target for being fair – most of the time. But not this time. Should have thrown the petition out in ten seconds, but he didn't."

"Any idea of why?" said Edward.

"My partner speculates he owes favors to somebody in Miami, but I'm really not sure what, who or why. That's going to be a problem. I'm thinking you can get the goods on Linda and her boyfriend. It's the kind of thing you do easily. In front of any other judge, it would be a slam-dunk. In front of this judge, I don't know. Depends on if he really does owe somebody a favor and how hard that particular somebody will push it."

"Got it," said Edward. "You have no idea of who The Judge wants to please. Anything else I should know about him?"

"Only thing bad I heard about him was he had a beef with a pretty court reporter a few years ago. Lady said she was his mistress and he owed her palimony or something. It went away several hours after she served him with papers."

"I think I got enough to start with," said Edward. "I'll be going to Miami for a day or so. Hibiscus put some good Voodoo on me, so I should be safe. Between a guy I know at the port, another guy I know, and my laptop, I'll be better informed when I get back. Oh, one last thing."

"Yeah?" said Chip.

"I told Roger he wasn't to share the details of how I solve his problem with you. But between us – same as always?"

"Same as always," said Chip. "You give me deniability and I'm happy. Nothing can come back to me. Ever. I do the legal stuff. You do the rest. Are you driving the pickup truck, or are you going to take the S-class Mercedes to Miami?"

Edward smiled.

"Got it," said Chip. "You're taking the Mercedes. You'll fit right in down there in a black Mercedes."

CHAPTER ELEVEN
A WIFE IN NEED OF A DIVORCE

Linda's cell phone buzzed. She looked at the caller ID and saw *RESTRICTED*. Her skin crawled whenever she saw that on her phone. Only two people ever did that to her – call from a hidden ID. Their self-importance dictated calling privileges were one way only – to her – not from her.

"Hello," she said.

"You need to come to my office. I have some papers for you to sign," said the voice on the other end.

"When?" she asked.

"In about an hour," he said.

"Can't," she said. "I'm at a job interview."

"McDonalds isn't that picky," he said. He laughed at his own joke. "You'll be done with whatever interview you got going on and be at my office in an hour."

She wasn't at an interview of any kind. But he didn't have to know that. "I don't know," she said. "I'm not sure I want to go any further with this. I'm not really happy about seeing Roger ever again. In court, or otherwise. I don't really care about the money. Can't we just ask for a divorce so I can be free and be done with this?"

"That wasn't our deal," said the man on the phone. "Besides, what kind of whore are you if you don't want to soak your old man for all you can?"

She hung the phone up.

It rang again. She let it ring four times.

Before it went to voicemail, which she had no intention of listening to, she touched the *accept* button but didn't say anything. She put the phone to her ear. The man on the other end had ice in his voice. "Don't you *ever* hang up on me again. You understand?"

She didn't answer.

"DO YOU UNDERSTAND?" hissed the man.

"Yes," she said.

"Good," he said. "Now we have that straight. So, come over to my office in an hour. You might have to sit in the waiting room until my paralegal lets you into my office. You understand?"

"Yes," she said.

"Don't be late," he said. "And don't ever hang up on me again. Your daddy won't tolerate it, and neither will I. Do you understand?"

"Yes," she said.

"Yes – what?" he said.

"Yes, sir," she said.

The drive wasn't long. The only acceptable thing about the man was the quick, easy drive to his law office. She parked her beat-up Expedition in a shady spot just outside his office and left the windows cracked open. Her air conditioner was broken. No point in letting the car get any hotter than necessary.

As he'd promised, she had to wait. One look at the receptionist and Linda read her mind. *The receptionist knows what's going on. She has to know.*

Linda felt her face burning as she sat on the most distant, high-backed, red leather chair in the waiting area. She looked around, hoping to find a magazine or something to take her mind off the visit. She hated being here. Hated it!

There were faux mismatched oriental rugs on the floor of the too-small reception area. A coffee table with a chip out of the wood on one of the legs and a box of Kleenex sat in front of her. Faded velvet curtains were coated in dust. There was dust on the windowsills too. A similar, fake leather covered – but mismatched sofa was tucked against the other wall. The only reading materials in the office where free shopper guides and coupon clippers. Even the end tables were mismatched.

The mousy paralegal-receptionist occasionally glared at her through half high glasses from behind a cheap desk at the other end of the room. *She knows about him. She has to know. Paralegal, my ass. The girl probably can't even type. I'll bet he pays her a dollar less than minimum.* Then, after reflection, she thought, *at least she has a job.*

He'd said eleven-thirty. Ten minutes after noon, a working man with a cotton long-sleeved blue shirt with his name on an emblem came into the office.

He walked to the receptionist and said, "I'm here a few minutes early. Is that okay? I'm supposed to sign off on the final today." He smiled when he said the last sentence.

"Sure, Mister Rodriguez. I'll show you right in."

As the receptionist opened the door, Linda could see R. Shuster Simon sitting behind an oversized desk in a recliner chair behind his desk. He had his hands, fingers-interlaced behind his head, elbows out. She saw dark, yellowed sweat stains on his long-sleeved white shirt at the underarms. She shivered. Through the open door, his eyes engaged hers.

Rodriguez walked into Simon's office and looked at Linda over his shoulder. He smiled.

She didn't smile back.

R. Shuster Simon, attorney-at-law, grinned at her like a Cheshire cat for five long seconds until the door closed behind Rodriguez. Immediately, she could hear indistinct male chatter begin. She couldn't make the words out, but she was sure they were talking about her. Of course it was possible the Rodriguez fellow was simply a divorce client – he probably was, but still, she didn't want the two men to be talking about her.

She had to concentrate to keep from hyperventilating. Her sugardaddy had started the ball rolling. When *he* had told her she should get divorced, be free of Roger at last, and have would enough money for school, it sounded like things were finally going her way. *He* said the time was right. It was *he* who had told her about Roger's brother getting run over. "Get the divorce now," *he'd* said.

"So, how much will this divorce cost?" she'd asked. "You know I have just enough to live on as it is."

"Silly girl," *he'd* said. "Any attorney worth his salt will do it on a contingency basis. He'll get a percentage of your settlement. He gets paid when you get paid. On this, I should know."

"What percentage of my settlement will this lawyer get?" she'd asked him.

"Normally about thirty percent. My guy will have to do the final settlement, but I figure if Roger is getting like a quarter mil, you could get a quick settlement of a hundred grand. Come to think of it, that would be if you go the long drawn out way. But eighty grand, quick and easy. No problem. Simon owes me a small favor, so I will tell him to do it and you'd just have to pay him twenty-five grand or so. You'd still be sitting pretty – so to speak."

"That much?" she'd said. "That's a lot of money for a divorce."

"Honey, that's the way the judicial system works. Look, the bum you're married to is getting a windfall. His brother, God rest his soul, probably didn't feel a thing. He probably didn't even see it coming. Or if he did, his last thoughts were, *A truck! A fucking truck!*, and bam he was gone. So Roger gets a truck full of money. You're entitled."

"Twenty-five grand's still a lot of money to pay," she'd said, "for a divorce. That's all I really want. And I want to see my kids when I'm back on my feet."

"Well, there's a way...," he'd said. "that maybe we could get him to cut the money thing to practically nothing. In fact, nothing at all if you play your cards right."

"How?" she'd asked.

All she had to do was wear a particular dress, *he'd* said. He described the dress. He'd bought it for her. Tell Simon she had a fantasy. He described the particular fantasy she needed to relate to Simon. Simon got off on being told about stuff like that. Simon would know what to do.

And that's how it started. She told Simon the fantasy. She let him grope her for a few minutes. Then, when he'd said the most filthy things a man can say and gotten completely aroused doing it, he made her put her hands on his desk, got behind her, pulled her panties down and made her ask for it.

She'd always fantasized about being bent over a desk and used. Simon completed that check-off, but not in a good way. But then, *as a formality*, he'd said, he'd thrust some legal sized papers at her and told her to sign them.

Of course, once wasn't enough for him, even if was more than enough for her.

So, here she was, sitting in his anteroom, waiting while the receptionist glared at her with the hatred a plain woman has for a sexually attractive woman.

All she was supposed to do was sign some papers for her divorce. He'd probably want another payment too. How many more, she wondered. She wondered if she told Simon she'd prefer to let him have his thirty percent, would he go for it? Probably not, she decided.

"Mrs. Cooley," said the receptionist, "Mr. Simon just buzzed me. He said you can go in now."

"Umm. Okay," said Linda. "But I think he has someone in there with him."

"He said to send you in. I'm sending you in," said the receptionist.

She knows. Damn it. She knows. God, how did I get in this mess! Linda opened the door and walked in. Rodriguez was standing in front of Simon's desk with a guilty, nervous look on his face – and there was an unnatural lump in his pants. He had a hard-on.

"Mr. Simon, you said you had some papers for me to sign?" she said, ignoring the obvious.

"Aaah, yes," he said. "I had thought they'd be ready by now. Evidently they aren't. But per our agreement, you can make a payment today."

"I don't think so," she said. "Besides, you're still busy. You can work on your friend's problem without me. Call me when you want me to sign those papers."

She turned and left the room.

As the door was about to close, he said to her, "No little girl. It doesn't work that way. You need to make a payment – today – times two. If I need to

71

make a call, I'll make the call. You know I'll do it."

She was never, ever rude. Ever. But in one instant, in a purely reflexive moment, she threw her right hand up, middle finger extended and kept walking to the elevator. She did not turn to look back at R. Shuster Simon.

She'd get a divorce some other way. She didn't know how, but she would.

Once back in the parking lot, she sat in her beat-to-hell Expedition, shaking like a cat dunked in cold water, unable to make herself start the engine or God forbid, drive. She shook with anger for ten minutes, arms crossed over her chest, squeezing herself. Anger gave way to tears. She cried for five minutes forcing a river of muddy mascara down her cheeks. Finally, as the crying gave way to hiccups, she took a deep breath and rummaged through her purse hoping to find a cigarette. She'd quit smoking. She was constantly quitting. This time she couldn't find a cigarette to unquit herself again, damn it.

Finally, after saying unladylike things her mother *would not* approve of, she found a stale, water-stained yellowed cigarette under the passenger's seat and gazed through the windshield at the playground fifty yards away while she decided what to do next. The cigarette was disgusting to look at, but she was desperate. Just as she got it lit, her phone buzzed. *RESTRICTED.* She ignored it.

It buzzed again. *RESTRICTED*. This time she accepted the call, and said, "Fuck you, Simon," then hung up.

It buzzed again almost immediately. She accepted, then hung up.

Again. This time, she accepted the call but didn't speak. She put her phone to her ear. The call wasn't from Simon. It was *him*.

"First, don't say fuck unless you are on your back and your legs are open," *he* said. "Second, you answer all my calls, all the time. Got it? So – this disagreement between you and Simon has made things difficult for me," he said. "For you too. I need you to calm down – now."

"He called you to tattletale on me, didn't he? That man is an asshole," she said. "He's gross, he has BO and bad breath and ugly skin. He's ugly, and he's rude. He called me a whore. I *will not* tolerate being treated that way. Worse, he had some guy in there with him. I'm not doing the both of them. And don't ask me to."

"I need you to calm down," *he* said.

"I am calm," she said. "I'm just pissed. I'm tired of being nice to your friends. This isn't fun anymore."

"So listen. This is important. Simon is an asshole sometimes. No big thing. You told me it was a fantasy of yours to be bent over a desk. In an office where the people outside didn't know. Didn't you?"

"Not every fantasy has to be lived out more than once," she said. "And it wasn't at all like my fantasy. I do stuff for you sometimes. You're different. I can go along with stuff for you, but this guy is an asshole. It's twisted too much and I'm done with it."

"I don't want to have to play hardball," *he* said. "but Linda, from time to time, I need you to just trust my judgment. We've come a long way. I take care of the rent. And the school thing is covered. Insurance stuff too. Covered a lot of other bases too. You know it would be silly for you to force my hand and end our arrangement. I need you to do something for me. You want to see you kids, right?"

Across the road, in the playground she saw a mother leading two children. *Awww. They're the same age as mine. Oh god, I have to see them. I just have to.*

She didn't speak. She tried to think. She wanted a deep dirty drag off of the nasty old cigarette, but it had gone out. She fiddled with it while they both waited on the phone to see who would speak first.

After a long second effort with a shaky lighter, she got it lit again. She sucked deeply, letting the smoke fill her lungs, letting the sting of the smoke and the numbing of the nicotine do its job. How a person could hate a thing and love it at the same time was a curious thing to her. How she loved that cigarette!

The mother across the street in the playground was pushing them in the park swings.

"Linda," *he* said. "Be a good girl. Don't make me mad. Please don't make me play hardball."

"What do you want me to do?" she said.

"Nothing much. We'll have this thing moving along in just a few more weeks," *he* said. "Go back into Simon's office and let him make a deposit. Take your panties off before you go in, spread your legs and bend over his desk. You told me he's quick. Think about something else. Think of Valmay maybe, or think of me and what we'll be doing tomorrow when I get down there. Be a good girl and moan like it's fun."

"I'm not doing that guy that's with him," she said.

"Don't have to. I made Simon agree to a compromise for today. He wanted you to – you know – give up a quickie for the other guy. Then he wanted to have you after. He'd really gotten his hopes up. He's been screaming about you to me and carrying on like a baby on the phone. Said you embarrassed him in front of an important client. But I told him today wasn't the day for that. He and I came to a compromise. Simon bends you over the desk. Rodriguez gets to know what Simon is going to do. He gets a peek at your charms and he leaves. Simon will make a deposit, you put your panties on and go home. That's about it. See? I'm on your side here. We really need to get Simon to complete this divorce. The process is started. First hearing went just as I predicted. Just hang in there and take one for the team from time to time."

"This is the last time," she said. "I can't stand that bastard."

"We'll see," *he* said. "We'll see. One other tiny little thing."

"What?" she said.

"Valmay said he's texted you. You haven't replied. He says he has some weed and a little something else for you to use when I get down there tomorrow. I'm looking forward to seeing you. I'll be there at about noon. Valmay said you haven't been over to pick up the stuff he has for you. Said he'd be happy to deliver it to you after he gets off work tonight. Kind of works into my plans anyway."

"I'm done with the coke. Forever," she said. "Weed too. I can't concentrate on my classes. I'm getting behind. And Valmay isn't as much fun as he used to be. I know you like hearing about it after he's been over to see me, but I don't want to do that anymore. I'm just sayin'."

"Look I don't have time to get into a long conversation with you right now," *he* said. "Get the product from Valmay. Pay him like always, on your back so he goes home smelling like you. If you don't want any of the other stuff, that's up to you. I like you a lot better when I see you and you have some weed and a shot or two, or a snort or two. So get it."

"Okay," she said.

"Good girl," *he* said. "Now go back in there and put on a first rate performance for our friend Simon. Make sure he thinks you love it. I'll tell Valmay to make your delivery after he gets off work. Don't bother to shower after Simon, or after Valmay. It'll be a treat for me to know what you've been up to."

"Okay," she said.

The mother and the two children were gone. The swings in the park were empty and motionless.

CHAPTER TWELVE
DANTE, A FRIEND WITH
A HOLE IN HIS HEAD

The receptionist in the downtown lobby suggested politely to Edward he should wait until someone came to escort him to the 32nd floor. Perhaps he could take a seat, she advised. Edward remained standing and smiled at her. Two minutes later, Dante himself came down to greet him.

"Damn, it's good to see you, Paul. What brings you back to Miami?" said the black man stepping out of the elevator. He smiled and extended his hand. He wore an understated two-thousand-dollar suit, a Rolex watch and a designer tie. The light scent of Bay Rum followed him.

"It's been a long time. Come on up to my office. I have some very nice Cubans we can smoke and I'll order lunch brought in, if you have time."

He and Edward Teach shook hands.

"Yeah, it's been a while, Dante." said Edward as the elevator doors closed. "Oh, and just for the record, I'm not Paul anymore. Changed my name a while ago. My passport says Edward Teach now."

Dante laughed. "Edward Teach the pirate? So now you're Blackbeard himself! It fits, but in a good way. Actually, I'd heard some of the story."

"A name is just a name," said Edward. "Sorry to barge in like this. After we get caught up, I have a favor to ask."

Dante laughed. "Are you kidding me? I owe you my life. Besides, of all the guys that became part of my life after I dropped out of school and learned what real work could be like, you're the one I wish I could see more often."

The elevator door opened at the thirty-second floor. Edward laughed hard as he looked at the lush furnishing in Dante's office. "Dante, I hate to be the one to tell you this, but playing the part of a stoner kid who dropped out of college to take a job as a deckhand on the barefoot cruise circuit is not exactly real work."

"Captain, working under you, it's pretty close to the real thing," said Dante. "Hey, I heard you went straight from the barefoot charter business to unlimited tonnage licenses, sometimes even pushing LNG from the Sea of Arabia to the Gulf of Mexico."

"Not exactly a straight course, but yes, that's where I ended up – for a while," said Edward.

"Mr. Pirate, you have to have balls made of titanium to want to move that stuff. I read up. One ship loaded with liquefied natural gas has ten times more energy than the hydrogen bomb we dropped on Hiroshima."

"Pretty much. But that's why they pay well to Captain and crew. So then, I'm assuming you know what the fastest thing on the earth is?"

"I sense a joke here," said Dante.

"Fastest thing on the earth is an eight-hundred foot ship full of LNG headed at the pierhead at two knots," said Edward.

Dante looked at the ceiling deep in thought, then smiled. "Okay. I think I got it. An eight-hundred foot ship has no effective steerage at two knots. So, unless you have enough time to direct the harbor tugs – which you don't – the world is about to end, if something fouls up. Right?"

Edward laughed a deep echoing laugh. "See, I knew you were a true seaman. So, you changed course and became a successful investment banker. I hope my tutelage helped just a little bit. Judging from appearances, you learned well, my friend."

"I did," said Dante. "So from tall-ships you went straight to the top of the mountain?" Dante pointed a Cuban cigar at Edward.

"Not exactly. There were a few bumps in the roads and dragons to slay in between," replied Edward. "Chief and I spent four years one month on a former whaling island near Patagonia while I studied for licenses and read up on deep draft boats. Tell you about that some other day. You look good. So, I guess after the incident in Rio, you took your parents up on the offer to finish school at UM.

"Forgive me for staring. I've been looking at your head where the whiskey bottle went in. It healed up nice. No scars, no marks where I stitched your scalp back on. I can barely make out an outline of where it happened. Hope you've been smart enough to stay out of waterfront bars since then."

"I have, thanks to you. Doctors back here in the states all commented on what a great job you did." Dante stood and looked out over Biscayne Bay. "Yeah, it worked out with my dad. No bad blood anymore. I kind of hoped you could work it out with your dad too, but life is life. Like you noted, I'm in investment banking now. Life is good."

Edward let his booming laugh go unchecked for a moment. "I never would have guessed. Thirty-two floors up. Best view in town and nice furnishing. I guess you gave up on the ambition of being a ship chandler. Obviously investment banking pays better than buying foodstuff and supplies for grumpy business agents."

"Listen," replied Dante. "I was out of town when your wife died. Terrible accident. No way they could save her, I guess."

"Four different guys tried to dislodge the chunk of steak from her airway," said Edward. "EMT's tried a tracheotomy and finally got it out with forceps, but seven minutes without oxygen to the brain is simply too long. Or it was for her. I felt like crap. Maybe if I'd been there, I could have saved her. Those idiots were clumsy. Just clumsy."

"Damn. You doing okay then?" asked Dante.

"Yeah. The truth is, we weren't doing all that good before it happened. I was in the process of ending it. Death and divorce are twin bitches sired from different mothers. She didn't deserve to die, but I couldn't live with her anymore. So for the most part, my grieving was done before she choked to death. Who really knows?

"Do you remember Chief? How eccentric he was? Just before Stella died, he cashed in his savings – he was always saving, saving, saving – quit the sea, and decided he wanted to be a real pirate – on shore. Saw a movie and went off the deep end. So to fit the image he had decided on, he bought a bar and a parrot – which is another story altogether. This woman he got the parrot from...."

Edward stopped talking. Dante had a huge grin on his face. He returned to his chair behind the massive mahogany desk.

"Actually Captain, I heard about Chief, and I heard about the girl too. Hibiscus is her name, unless I got it mixed up in my head. I lost track of you about the time you changed your name. Just one question, me being nosy and all. This girl, Hibiscus. Did she really fall in love with you and put a hex on your wife to kill her?"

"She thinks she did," said Edward. "Sometimes it's easier just to let a crazy person think what they want." Edward turned from looking out of the window, and sprawled on the leather guest's chair in front of Dante's desk. He re-lit his cigar and inhaled lightly. Exhaling, he said, "Look, I came to ask for a favor."

"Ask," said Dante.

"I'm not a Miamian anymore, and when I was, I wasn't particularly connected to the scene. I'm guessing you still are. I'm looking for a guy. Supposedly he's very upscale and into the party scene. Name's Valmay. He sells drugs and girls. Some of the girls are a bit young – as in underage."

"So you call on me because I'm black and I like the girls and I'm single and rich. Right?"

"If it walks like a duck and quacks like a duck...."

"I used to walk the walk. Still do the nightlife some. But this isn't Rio. I still like the ladies, but they gotta be old enough. Drugs don't do it for me. So can't help you there. Name of Valmay doesn't ring a bell. Sounds Haitian maybe. So you want me to chase this guy to the ground for you? Tell me more."

"I thought you might know him. Be good if you do. If not, hoping you could ask around. He's a good-looking dude. Early thirties, slim, very black, carries himself with confidence. I was told he's upscale. Maybe it's a recent change for him. Not sure. The upscale part, that's what made me think of you. He's been in Miami about three years. Might have been here before he moved down from Tampa with a certain girl," said Edward. "I have a bead on her and I want to know about this Valmay guy first if I can."

"No doubt you ran a background check," said Dante. "What did it show?"

"Curious," said Edward. "Whatever was on his criminal record – is gone. Expunged. Like it never happened. Dude might be connected to someone with legal clout. Not even a picture of him when he got arrested up in Tampa on drug charges...and I got it on good authority he was arrested on a cocaine bust."

Dante said, "Got it. Dude has pull, then. Like I said, I don't know him, but there's guys around I could ask. This guy, I'm guessing he's still into coke if he's dealing. Lots of party people are still doing it. I'll start with that. I'll check out big players who sell coke. Youngsters use ecstasy. That, and oxycodone. Crack and meth is for those on the way down. As for escorts, not so much. Girls go independent now. Upscale girls look for sugardaddys – internet and all. I've been known to keep a girl for a month or two, myself. I'll check around and get back to you. The phone number you used to make the appointment with, is it still good?"

"Better than yours," quipped Edward handing Dante his card. "I had to track you down the hard way."

"Long story there," said Dante. "Had to de-list. Some girls can't take no for an answer. Anyway, I got your number. I'll be back what I can get on this guy, probably a day or so. You want to do dinner? I know some places. And hey, you had to be knocking down a quarter mil a year when you were moving LNG. Hope you invested well. I could help put some of it to work if you want."

"No thanks," said Edward. "I keep most of my savings in gold. No pirate jokes either, okay? If a man has enough gold, he doesn't need to worry about investments. The bar pays its own way, and I don't have many expensive vices. Don't have to look at the Dow, and gold is always pretty to look at. And I'll have to pass on the dinner too. I'm going to wear out my laptop doing some searches on my two Miami targets. Call me."

CHAPTER THIRTEEN
SEARCH, BRIBE, AND GOOGLE

From Dante's office, it was a short drive to South Beach, then to Ocean Drive. There, among perfectly manicured spacious lawns and tall flowing palm trees, he drove directly to *Hilton Bentley* on Miami Beach.

An immaculately dressed young man opened the door of Edward's Mercedes. "Sir," he said. "Are you checking in? Can I help you with anything?" The young man had only a trace of a Cuban accent.

"Thank you, no," said Edward. "The head bellman. I believe his name is Enrique. I inadvertently forgot to give him something." Edward held an envelope in his hand.

"Of course, sir. I'll be happy to see he gets it," said the valet.

"I'm sure you would," said Edward. "But I'd prefer to give it to him myself. Could you direct me to him?"

"Of course, sir. He's at the bellman's station, right through that door. You can leave your car here if you like. I believe he's at the station. If he's not, someone there can summon him for you."

Only one man inside the luscious lobby could have been Enrique.

Edward put on his most engaging smile and walked up to him.

Enrique met his smile equally.

"A good friend of mine," said Edward, "stayed here recently. He particularly remembers you had full command of all circumstances. He told me you might be able to help me."

"Of course. Whatever can I do to help you, sir?" said Enrique. "I don't remember your face. Are you a guest here?"

"No, not for a few days yet," said Edward. "I'm looking for a man who arranges things. He's a nice dresser, black, has dreadlocks and is often in the company of an attractive young woman. He's been highly recommended. I believe his name is Valmay. Do you perhaps know how I might find him?"

"I'm not sure if I know such a man," said Enrique. Enrique looked quickly to his right, then to his left to see if they were being watched or listened to.

Edward held out the envelope. "Of course. Here's my card. If by any chance you know any way, or can find any way, I can find Valmay, I would appreciate it a great deal."

Inside the Envelope there was a gold embossed calling card that simply said, *Edward T. Acquisitions.* One line below there was a 305 area code phone number. A fifty-dollar bill was attached with a paper clip.

After the *Hilton Bentley*, he visited, *Turnberry Isle* Miami, then *Mondrian South Beach,* then *The Tides South Beach,* then six more upscale, expensive places where the head bellman or the concierge might have heard of Valmay or the services he provided.

When he was done, he'd spent five-hundred dollars and nobody had heard of a high-dollar player who sold drugs or women with a name like Valmay. The bellmen took Edward's card and made notes in their notebooks.

CHAPTER FOURTEEN
ELIMINATE THE IMPROBABLE

One by one they checked in as they'd promised. By four in the afternoon the following day, Edward had heard from all of them. They looked, because there was a cash bonus. They all reported no joy. They'd keep their ears open, but made no promises.

Edward got up from the work table in his motel room, closed his laptop computer and stretched. Beside him was a yellow tablet with some notes penned neatly under the heading, *Linda Cooley.*

He put on a pair of comfortable sneakers, white yachter's slacks, and a Columbia fisherman's shirt, slid his cell phone into his pants pocket along with a moneyclip and left his comfortable motel room near his favorite marina.

If one door won't open, try another.

Target number two was within range. Time to inspect the surroundings. He settled into the front seat of his Mercedes, set up camp and started scanning with a pair of small binoculars to see if he could find target number two.

Just as he decided it was a good place to watch a subject from, the cell phone jingled in his pocket.

"Yo, Edward," said Dante. "Time to report in to the Cap'n of the ship. I've put feelers out everyplace I could."

"Came up with zip?" said Edward.

"Less than zip," said Dante. "I even went above and beyond the call, seeing as it was you who asked. Only one guy by the name of Valmay comes up. And he sure ain't an *important playah*. More like a wannabe playah. I think maybe somebody gave you some bad intel. Either that, or this guy moved elsewhere. It happens."

"Probably right," said Edward. "I do appreciate the help though. You ever want to come slumming up Sarasota way, let me know. Drinks are on me, and I got the use of a Beneteau – forty-seven footer. Give me the info you got on the wannabe playah."

"Cap'n Teach, you tempt me. There are times with I truly miss the days on the water and the nights under the stars. I really do."

He gave Edward information on a guy who might or might not be named Valmay and ended with, "Let's stay in touch."

Edward put his phone down, picked up his binoculars again and scanned. Target number two had to be close by.

Minutes later he muttered, "Bingo. There you are, my pretty."

He'd found Linda Cooley.

CHAPTER FIFTEEN
WHO'D I JUST HIRE?

Rosemary walked into Chip's office. "That guy, Roger. He called again. Said he just wants a few minutes. I told him that your time was billable. He said he knew. Said it wouldn't take long. Can I set him for four this afternoon? He said he gets off work at three and…"

"Sure," said Chip. "I thought he might call. See if you can get Edward on the phone for me before Roger gets here."

Roger was five minutes early. He started right in.

"This guy we got working for us, the pirate-looking dude, Edward…." he began.

"Edward Teach is working for you, not for me," said Chip. "Evidently Rosemary saw fit to give you his name, not me."

"Yeah, right. Whatever. I'm in for this, but is he really smart enough and bad enough to pull this off?"

"He is…," Chip paused to stress the remainder of his remark, "…. perhaps the smartest man either one of us will ever meet. He retains everything he reads. He reads a lot. He puts stuff together in his head pretty good too."

Roger pondered on Chip's reply for a few moments, then said, "Okay, I hear you. But can you give me a short bio on the guy? Like they do on the History Channel?"

"It's interesting, but it wouldn't make any difference," said Chip. "on how he does what he does. He likes his privacy. And you probably wouldn't believe me."

"I make a lot of mistakes what with me being impulsive," said Roger. "I hired him for a lot of money when I was pissed at the judge after the hearing. But I been thinking. Is this guy legit? I just want the fast version. I want to know that my judgment to hire him is solid. If you don't tell me, then I gotta go snooping around. I'm getting better at snooping and tailing guys than I used to be. But sometimes I'm not so subtle, ya know? I might fuck it up and this guy Edward might want to rough me up for being nosy. And I might not want to get roughed up so easy. Or I might stumble on something that hits a nerve and he finds out and quits on me. I got a lot at stake here. I don't need Linda back. We ain't a fit. Dewey isn't as smart as Linda, but she's sweet. You know how much money is at stake. Just tell me, and I go back to being a dumbass painter, boss. Okay?"

Chip smiled. "You'd mess it up bad if you start looking. Edward Teach is....different. I figured that's what you wanted to talk about when you called Rosemary to make the appointment. Asked him if it was okay. He gave me limited permission, but only limited."

"I figured," said Roger. "So tell me, and if it sounds solid, I'm a friend to you and to him forever.

Provided you don't scare me too bad with the facts."

"Fast answer," said Chip. "He was born with another name. Dad was an evangelist preacher. You know, the kind that convinces people to fall on the floor frothing at the mouth. But practically from the day of his birth, Edward's dad took note of his ability to learn, remember and process almost anything and everything he was exposed to. He pressured him, set him up to get the best of everything. Kid could have been anything. His dad wanted a prestigious doctor. So, Edward became one. Three years ahead of his academic peer group, he excelled at everything. Well, maybe not religion or music. The man has a tin ear. On the last day of his residency at Johns Hopkins, he walked out and wasn't found again."

"Johns Hopkins," said Roger. "That's a famous hospital up in New York or someplace, right?"

"Baltimore," said Chip. "The thing is, he decided not to complete his residency. Quit one day shy. As a result, he isn't board certified to practice medicine – by his own choice. My guess is, his Freudian brain quit that way to get even with his dad about something, but what do I know? The thing is, he could have been. Most guys take like twelve years from high school until they're board certified. He did it in nine, but walked out one day shy. Almost unbelievable. He disappeared. Didn't tell his family where. He just disappeared. To this

93

day, they don't know where he is or what happened or why."

"Wow," said Roger, "For real? So where'd he go?"

"Mmm…don't know the exact details, but short version is he became a seagoing bum. Worked on the barefoot cruise circuit. You know, big tall sailing ships where the customers help the crew sail to little known Caribbean islands and pay their Yuppie asses off to do it.

"Cream rises to the top and in just three years, he was the captain of a sizable vacation boat that catered to adventuring party people with money."

"Wow, he did that for like….how many years?"

"Almost twenty," said Chip.

"Twenty years?" said Roger. "I bet he got all the pussy a man could want. He's got the look. I wouldn't get married either if I was him. And that girl Hibiscus, she's got some kind of mojo."

"Well, there's more, and it's interesting. But all you need to know is he's a man of character. Just remember he's the kind of man who defines what character means. He was married. His wife died, and I doubt he'll ever get married again. His wife became fat and ambitious immediately after she got a ring on her finger."

Chip was on a roll. "She pushed – just like his dad did, and for a while Edward climbed the ladder to success. He was successful but not happy after he became licensed to command commercial freighters, and continued up the food chain until he got unlimited tonnage certifications.

"Just when Edward was about to divorce her to return to the sailing boats, a friend of his, who was two-parts shy of being a million parts odd – died. The man left the bar and the parrot to Edward."

"So that's how he got the bar?" said Roger.

"That's about it. Except the part about Chief dying. When Chief died – Chief was the guy who really wanted to be a pirate. He bought the parrot, whose name has always been Blackbeard, from a witch in Kingston.

"A real witch. Not a pretend witch. You met her. She knows more about potions, herbs, roots, and drugs than all the PHDs in the country of Columbia. She bought the parrot from an estate of a friend of Chief's before Chief could get there, for who knows what reason. She and Chief both believed Blackbeard the parrot, was Edward Teach's honest-to-god parrot. She also claimed – claims – she was Teach's mistress from the 1700's. Nobody listens to crazy people, so everybody humors her.

"Anyway, Chief bought the parrot from her. Can't tell you why she agreed to sell the bird to Chief. He bought the bar in Siesta Key, quit the sea, and tried to run the bar."

"No shit?" asked Roger. "You swear this is true?"

"Chief was real. I handled the purchase contract. That's how I met him. The guy was covered in

95

tattoos. Covered. Scars all over his face. Dressed and talked like a pirate all the time. After he bought the bar, he actually asked a doctor to amputate his leg so he could get a wooden leg. Said he had pains in his leg at night and the doctor should cut it off. It's an image thing I guess. Wooden leg, parrot, rum and attitude."

"You swear?" said Roger. "You're not fucking with me about this?"

"Nope," said Chip. "The rest is just about as interesting. So, Chief buys the bar, but it wasn't going to work. Everybody saw that right off, including Chief. It lost money from day one. The witch girl from Kingston, who is Hibiscus, shows up a month later and puts some good Voodoo on Chief and business picks up. I don't believe in Voodoo. I suspect the reason business improved was Hibiscus is hard not to like, and customers came to see her more than any other reason. So, Edward visits Chief and Hibiscus meets him and falls for him.

"Remember Edward's name is still something other than what his mom and dad gave him, but it wasn't Edward.

"Hibiscus believes he's her former lover, Edward Teach. Only Edward was still married and he wasn't interested in Hibiscus, or if he was, he didn't show it. All men are interested in her. All men."

"And….?" said Roger.

"A month later Chief dies from cancer that had no major symptoms until two weeks before he died.

96

He tried to get his doctor to amputate his leg one more time, and during in the examination, the doctor discovered the cancer.

"Chief came into my office the day he got diagnosed, had me draw up a quitclaim to the bar in Edward's favor, showed me life insurance the bank had made him buy, but I already knew about the insurance.

"He had me draw up a paper about Blackbeard, but it was just a piece of shit paper. Not legal, because parrots can't own a bar or a liquor license. And the bastard died two weeks later.

"Two weeks later still, Edward's wife chokes to death on a piece of steak in front of a dozen people," Chip added.

"Hibiscus put Voodoo on everybody, it seems. Now, don't get me wrong. I don't believe in Voodoo. Neither does Edward, but he isn't a man to ignore fact versus fiction either. I know for a fact Hibiscus tried to put a love spell on Edward, but he's not buying in. To him, their relationship is part business and part sexual release.

"But, to make the break in his life complete, Edward changed his legal name, took over the bar, and told Hibiscus if she was a real witch to keep her charms in check." Chip leaned back, assessing Roger. "They sleep together, you know."

"Ya, you just said. Besides, he told me," said Roger. "You swear this is all true?"

"It's true. I swear. Now, like I said, it doesn't mean Hibiscus really is a witch. She isn't. There's no such thing. In spite of her apparent extensive knowledge of tribal chants and herb potions and drugs, she's just mixed up. She just thinks she's a real witch. She has papers, but they're not legit. But it's not my job to learn such things. She's been to Haiti, Louisiana and a lot of other places where the Voodoo mystique is popular, and she's as clever as a card shark on a river boat. I heard her mimic Oprah once, and she totally loses the Jamaican accent when she wants to. Her papers are in order, but her life before she moved here is a total mystery. She really believes. That makes her dangerous.

"It's a pure coincidence about Chief and Edward's wife dying, and the circumstances making him a private investigator, but believe me, the man has talents and knowledge you wouldn't believe.

"One last thing," said Chip. "I got limited permission to tell you what I just told you. Limited. That means *you CAN NOT* start discussing him with anybody. Anybody. He'll fire you and me both if you let on I told you this story. As gifted as he is, he's entitled to be a little strange. So, just humor him. Don't bring up his past unless he mentions it first. And be warned. Hibiscus really does have something that makes men want to fall in love with her. All men. You get my drift?"

"Yeah," said Roger. "You already said. I see she got to you too. I'm thinking I need to keep myself to Dewey. Got it. No more questions. He wants me to know, he'll tell me. I don't know whether or not you're shitting me about Edward, but it don't make any difference so long as he gets me out of this thing."

"I think your thirty minutes are up," said Chip. "We'll be in touch."

CHAPTER SIXTEEN
BASIC BOY-GIRL
INTRODUCTION

"You ran an ad," Edward said to Linda, "on Backpage. On the internet. "

Hours of computer research yielded a great deal of information about Linda, although Valmay, or at least the Valmay Roger had described, was still unfound. So, Edward had concentrated on Linda. Linda would eventually lead him to Valmay.

By the time he called her, he knew every website she'd visited, when she'd visited it and how long she'd stayed on it. He knew who was on her Facebook account. He knew how many email accounts she'd had, and what personals ads she'd run or responded to. He also knew her phone numbers. Her bank accounts too – overdrawn all. He knew a lot about Linda, but still he wanted to know the woman.

Linda said, "Huh? Excuse me? Who is this? Oh. Yes, God that was a long time ago. I'm sorry, I ran that thing and so many men were rude I quit answering the replies. Is my phone number still out there? I thought I took the ad down."

She had indeed taken the ad down. But Edward didn't need to tell her that. Nothing really dies once posted on the internet.

"I'm Edward. There was a link," he said. "I followed the link. I'm not a creep and I'm not rude.

I'm a very nice man. Can I talk to you for a minute?"

"Okay," said Linda. "You have a great voice – deep, commanding – like you're used to telling people what to do."

She dangled her feet off a dock looking at a row of sailboats at their moorings, and held her cell phone between her ear and her right shoulder. Her sandals were nearby. If she stretched her legs just a little bit, she could get her toes to make circles in the water as she moved her feet. There were lots of sailboats to look at. Most of them had a ribbon of green slime growing along the waterline, indicating non-use.

"Yeah, I've been told," said Edward. "I'm sort of a traveling man. Spent some time at sea. I have to tell people what to do. Part of my job, I guess. I like your ad, don't want to do the escort thing, thought maybe we could talk about how it could work. Thought being a sugardaddy was better. Maybe we could meet up?"

"Maybe," said Linda. "I don't really like to talk about or think about stuff like that. What do you have in mind?"

"I was thinking about lunch, if you have time." He said.

"Maybe," she said. "I'm at the Marina Del Mar. Where they keep the sailboats. There's a bar and grill there. You know where it is?"

"I'll be there in an hour," he said. "I'll find you."

Edward closed his phone, picked up his binoculars, and let his eyes be his only input for a moment. A bit of observation was in order.

CHAPTER SEVENTEEN
WATCH, WAIT, THEN MOVE IN

During the phone conversation, Edward watched her without binoculars. A man of the sea, he was constantly looking for little things that might have an effect on his intended course.

He'd been talking to her on the phone and watching her through the windshield of his Mercedes, parked far enough away so it wouldn't be obvious he was studying her.

If she hadn't answered the phone, he would have tried a blind introduction. He'd followed her, tracking the position of her phone for more than a day. He learned she didn't seem to have a consistent pattern. Linda seemed to be anything but predictable.

The computer helped, but it could only tell him so much about her. He wanted to know the woman.

He said an hour. But instead of approaching her at the end of the hour, he sat and watched her from his car. He was of the opinion detailed observations were underrated. And so he observed. Then he observed some more. He waited fifteen minutes past the time when they were to meet just so he could watch and observe her actions regarding a possible standup.

Clearly she wasn't a woman with a great deal of patience. She fidgeted, looked at the time on her cell phone and paced, evidently trying to calm herself. She bit her fingernails. She adjusted her blouse so her breasts showed more prominently. Her low-cut blouse showed nice natural cleavage. She brushed her glossy long black hair quickly, then put her brush away as if she didn't want to be caught doing it. She stood, stretched, then touched her toes a few times. Tight jeans looked good on her too. She wore flip flops. She wasn't a skinny waif. More like a sturdy built Midwest girl should look, in a Marilyn Monroe way. She could have called him back to see if he was going to show – he'd let his number go through when he called – but she didn't.

Twenty minutes past the meeting time, Edward strode up to her. "You look like a lady who could use some lunch," he said.

"Are you Edward?" she said.

"I'm either me, or I'm a ghost of me," he replied with a smile that was meant to disarm her.

"Hi," she said, straining her neck to look up at him. "I recognize the voice now. And you're tall to match. Wow, exactly how tall are you?"

"Not tall enough to get into the NBA. Besides I'm too old and too white." he said. "But tall enough to have to duck my head in places where other people don't have to. You in the mood for a bite to eat?"

"Sure, why not?" she said.

They walked to an outdoor patio at the marina. She ordered a bottle of dark ale. Edward had a draught beer. When the waitress came back, he looked at Linda and then the waitress. "Is the paella good here?"

The waitress beamed. "It's one of our best dishes. It's very good. Would you like a portion for two?"

He looked at Linda, and raised his eyebrows. She smiled a quick smile that showed teeth and let her eyes say yes.

"Paella it is," he said. "The house salad too, and some Cuban bread please. And bring the lady another ale."

The waitress beamed. For a moment, her body language suggested she wanted to hang around, but she caught herself and left in a hurry.

"You ever do this before?" he asked. "I mean the ad."

"I'm supposed to say no, like I'm a virgin or something," she giggled. "But obviously I'm not. It wasn't one of my brightest ideas. Like I said, I thought I took it down. I'm still trying to find myself, ya' know? You just happened to catch me at a time when I was susceptible to talking to someone. So, how about you?"

"Well, I've had girlfriends I've taken care of. Same thing, I suppose, as being a sugardaddy. Everybody pays for what they want. Why not this? The ad you ran said sugarbaby. I thought it might save time. Are you still looking?"

She laughed. Her laughs weren't silly girl laughs. They were laughs that telegraphed the thought she was happy to be with him, yet they'd just met. They suggested past intimacies, future intimacies, and they made it clear she liked to laugh. He liked to hear her laugh.

She didn't answer the question. Instead, she drank deeply from the bottle of ale, like ale was her best friend. She didn't use the glass. She didn't intentionally put the bottle to her lips in a sexually suggestive way, but Edward felt a twinge of arousal anyway. After she drank, she held the bottle in both hands, like a child holds a security blanket.

She said, "I think I'm supposed to say something. But I don't know what. Are you married?"

"She died," said Edward. "Not looking to get married again. Ever."

The waitress brought their order of paella and they waited until she had set it out for them.

"Oh, I'm so sorry," said Linda. She said it like she meant it. "Most of the guys who answered the ad are married and want a girlfriend on the side. Sometimes they lie and say they're divorced or separated. And they're usually overweight, bald, old and lonely. Some lie about it, but most just want to play – you know." She didn't pick at her food, or pretend to be coy. Instead, she picked up a shrimp and bit into it hungrily. "Mmm, good."

"Does that bother you?" said Edward. "About them being married?"

"Mostly no. I mean I don't want to hurt anybody – ever . I think marriage is a horrible idea unless you want kids, and then...oh never mind. I don't

106

want to be treated like a prostitute, if that's what you're asking. I mean, I suppose that's what it is when you get down to it, but I won't date a guy I don't like. And to tell the truth, I'm not really looking to date right now. I have some issues to resolve. Social rules are arcane don't you think? Do this, don't do that. Drink this, but don't smoke that. So, what are your vices?"

"I'm unconventional about things," said Edward. "Pragmatic. Antisocial, I suppose. I go against the grain, sail into dark storms to see what will happen. Are those vices?"

"Not to me," she said. "So, what's your take on being a prospective sugardaddy?"

Edward smiled, "Like I said, boyfriend-girlfriend, husband-wife, hooker-client, there's very few distinctions. Money, companionship, sex. It all gets mixed up. So if you and I make an arrangement, it wouldn't be a monogamous thing for you, I'm guessing."

"It depends," she laughed. "It could be. For a while anyway. I'm not the marrying kind. Did it once and it turned us both into miserable people. I'm probably not the monogamous kind either. Is serial monogamy a crime?" She laughed. "I'm guessing – but I don't think you're monogamous either. So, what kind of work do you do?"

He smiled. And waited and said nothing.

When it was clear he wasn't going to say anything, she added, "It depends on if we have a good time together. Something tells me we might have fun. How long, is another matter. I have a thing for older guys who are tall and have big hands and long fingers. And there's the other thing I don't like to talk about."

"Money," he said.

"I don't like to talk about it. I mean, I'm broke. Have bills to pay. I'm horrible with money, but I don't want to be one of those girls who's just out for your money. I know it's screwed up. I'm not very good at this, am I?"

"I'm still here, so I guess you're doing okay," he said. "So, you don't want to talk about money, and you don't know what kind of an arrangement you want to make. But you think you might like me. Right so far?"

"Uh huh," she said. "I'm looking for a real job too. Just in case you know somebody who wants somebody like me who's good with customers and cares about doing the right thing. " Her eyes said things Edward hadn't heard in a long time. He decided a man could get lost in those eyes and in her smile.

"Suppose you tell me about your current arrangements," said Edward.

"Suppose," she said, "we finish eating this delicious paella first. I wasn't hungry a while ago, but right now, I'm starving. I'm dying to try one of the mussels in here. Besides you were late and it won't hurt you to wait on me for a bit." She laughed again and shot him a genuine smile.

When they'd eaten most of the paella, she brought up her current situation. "Well, it's not like I'm seeing half of Miami, but if my life ever got put into a book, it would be a best seller. If I was somebody in a former life, I was Mae West. Only I'm not famous, or an actress, or blonde. But I have all her sexual impulses. I'm sort of seeing somebody, but I can't talk about it. It's time to move on, but some things are easier said than done. Don't you think?"

"What I think," said Edward, "is I'd like to extend this conversation. I really would like to know you better. I have a little bit of work to do this afternoon. Research sort of. It might take a while. How do you feel about breakfast tomorrow morning?"

She looked disappointed for a moment, then brightened. "Sure, that would be nice. I generally get up and run just before daylight. Not a long run. But it's so nice being out before everybody wakes up. Maybe after a run and a shower?"

"Maybe you could tell me where you go to run, and I'll join you," he said. "I'm still good for about two miles."

CHAPTER EIGHTEEN
NO-LIE RULE

"I'm going to invoke the no-lie-rule on Roger," said Edward.

After spending four days in Miami, he'd headed back to Siesta Key. They were sitting in Chip's office drinking a beer after Chip's last client had gone home. "He lied to me and I'm done."

"You have to be kidding," said Chip. "I got the impression he's painfully honest. I know he exaggerates some, but an outright lie?"

"He hit Linda. He implied, and you implied, he only hit men. Men I can tolerate getting thumped. Women, not."

"Okay," said Chip. His face telegraphed concern and doubt. Clearly, he wasn't prepared for Edward's announcement. He waited a moment, then carefully asked, "Edward, you never hit a woman? Ever? Not even in the strange dives you went into in all those foreign ports?"

"Pushed a crazy woman off me hard enough to send her across the room once. In Buenos Aries. She had a knife and was trying to give me some kind of tattoo. That was self-defense. Doesn't count. I don't do tattoos. What Roger did to Linda, and what he did to her after he hit her. That counts."

"I don't know what that's supposed to mean. Okay, so I'm guessing you got her side of the story. So what happened down in Miami?"

"I went for a morning run with her. She's broke as hell. Reason she's broke and in debt has a lot to do with Roger. Sometimes on and sometimes off with the drug dealer. He's just a black asshole nigger with dreadlocks, a long willy, and ghetto charm who deals drugs, and happened to be handy...."

"Whoa, strong language from a man as fair minded as you," said Chip. "I heard you slap men in public places for talking like that."

"If the glove fits, you can't acquit," said Edward. "You know I'm not a racist. This guy is a piece of trash, regardless of the color of his skin. Good-looking dude, though. I could see how a girl could get a momentary heat. I haven't met him personally. Just watched him from a distance for a few hours. You had his name right. Valmay. Has five kids with a baby-momma and collects welfare on all of them. Baby-momma knows about Linda and hates her but knows to keep quiet. They don't all live together. He just visits Linda once in a while, gives her drugs and she pays him with sex. I don't think she hates it. I'm guessing it part recreational, part boredom, part silent retribution against Roger, and part self-flagellation for her. He pokes a lot of women, but he's particular about who gets to share his bed. He thinks he's God's gift to women. Likes white women. Linda in particular. Linda and college-aged kids. . . . "

"So, he's just as just as monogamous as you are, I suppose," interrupted Chip. He took a long drink from the bottle of beer.

Edward didn't smile. After a long count of ten he resumed, "He's thirty-one. Makes him four years older than Linda. Works as a fry cook at a restaurant on the water. Sells drugs to the manager, the owner, the servers, and a few customers. It makes his job solid for as long as he wants. He's not above smacking a woman around to get what he wants. Likes to play rough. Speaks Ebonics slang. Has this bad-boy image to protect. Owns three or four cars, all pimped-out with unnecessary shiny trim, oversized wheels that appear to be moving when he's at a traffic light. Wheels and tires are worth more than the car. One or two of them run, the others are missing a vital part. You could spot his cars a mile away. Guys like that make it hard for any man with black skin to get a chance at beating the race stigma."

"I'm listening," said Chip. "I take it you and Roger are in agreement about Valmay, except Roger thinks he's gone upscale, and from what you say, he hasn't. He's a piece of shit. So, what's Linda's story? Why do you want to drop him? I take it you had some time to hear her side of the story? Obviously there's more to it than what Roger told me. Oh, and what about the angle of getting her busted on solicitation and tying Valmay to it?"

"Solicitation won't work. She's pliable to an extent, but I don't think Valmay's actively pimping her.

"Back to the reason I'm dropping Roger. You probably got the back story version from Roger. No big deal there. Nice girl from Nebraska. Good family. Only one mental issue that counts. It might, or might not, give her a serious daddy complex. So, she comes to Florida to dry out after flunking out of college twice. She can't resist rock groups, baseball games, party scenes, or dancing. An adrenaline junkie for sure. That kind of girl.

"Nobody dislikes her, except maybe other girls who feel threatened. She's kind of like Hibiscus. Every man wants her. Women probably tend to hate her on sight. She smells nice, but in a different way than Hibiscus does.

"So she comes to Florida. She meets Roger who is charming and disarming and who takes her dancing. I guess he told you, like he tells everybody about how he likes to dance. Evidently he goes dancing five nights out of seven. Drinks scotch neat like I do. Dances barefoot, no matter what, and asks every girl who dances slow with him if she needs to be fucked and can he be the guy to do it to her."

Chip laughed. "He didn't tell me that. But it kind of fits. He's ballsy enough to say that."

Edward continued, "So, they meet, she'd had a few drinks, and she took him up on his offer. They hit it off. Ended up living together. All went well for a while. Roger claimed he'd had a vasectomy, which was a lie. They agreed to an open relationship, which she didn't take him up on – meaning she was monogamous to him. He wasn't."

"Again, this sounds strangely like you and Hibiscus," observed Chip.

"Don't try to sidetrack me," said Edward. "So, they go dancing almost every night. Roger grows some pot on the side. Did he tell you that?"

"No," said Chip. "He neglected to mention it."

"Well, anyway, Linda has been a toker since college. Says it keeps her from being hyper. Her head is wired different. But in a good way. I'm intrigued by her. So, Roger kept her supplied. Or part of the time. Anyway, she eventually gets knocked up and quits with the booze and the weed while she's pregnant. Roger persuades her to stop working to stay at home and raise the twins. She gets hyper – being cooped up like that, especially since she uses weed to keep herself mellow and she'd been cut off.

"At first he tried to accuse her of getting pregnant with somebody else, but when the boys were born, it's clear they're his and he's a proud poppa who lied about being vasectomy safe.

"The whole time she's pregnant, he continues to go dancing most on every day whose name ends with a *y*. They got married a week before the twins were born. She didn't say whose idea it was. Roger clearly enjoyed the way his life was going. He didn't make a lot of money, but Linda was there to keep his bed warm, plus he got to be a dad with a hot meal on the table every night. He had a good deal. She didn't. You get the idea."

"So, where does the breakup come in?" asked Chip, "Or is this really going to be a long, long story."

"So, he gets her pregnant again. After the third baby is born, she wants to go back to work, to school, and she wants some time to socialize too. He gets crabby about it. But the deal they make is she goes out once a week to dance too, and he stays home or gets a babysitter and goes with her – when they can afford it, which she says never happened. Part of the deal was, he goes out once a week, which turns out to be twice, sometimes three times a week, and she stays home with the kids. She swears she was a good mom, but she needed more out of life.

"So, one day in May three years ago, it's her turn to go out, and Roger says no. She goes anyway, leaving him to babysit the kids. She had a few to drink, which seems to be a problem for her, and she's been buying weed from the Valmay guy who keeps telling her how he needs to give her some of his foot-long blacksnake. She claims she was tempted – just to satisfy the bucket list a hippy girl is bound to have – but didn't partake before then.

"She comes home, slightly inebriated – more likely shitfaced drunk, and Roger throws her out. She makes a scene in the front yard and Roger smacks her around. Gives her a black eye. Throws her clothes in the yard and says he'll kill her if she doesn't leave.

"She drives away leaving the clothes in the yard. Cop pulls her over. She has a bottle of beer between her knees and she's crying between sips. He asks her to get out of the car. She says, no thank you. He asks if she has a beer between her legs and she says, *No officer. What I have between my legs is a wonderful green cock named Heinekens I suck on and who doesn't smack me around and won't get me knocked up again. I should have been born a man like you. Would you really like to see what I have between my legs?*"

Chip laughed, nearly spewing the beer he was drinking.

Edward smiled. "You know, I really believe her."

Chip said, "So obviously she got arrested. I found the DUI and resisting arrest charge. But didn't know the circumstances."

"This is where Roger turns into the asshole," said Edward. "He wouldn't bond her out of jail or pay for a lawyer. She was totally homeless and on her own. She'd bailed his nasty ass out of jail three times for getting into bar fights. He hung up on her when she called, and wouldn't pay the cell phone bill, and it got turned off. Laughed in her face about the DUI.

"So, the drug dealer Valmay is the one who eventually bailed her out about a week later. She got in trouble in high school back in Nebraska and

116

the court here in Florida counts that. She still owes attorneys who didn't do a damned thing for her. She's on probation. Lost her license. And she doesn't know where to turn. She doesn't really want to go back to Roger, no matter what the court papers say. She really does want to get back in school. She feels awful about leaving the kids, but she doesn't have any way to raise them as a single mom. So, Roger lied to me and I'm done with him."

"You slept with her, didn't you?" said Chip.

Edward smiled. He took two slow breaths. Chip could wait for two breaths.

"Not yet, my friend. Not yet."

"The *not yet* answer have anything to do with Hibiscus, or the fact Linda is legally a married woman? Or the fact she's the wife of a client?" asked Chip softly.

"Nope. I have no scruples when it comes to sex and pretty women. You know that. Well, okay. I have very few scruples. Your wife is out. Rosemary's grey hair and widowhood notwithstanding, she's a loyal employee of yours. She's out too. The wife or a girlfriend of a friend is off limits. The rest get a count of two. Two seconds to determine if I would or wouldn't. And she's damned good-looking, so it was a short two seconds.

"Like Valmay, I tend to value quality. Besides, you already know, Blackbeard keeps me supplied with all the pretty girls I need when I feel the need for variety. I make 'em show ID if they're close to the border, so I don't get busted for underage, but if they look nice, you know me.

"I'm thinking Linda would be something different. So, I'm waiting. Besides, it's best to decant a fine wine before drinking it."

"Got it," said Chip. "She decanted. Just don't get drunk off this particular variety."

CHAPTER NINETEEN
FIRE THE CLIENT

The phone call Edward made to Roger was short and sweet. "Get your ass to the bar this afternoon after work. We have to take care of something."

Roger read his tone of voice and said, "Sure boss, I'll be there at four-thirty. Anything...."

Edward had hung up already.

At four-thirty, Roger walked into *The Eloquent Parrot*, sat at the bar and waited. No waitress, no Edward, and no Hibiscus in sight, although a few customers were playing darts and drinking beer.

Seconds later, Edward strode through the bead curtain and walked up to the other side of the bar. He wasn't smiling. Roger was.

"Your bar tab comes to forty dollars and change, plus a tip. That includes your dancing visit the other night while I was down in Miami. You can pay me now. I'm ending our agreement. I'm not decided on the twenty-grand thing yet. You lied to me about Linda. I warned you about lying."

Roger kept the smile, but slid off the barstool. He didn't reach for his wallet. He clenched his hands into fists on top of the bar. Edward, on the other side of the bar, didn't break eye contact, but his hand slowly slipped around the ax handle he kept there for handling unruly customers.

"So? What lie?" said Roger. "Yeah, I been thinking I ought to own up to a few things. I'm not a saint. But neither is she."

"You neglected to tell me about growing pot to sell."

"I quit growing it when she got pregnant. I only sold it to wetbacks anyway," said Roger. "She got knocked up, she swore off pot. I quit growing. Was too risky anyway."

"You slapped her around, the night you threw her out," said Edward. "Gave her a black eye."

"I did. Well, I slapped her once. Knocked her down. Baby sitter cancelled. She threw a fit. I told her not to go, but if she had to go out, she should take a taxi instead of driving if she was going to have a drink. She promised me she wouldn't drink. Drove home drunk anyway. I shouldn't a hit on her. Just slapped her, I swear. Then she said some crappy stuff, and I boiled over. Whenever she has something to drink, she gets started spewing nasty stuff and won't shut up. Keeps saying stuff, on and on and on. Stuff a woman shouldn't say.

"Edward, she just wouldn't stop. Said I was lousy as a husband and lousy as a father – which I ain't. Said stuff about sex between me and her which a woman shouldn't say. So, I told her to go to hell and never come back. She wouldn't shut up so I slapped her, and she finally shut up."

"So, she didn't run off on you," said Edward. "You lied."

"She ran off with that *n*.. with that drug dealing, *Nnnni*…you know."

"The guy she went to Miami with, is a piece of shit," said Edward. "But the piece of shit bailed her out of jail, which you didn't," said Edward.

"Boss, I swear on my kid's lives. I swear. I only wanted to punish her so it wouldn't happen ever again. Teach her a lesson to never forget, I really did. I wanted to leave her in jail for a week, to show her she shouldn't drink and drive again. But when I went to bail her out, this Valmay guy had already done it. I swear. And when I tried to find her, I find she's living with him and moving down to Miami," said Roger. "I knew it was over."

"And you lied to me about Valmay being a major drug dealer, pimp player and her prostituting herself and underage girls," said Edward.

"Boss, that part is true. She told me. She said Valmay had gotten a better job working on the water and was selling shit to upscale dudes. It pissed me off. She said she had her own place and he was welcome to come bone her anytime he wanted, on account of he bailed her out and not me. She said she liked it from him. When she gets mad, she starts saying stuff that makes a man crazy. I swear," said Roger.

"So when did all this happen?" said Edward. "What you say she said to you."

"On the phone. It was about a week after she ran off to Miami with him. I called one night. She had the phone turned back on by then. I'd been calling every day, just to see if I could find out she was all right, you know? I wanted to try to make up with her, but she was mad at me and I guess he was there with her and they were partying and having sex. She was probably drinking. Wasn't a good phone call for either one of us. Never talked to her again. My pride couldn't take it. Maybe her pride made her say stuff too."

"You swear she said those things?" said Edward.

"I swear. She said them. And I'm not proud of it, but I drove down there and by chance, I found her Expedition and followed her around for a day. She had a suspended license, but she was driving anyway. That's when I saw that asshole, Valmay. He was all dressed up and got in her car and they drove off to the hood. I barfed my lunch at the side of the road and came on home.

"Look, I saw what I saw. But I can't pretend I really believed everything she said either. Maybe she was drinking or was still mad at me. Look, I didn't own up to hitting her, but I never said one way or the other. Anyway, it was the only time ever. But I would have taken her back. Truth is, it wasn't going to work out between me and her. She's from a good family. I'm just trailer trash trying to make do. She deserved better. But she damn sure doesn't deserve to be with that *ni...ni...n*...drug-dealing asshole. See??? I didn't even say the *N* word on account of you. I'm trying to follow the rules. If you fire my Irish ass, then I got to do this on my own. My kids need me here,

122

not in jail. You know I'll fuck it up if I do it my way. I'm asking...."

Roger dropped the painted smile. Edward put the ax handle down behind the bar.

"There *is* something you can fix – without going to jail," said Edward.

"Name it," said Roger.

"You lied to Linda about having had a vasectomy. You told Dewey the same lie, didn't you?"

"Guess I did," said Roger.

"Fix it," said Edward.

"Ok, I'll tell her when I get home. I swear," said Roger.

"No. Telling her won't fix it. Get the vasectomy," said Edward.

Roger sat back up on the barstool. He didn't smile. He and Edward looked at each other, eye to eye. For a full minute, neither man blinked. Finally Roger smiled and relaxed.

"Okay," he said. "I'll tell Dewey when I get home I'm not exactly safe that way. I'll tell get her to find a doctor who can snip me. I'll get snipped. I'll get some rubbers on the way home to use until I get cut. So, do we still have a deal?"

"It's possible. One other thing we need to talk about...."

"You slept with Linda," said Roger. "I can tell. Can't say I didn't see that one coming from a mile away. You're the kind of guy she would go for.

She likes 'em big and tall. Can't blame you for wanting her. She's a lot of woman."

"Nope. Not yet. Probably will though. Got some details to take care of first," said Edward. "You two are done. You said so. You got a problem if we get intimate?"

"Be easier for me to handle," said Roger, "if you would smile when you say it. I think I could be okay knowing about it. Especially if you take that guy Valmay out. The one thing makes me crazy is to imagine her and him doin' it."

Edward smiled.

Roger smiled back.

Roger said, "So, do I need to settle the bar bill now?

"No. We'll take care of it later," said Edward. "You still got a tab running. I think I can say Valmay's days with Linda are just about over." He turned and went back through the beads.

Roger sat for a moment longer. He looked over at Blackbeard and said, "Thanks Bird. I'm glad you didn't say something to mess it all up. I was in deep stuff there for a minute." He took out his billfold. He thumbed through his money, then opened the plastic folder where he kept his pictures. He took the picture of Linda he'd been carrying since they first met and pulled it out tenderly. He looked at it, sighed, then carefully laid the picture on the bar in front of Blackbeard, turned, and left.

From the end of the bar where she'd been watching and listening, Hibiscus moved towards

Blackbeard like a black ghost. She picked up the picture of Linda and stared intently at it. Looking casually over her shoulder to be sure she wasn't being watched, she palmed the picture and walked away.

As she moved away from the bar, Blackbeard whistled. Then he recited a few lines from a Crosby, Stills and Nash song that played on the jukebox from time to time.

So we cheated and we lied. And we tested
And we never failed - to fail
It was the easiest thing – to do.
You will survive being best-ed
Somebody fine - Come along-
Make me forget about loving you.

CHAPTER TWENTY
TAKE THE LADY
FOR A SAILBOAT RIDE

"That day we met," Edward said, "you were dangling your feet in the water and looking at sailboats. You like sailboats?"

He was driving down Interstate 75, headed towards Alligator Alley, then on to Miami, while talking to Linda on the cell phone. She had just finished her early morning run. They'd talked on the phone once or twice a day ever since they met – just so he could be sure she was doing all right – or so he said.

"God, I wish. I've never been on a sailboat. Been dying to go out on a boat ever since I got to Florida. Funny thing is, I moved here from Nebraska so I could get away from snow in the winter and be near the water all year long. God, I love the water. I'd do anything to go out on a boat. Any boat. You have a sailboat?" Her voice went up hopefully as she asked.

"Better yet," said Edward. "I have a friend who has a sailboat. It's always better to know a guy with a boat than to own one, believe me. He keeps it at the marina where we met. I was thinking about picking up some Cuban sandwiches, a soda or two, and going for a sail this afternoon after I take care of a little something. You interested?"

"Are you kidding?" she laughed. "Where, when, and what do I wear? I'll bring the beer."

"Slip number C-169. About three hours from now. Bring a swimsuit if you want, and probably a long-sleeved shirt. No beer. No drugs, not even weed. Might want to bring some sunscreen though. You have nice skin, but there is such a thing as too much sun."

She laughed. "No beer? You didn't mind buying an ale or two for me when you bought me lunch."

"No beer," he said. "I was plying you with liquor so I could get to know you. That was different."

He hung up, then looked at his watch. He had plenty of time to see a man and still make his date with Linda.

CHAPTER TWENTY-ONE
WHO-YOU?

"Hey, buddy!" Edward's voice boomed.

Valmay jumped as if he'd been shot.

Edward was standing in Valmay's back yard inside a mismatched wooden fence with barbed wire strung along the top.

Just before Edward called out to him, Valmay had his head down as he was getting ready to put the key into the car door of his current ride, a five-year-old Honda Civic with a dropped chassis, low profile tires on oversize chromed wheels.

"I bet you think you look good in that car," said Edward. "Actually you just look silly. Trying to be bad, I mean."

Edward figured it was early in the day for Valmay, twenty minutes short of high noon. Men in Valmay's line of work tended to sleep late.

"Huh?" said Valmay. "Who-you?"

Edward smiled. His timing had been dead on. He'd surprised Valmay. Nobody should be in a man's backyard but him and his cars.

Valmay patted the knife he had clipped in his shorts like a gunslinger from the old west patted his gun – a *tell* for Edward. No doubt about it. Valmay wasn't a playah, he was a low level dealer wannabe.

From the size of the knife clip and the way Valmay patted it, Edward was pretty sure he knew what kind of knife it was. He had one just like it.

Years of time on boats with a rough crowd and time spend it foreign ports had taught him about knives.

Razor sharp and heavy, it opened with a fast, spring-loaded click at the touch of a lever and at four and three quarters of an inch long – it was legal to carry. Cut a man once or gut him if necessary in a fight – then get rid of it. Valmay probably used it to intimidate and threaten women too.

"Need to share something," said Edward.

"Wrong dude muthafuckah. Get your nasty, white ass outtta mah yard,"

Edward smiled, then let it go. "Actually, you're right. I'm not your buddy. I'm a teacher. Got a few important things to share. Then I'm gone. What you do after is up to you."

Valmay didn't respond. He pulled his droopy shorts high enough to get a firm touch on the knife, adjusted his white wifebeater tee shirt to cover the front of his shorts, and glared at Edward. Fifteen feet separated them. About the right amount of distance and time to get the knife out if needed. Edward saw the motion and mentally shrugged it off. He had a knife too – and training. And experience. Valmay would not fare well if he went at Edward.

"You been banging a friend of mine," said Edward. "Girl named Linda. You been selling her favors to guys that likes white pussy. You been selling drugs and shit. You're done with all that. Remember you heard it here first. A man's nuts cause him a lot of problems. I can fix that for you if you don't start behaving."

"Wrong mothafuckah! Ain't nobody talk lak that to me. Get your stinking cracker ass off my place before I cut your throat," said Valmay. "Law says I can."

"See there? I knew you'd say that." Edwards smiled with his mouth, but his eyes stayed cold. "I'm the law now. Law is giving you a last chance. Last chance or not, I'm sure you're going to ignore what I want to teach you. So, I'll jump right to the good part. Here's what's going to happen," said Edward. "You're going to stop. One way or another, my black brother, you're going to stop. Don't go anywhere near Linda. Ever again. Ever. Don't call her. Don't text the girl. If you see her by accident, then you run the other way like hell. Like I just told your black ass. One warning is all you get,"

With that, Edward Teach turned, opened the rickety wooden gate that now had a broken hasp and lock, and vanished.

Both men knew he'd be back. Both had different outcomes planned for their second meeting.

CHAPTER TWENTY-TWO
FIRST SAILBOAT RIDE – EVER

The sun warmed their skin as the wind steady at fifteen knots kept them comfortable. A few white clouds skidded above as the sails billowed fully.

Edward brought the Cuban sandwiches and a six pack of diet Coke. He'd also thrown a towel and some other bare essentials into the cabin below. Linda had foregone the beer, but she'd mentioned it again just to be sure he meant it.

It took him only fifteen minutes to get underway.

They were sailing north along the coast, two miles out, nicely making way – going nowhere, or anywhere they wanted, or so Edward said. They were on an almost new thirty-eight foot boat, under full sail.

"I brought a swimsuit," Linda said, "but it's one of those swimsuits nice girls don't wear in public places." She laughed nervously. "I've never worn it before."

"And you want to put it on, but you're being coy about it, and I'm supposed to convince you somehow," he said, "so you don't feel guilty when I'm overcome with lust and ravish you repeatedly as I become drunk at the sight of your minx-like charms."

"I was hoping," she said. Then starting another topic, "Do you talk like that often?"

"Only when I'm under the influence," he said. "No beer necessary today." Edward gestured to the hatch. "Go below and change if you like. Take your time to check out the layout of the cabin. I think you'll be impressed. The boat is equipped for long voyages. Overnighters too."

"Are we going to spend the night on the boat?" she said.

"We might. Let's see how this afternoon works out. There's an inlet a few miles up, then there's the intercoastal waterway. I'll bet I could find a place to anchor. That is, if I am overcome with lust at the sight of you and your alleged swimsuit. And of course, if you are similarly inclined."

She laughed. "Captain Teach, I like you. I like you a lot. Oh, look there!"

As she spoke, a pair of bottle nosed porpoises jumped playfully close to the boat and surfed in the abbreviated wake of the boat slipping through the water.

Linda squealed and giggled as she watched them frolic. She crawled carefully on the bench seats in the cockpit as the boat tilted slightly, then stood close to Edward, who was standing behind the large stainless steering wheel minding the sails. Without saying anything, she held on to his bicep to steady herself and leaned close to the rail so she could watch them play. Wonder and joy lit her face.

She released her grip for a moment when she became so enraptured she jumped up and down and clapped her hands in glee.

The porpoises seemed to know they had an audience and cavorted with each other and the boat, showing off, sometimes jumping clear of the water, sometimes simply surfing in the wake of the boat.

The porpoises stayed with them as they sailed north, eventually leaving them with a backward dance, heading for another boat on the horizon.

By the time they reached anchorage, it was clear no swimsuit show was required to convince either of them an overnight stay on the boat was absolutely necessary.

CHAPTER TWENTY-THREE
BEHEADING A COCK

In Tampa, two blocks south of Interstate 4, just a little bit west of the Ybor district, the projects begin. For the most part, what happens in the projects doesn't concern the police or the middle-class residents of Tampa. Cubans, blacks, and islanders blend and merge cultures including illegal gambling on animal fights. Cock fights, dogfights and occasional unlimited testosterone moments when bare-chested men go at it until one of the contestants is pulled from the impromptu ring – unconscious, were there part of normalcy.

Just before dark, a tall, attractive, black woman with short hair, a hibiscus behind her ear, and an empty fishy smelling wire-bound crate that looked like a ghetto cat carrier in her hand walked into a cigar shop not far from the bus stop. Her posture, facial expression, and gait all screamed *attitude*. She asked the proprietor if Willy was in the back. Willy was in.

"I wan' de meanest, baddest cock in de place, mon," she said to him. "And don't even go dere about tryin' jookin wit me if you want any wet wet for de next ten years. I put a sure hex on you if you do, make you buddy soft lak bread not cooked. I not in no mood for funny tonight."

"Momma," Willy said, "don't come round here telling me what I do. I don't care shit about what Voodoo you got. It doan work on me. I got one fine

134

fighter and one scrappy gonnabe. Not for sale." He slapped his hands together twice in a rubbing motion as if to knock dust off of them.

Fifteen minutes later, the woman walked out of the store with a fighting cock in the wire cage. The bus driver wouldn't let her on, but a cabbie agreed to take her home if she paid upfront. It was a long, expensive ride, but she paid.

Two hours later back in Siesta Key, behind *The Eloquent Parrot*, Hibiscus donned her ceremonial garb and approached the crate. She skirted her neatly tended herb, vegetable, and flower garden, and repositioned the crate until it was just so. The thoroughly irritated fighting cock glared at her as she knelt before the cage in mediation. After a few moments of meditation, she put her hand into the crate, suffered a sharp bite from the bird, ignored it, grabbed the rooster by the neck and pulled it out. Her face bore no emotion, no anger. Indeed, she intended for the bird to bite her.

She swung, then twirled the bird in a circle, like a softball pitcher before the throw. One full revolution, then she reversed and wrung its neck breaking it, so it began to flap its wings in a death throe like the devil itself. No noise came from the mouth of the bird, for Hibiscus had clamped her hand tightly over its beak. The only sounds were the frantic flapping of wings and the muted base notes from the jukebox playing inside *The Eloquent Parrot*. Somebody had found In-Godda-da-Vida on the jukebox.

While the bird thrashed and quivered, she pulled a straight razor from a pocket sewn into her robe, held the bird down with one knee, swung the blade open, placed it on the underside of the bird's neck, then pulled sharply up and away – liberating the head of the rooster from the writhing body. She grabbed it by the neck and directed the nubbin spewing blood into a wine glass she'd taken from behind the bar. As the blood flowed, she put the cock's head into the drawstring leather sack she used as a purse, then removed the feet and claws with the razor and wrapped them with a yellow shawl. She put them into the purse too. When the glass was half filled with steaming purple-black blood, she placed it on a small shrine in her miniature garden.

Reverently holding the now limp carcass of the dead fighting cock, she opened the wirebound crate wide. As she walked back to the garden and her shrine, she put the carcass of the bird - breast up - into the rectangular crate. She began to murmur a chant as she tied the bird inside with a piece of thread.

She tied the bird, one leg first, then the other, to opposite sides of the inside of the crate. Then she tied the stubby wings similarly, so when she was done, the bird was spread-eagled, headless, and upside down. Carefully, she plucked the small underbelly feathers out from the tail up to the ribcage until white skin showed, inviting an obscene invitation to view the bird's anus and stubby tail.

"Somebody not gonna lak dis, I tink. White powder bad for white ho's, I tink. Hard lesson to learn, I tink."

With the bird tied in this obscene position, she took out the picture of Linda that Roger left on the bar. Sticking it through with a long hatpin, the then jabbed it into to the featherless belly of the cock. Satisfied, she threaded the metal tang that served as a cheap hinge and closed the crate.

She returned her attention to the blooded wine glass at the altar in her garden. Kneeling reverently, as if she was in church, in front of the wine glass, she said the Lord's Prayer in English – backward, quite quickly, one word at a time. Then she massaged her wound, and squeezed and squeezed it until it began to flow again. She added her blood – a few drops only – to the contents of the glass. Then she said the Lord's Prayer forward, in French Creole.

CHAPTER TWENTY-FOUR
TEN FEET SHORT

Edward kept his cell phone turned off all afternoon as he and Linda sailed and played together. He often kept his phone off for hours or days at a time. The smartphone, a miniature computer really, was a useful tool, but the battery ran down quickly, so he often preferred to leave it turned off.

After the bottle-nosed porpoises abandoned them, Linda needed a kiss. Edward obliged her. One kiss led to another.

Laughing after ten minutes of kisses, he said, "Maybe you can go forward and loosen the anchor from where it's secured. I can drop it into the water from here in the cockpit."

They were just outside the channel in the intercoastal waterway.

"Show me," she said, "how you do all this by yourself. What do the different colored ropes mean?"

Edward turned the boat into the wind, letting the sails luff loosely.

"In a minute," he said, "the boat will drift backwards. The anchor will hold the bottom and I can furl the sails. If the boat doesn't take anchor, we can tighten the sheets and sail back to where we want. Then I try again." He pointed to the lines that rattled along the decks like agitated snakes. "Sort of a safety measure."

At that moment, the boat pointed into the wind and stopped. She'd caught tight on her anchor.

Edward loosened two sets of lines, and tightened two more. First the jib sail, then the main sail rolled up onto themselves.

"See? Not hard at all. It takes a minute to figure out which rope – they're called lines on a sailboat – does what. But once you know that, you can do practically anything you want without leaving the cockpit."

Linda's eyes focused on his. "Are you going to…?"

"Yes, I am," he said. "Come here, little minx."

She giggled.

Sometime after dark, and some highly effective lovemaking, they remembered to be hungry and devoured the Cuban sandwiches and soda before resuming hard, sweaty, sex play.

The following morning they made love again, more slowly, but with sure intensity until they were sated. Again, as they had the day before, they discovered they were hungry afterward.

Fortunately, Edward had some additional provisions stowed away. And they made do with what they found.

After they'd eaten a breakfast of fried canned spam, strong coffee, tinned crackers and a granola bar, Edward took a moment to power his cell phone up. He found three messages, one was from

Rosemary, two others from Chip. All said the same thing. He needed to call in – immediately.

He excused himself to go up into the cockpit to deal with whatever Chip wanted, leaving Linda below to clean up.

"Something's up," said Chip when he and Edward made cellular connection. "I got a call from Judge Bean's clerk. He had an opening on his calendar in three weeks and Linda's attorney affirmed he's ready to proceed. They scheduled it over my objections. If we aren't ready, he plans to award Linda attorney fees and fifty percent of the upcoming settlement.

"It gets worse. Since we actually received Roger's claim to his brother's estate, which it now seems I'm required to probate, they want temporary custody of the kids, and four thousand dollars a month for child support. Roger doesn't even gross that amount! They refuse to give us an extension. I've spoken to his clerk three times. She said if I ask again, the judge will find me in contempt. Obviously, I haven't told Roger about this."

"Edward, Linda's lawyer, Simon, and the judge both assume I'll have to default and then appeal his decision. Of course I'd win an appeal, but in the meantime all hell would break loose.

"Doesn't make any difference, I guess. We both know I'm not going to go to court with a hand full of dry air. But I need help."

Edward heard Linda humming below. He closed the companionway to ensure he could continue the conversation without being overheard.

Linda heard the companionway close and took a moment to power up *her* cell phone. There was a message from Valmay. *juss got sum sweet white. Somthin extra 4 u 2 C u tonite aftr wrk.*

She shook her head and laughed, then closed the phone with a loud click. Edward was talking to someone on the phone up in the cockpit. She couldn't hear what was being said, and didn't really care. She started humming a tune she liked but couldn't remember the name of. For the moment she was happy. Valmay could wait forever for all she cared.

"The sudden rush plus the ridiculous amount of four thousand a month says a lot," said Edward. "This judge has got to be on somebody's payroll. I can't get Linda to talk about her other life. She's too frightened to end whatever arrangement she has going with her puppet master. Barely admits the existence of Valmay. Says she wants out, but won't say who the main guy is.

"It isn't Valmay. He's her go-to guy for drugs and some recreation. That's all there is to him. I gave him fair warning, but I'll probably have to be more persuasive. I'll be done with my persuading in a few days. Do I need to come back up there in the meantime?"

"This is your case," said Chip. "It's your call. How's the honeymoon going?"

"Smartass!" said Edward. "Actually, she's genuine. The real thing. Very sweet. Too bad there aren't more girls like her. We'll probably be here the rest of the day. I need to ride her hard until I find out who her daddy is. Don't take that statement the wrong way either. If I find who her arrangement is with, it might help lead us to the judge's connection. Worst case I'll get back to Siesta Key this afternoon, or if things continue to go well, I'll be back there tomorrow or the next day. I hope I have some answers. It depends.

"Regardless, I really need to get back to my place so I can research more about The Judge. Maybe I can do some magic and figure who or what has leverage over him. I need some time with my computer at home. The laptop I have with me doesn't have all the tools I need."

"Linda, I'm sorry, but we gotta head back," said Edward after the phone call. "It's going to be a fairly easy sail, and we can sit in the cockpit and talk some. There are some things that need to be aired."

"Do we really?" she said. "I'm in heaven right now. Please don't spoil the moment. I know, I know, you have to get back to wherever it is you go I have no clue about yet. So, are you going to tell me about the mysterious you?"

"No, and we aren't going to play mysterious Linda much longer either. Time to play hardball. Sorry. I have some questions."

"We'll see," she said. "I don't really like the term *hardball*. I want to know more about you too. We can trade questions, maybe?"

"Trade questions? I suppose that's fair. Me first. Your bone formation. Suggests Native American," he said.

"Wow, you're good," she said. "My dad's curse. My mom's more Irish."

"You like to drink, but you don't handle it well," he said. "You smoke weed on a regular basis and it hurts your schoolwork and any jobs you get."

"Ouch," she said. "Okay, it's true. Still a daddy curse. An Indian thing, you know. So, what about you? What's your background? Errr, besides having a dead wife?"

"No siblings, two parents like everybody else. We don't talk. Religious differences. I don't believe. They do.

"You're delightful to be with, when you're not drinking. So why drink?" he said.

"I drink because...," she paused. "Because I just do. No fun to be the only sober person in a party. Drink, drugs, both the same mostly." She shrugged, and looked at him through the corner of her eyes, not directly. "I'm in control of the drugs, so don't start in about it. Weed is safer and better than alcohol. I'm ready to give it up, but not right this minute. I only do the other stuff once in a

143

while. Sometimes I need something to let my inhibitions go completely away so I can party. I can't not party, ya know?

"We agreed, I get to ask questions too. Do you work on a sailing boat, or the commercial kind?"

"I used to do the sailboat thing. Then commercial. Not anymore. I do something else now," he said. "That day we met. You told me how you got to Miami. About the husband Roger who threw you out. You told me you had to leave your kids behind. How much does that bother you? Leaving the kids behind, I mean."

"A lot. A whole-fucking-lot. I know Roger is a good father. I just haven't figured out a way to share the kids. Sometimes, I think about driving up to Tampa and just snatching them away, but that's stupid. I couldn't even take care of them. So I don't think about that. I thought you said you wouldn't judge me." She got up from where she'd been sitting and moved to the other side of the cockpit, crossed her arms over her chest and put her feet together.

"I'm not. I won't. I don't do that. Look, this isn't easy for me. I have some stuff to tell you, but I need to know some stuff too. Do you *really* want your kids back?"

She spun on the boat cushion turning her back to him. "Of course I want them back! Of course. But I can't. I know that, okay? It eats me up inside. I'd be a rotten mom to them. Roger is a good dad, I know that. I just told you. Stop it with the torture.

144

Why are you tormenting me like this? Why can't we talk about something else?"

"I told you, I fix things sometimes," he said.

"Not this, you don't. Who the hell do you think you are anyway, Edward Teach? A person with real feelings wouldn't ask me this stuff! Why are you making me talk about this and ruining our day?"

"Sure, I have feelings. And yes, sometimes I'm a bastard. But I'm not being mean. Really. I have a reason to ask. I think I can do something…."

"Is that so?" she snapped. "Why rub my nose in my shitty life? It's my own damn fault, I know. I own that. But…"

"So, what do you want?" he asked. "You want your husband back?"

"No. We aren't good for each other. He's a fun-loving, Irish jokester from the wrong side of the tracks who likes to drink scotch some and dance a lot. He works really hard – for a really nice guy, and when he isn't working he likes to dance barefoot you know, and he thinks he can sing Irish drinking songs, but he can't carry a tune no matter how drunk he is. He loves the kids. I love the kids. There's no way I can be a mom and a student and have a job and take care of them and be anywhere near to him without being mad at him for being happy all the time.

"No, I don't want him back. I'd just like to see my kids sometimes and hug them till they cry out. Just sometimes, ya know?"

"So, let's work on this. You got a lawyer?" he asked.

"Of course," she snapped. "I got lawyers hanging on coat hangers all over the place. They all send me bills on a regular basis, trust me. I got lawyers. I got a lawyer I pay a hundred dollars a month to – that will never get paid off on account of my DUI. I got a lawyer trying to expunge my assault charge for resisting arrest – which I didn't do. I got a lawyer for my unpaid bills who charges me more than my unpaid bills amount to, and I can't even afford to pay him to file bankruptcy. I got a lawyer who is skinny and ugly and had acne when he was a teenager and he still does, and he's filed papers to get me divorced from Roger, but he never will. He has roaming hands and bad breath and I let him take me to bed when he wants because my special friend says I should. So I do stuff and I drink and use some drugs so I can do it. And you know what? I'm still broke and I'm still married, and I still can't see my kids even once in a while, and you aren't going to change any of that." Her voice broke with the last sentence.

"So tell me about your special friend," said Edward.

"Fuck off," she said. "My life is my life. You're blowing a perfectly good day and a perfectly good chance of keeping me around by asking all this stuff."

Edward sat and said nothing. She was shaking with anger and in no mood to be talked to.

Linda stormed down into the cabin and said nothing.

After fifteen minutes, she came up from below and said, "Take me home, and don't talk to me anymore. You're just like all men. I hate you."

"I'm very much in the process of taking you back," he said. "Sailboats are slow. Look, I have something you need to know…"

"I'm totally not interested," she said, keeping her back to him.

Another forty-five minutes passed without a word being said. As the marina came into sight, Edward said. "I'm going to bring the boat in. I can take care of the docking process by myself. Just sit still until I finish tying up, okay? If you try to help me, you could mash a finger, or twist an ankle, or hurt your leg. Happens a lot. Just wait, okay?"

Linda didn't respond.

One at a time, Edward furled the sails. Then he started the small diesel engine to bring them in.

He could see her tensing up, getting ready to disembark, presumably without a parting word. He pulled the motor into neutral then gently slipped into reverse, bringing the boat to stop ten feet from the walkway of the boat slip.

"One more thing I need to tell you," he said. "You won't like it. But I need to be honest with you. I like you. I like you a lot. A whole lot. I really, really do want to help. And I can. I really can. Probably in a different way from the arrangement you have now, and at first it might seem strange.

"Look, before I met you, I took on a client. He's the reason we met. I'm trying to do the right thing here."

"You son of a bitch!" she spat as her eyes opened wide with comprehension. Her face was contorted, bright red. "You're working for Roger, aren't you?"

"I am," he said.

"Put this boat next to the walkway, so I can get off, or I swear to God, I will jump off and swim home," she screamed. Tears streamed down her face.

Edward wordlessly slipped the boat into gear. As soon as the boat was within jumping distance, Linda got up and walked to the bow rail where she vaulted over and landed on the walkway. She walked with measured deliberate steps the first one-hundred paces, then ran as hard as she could until Edward couldn't see any more of her. He looked to see if she'd glance back over her shoulder. She didn't.

Nice job Cap'n Teach, Edward said to himself as he watched her turn the corner. *Nice damned job!*

As she turned the corner, she opened her cell phone and texted Valmay back. *tonite is fine. Bring white. I need.*

CHAPTER TWENTY-FIVE
LUBRICIOUS LIBATIONS

Six hours later, Edward strode into Chip's office in Sarasota. Rosemary looked up and smiled. She always smiled hopefully at Edward.

He didn't smile back. "He in?"

"He's dictating some notes for me. I can...."

Edward didn't let her finish. He walked to Chip's office, opened the door, then dropped into the leather sofa to the right of Chip's desk.

"I don't suppose," said Chip, "this would be the best time to say something snappy about protocol and being nice to Rosemary or letting me do my job without being rudely interrupted."

"No, it would not," said Edward. "Now is the time to look at the clock on the wall. It's five o'clock somewhere and I am tired and in the mood for a scotch."

"Just guessing," said Chip. "Did the honeymoon come to an abrupt halt sometime after our phone conversation?"

"It did. Abruptly. I repeat, it's five o'clock somewhere," said Edward. His face had not even a hint of a smile.

"It's four o'clock here. Close enough. I'll buy the first drink. After that, we need to go to my favorite watering hole. I'm sure we'll both brighten our moods when we see Hibiscus."

"A drink first," said Edward, gesturing to the sideboard that had a decanter with scotch in it and glasses ready to pour it into. "I need to talk for a minute. This all doesn't add up."

An hour later, Edward, Hibiscus, Rosemary and Chip were at the captain's table at *The Eloquent Parrot*. A *reserved* sign lay on its side. The table itself was on a raised platform, a holdover from a time when live bands had played in the bar.

"This entire conversation is off the record," said Chip, looking directly at Rosemary. "Cindy is not to hear a word about it, directly or indirectly."

"Boss," said Rosemary, "So long as you don't flirt seriously with Hibiscus intending to sample Edward's private treats – ever again, your wife will not hear it from me. My lips are sealed forever. Edward, however, is free to proposition, or flirt with whomever he likes." She smiled hopefully at Edward.

All four broke out into laughter, Hibiscus included. With only a raised eyebrow by Chip as their signal, they lifted glasses, to touch together in an unsaid toast. Chip and Edward were drinking Scotch. Edward preferred unblended single malt scotch, Glenlivet. Chip was happy with Johnny Walker Red. Hibiscus was drinking Jamaican ginger ale, and Rosemary was drinking iced tea.

"Boss?" said Rosemary, "We're engaged in a conspiracy of some kind, I'm guessing. Your wife isn't allowed to know about it. But, exactly what's the conspiracy?"

Chip said nothing. Edward said nothing and let his eyes glaze over. Hibiscus touched her bare foot to the inside of Edward's thigh and said, "My Cap'n been to see de wife of a frien'. Took her to bed, he did. He doan feel bad bout doin' it, but it not turn out de way he wan'."

Chip didn't ask Hibiscus why she presumed to know all this. He simply nodded. "Four heads are better than one, Edward. Lay it out for us, maybe there's a solution."

"I broke one or three of my own rules," said Edward. "I knew better. Should have approached Linda directly with the truth the first time I met her, like I did with Valmay. Direct is better. Always. But I didn't. Perhaps I was planning to set her and Valmay up like you and I discussed. I don't know. I was direct with Roger. That part was okay. Maybe I was afraid of . . . ."

"So, Linda doesn't know you're working for Roger?" asked Rosemary.

"She does now. And she's pissed about it. Big time. Probably thinks I stabbed her in the back, which I haven't. I mean, I needed to know about the circumstances of her fight with Roger. Needed to know it's over between them. Needed to know about her status relative to her kids. She wants and deserves visitation, somehow. I thought if I got her to say all that, I could propose an idea to her and she'd redirect her attorney. But something tells me she's only marginally aware of what her attorney's strategy really is.

151

"But more than that, I needed to know who her lover-sugardaddy is, which I don't because she won't even think about talking about it. And I haven't a clue about why Judge what's-his-name...."

"Edward, you never forget anything," said Chip. His name is Judge Bean."

"... why Judge Bean has taken such a hostile attitude," continued Edward. He picked up his glass of scotch, let a spoonful of it spill into his mouth and rolled it around before swallowing it. It wasn't his first drink. He slurred the last few words.

Rosemary said, "It's clear as a bell to me I'm driving Chip home. Am I going to drive you home too, Edward?"

"I takin' care de Cap'n tonite," said Hibiscus. "He gonna need some of my magic I tink. Up in my room."

Ignoring the women, Edward continued, "She said she was sleeping, or had slept with her lawyer. A disgusting man, she said. Because her friend said to."

"You have to be kidding me," said Chip. "R. Shuster Simon, has got to be one of the slimiest, dirt-bag lawyers I've ever sat in the same room with. If he even thinks she has some money coming, he'd go for that first. Why would her sugardaddy make Linda take him to bed? That's messed up! And for her to comply proves he has a powerful hold on her. Simon is disgusting!"

"She a pretty girl," said Hibiscus. "Doan need no ugly man."

Edward turned to Hibiscus. "How do you know what she looks like? Have you seen her?"

Hibiscus stared wordlessly at him.

"Roger has a picture of her in his billfold," said Chip. "Did you see her picture, Hibiscus?"

"Not so important da picture," said Hibiscus. "Good prayer. Bad prayer. Dat important. Maybe de girl not such a bad girl — you know? Some lesson maybe, nothing dat kill her forever."

"Yes or no, Hibiscus," said Edward. "Did you put a spell on her?"

Hibiscus looked at him with large liquid eyes. Her foot ran up his thigh to his groin under the table top. She put her hand on his arm. "No diff-er-ence," she said. "You doan believe in dat stuff."

Rosemary's eyes got big. "Oh my GOD! You did. I think I have to go to the lady's room." She got and left the table.

Chip took a strong hit of scotch from his glass. "Something tells me my ride home is leaving shortly. Now, it's probably the scotch talking, but I have to say something anyway."

"No holding back now," said Edward, glaring hotly at Hibiscus. "Hibiscus is putting Voodoo everywhere but where I need it and I'm very drunk and very tired. What sage advice do you have for an old sinner like me?"

"No advice," Chip said. "But consider the possibility, however weird it might sound. What if our not so friendly Judge Bean is in fact Linda's lover, and the man who has this strange hold on her and who pointed her to the disgusting R. Shuster Simon, Esquire?"

"Dat could be," said Hibiscus. "I need a picture of dis mon."

Edward said nothing, broke his glass-etching stare, clenched and unclenched his fists. He got up and ambled towards his office. He walked as if he was on a ship in a storm, wandering back and forth across a pitching deck.

Hibiscus followed after him.

Rosemary came back to the table from the ladies room in time to watch them depart. "I have never seen that man drunk before," she said.

"It's time to take me home, Rosemary," said Chip. "I have not had quite as much to imbibe as yon Captain Edward Teach, but I am not far behind. The effects of lubricious libations, are steadily giving great warmth to my soul. So I surely must be chemically challenged too. Cindy will *not* be pleased! I think I shall blame it on you this time." His voice was slightly slurred.

Rosemary giggled. The sun hadn't set and both men were down for the count. At least for several hours.

As the door closed behind Chip and Rosemary, Blackbeard said in a loud voice for the patrons of the bar to hear, *All vodka corrupts. Absolute vodka corrupts absolutely. Scotch whiskey makes you frisky.*

154

CHAPTER TWENTY-SIX
CAN'T UNDO A HEX

Rosemary's opinion notwithstanding, Hibiscus had other ideas about Edward's immediate needs. Following Edward to the top of the stairs where she lived, she walked behind him into her living quarters until the door closed behind them.

Expecting him to bed her, she started to walk to the low pallet made up neatly covered with hand sewn quilts where she slept. He caught her halfway there, spun her around and slapped her hard across the face.

"Undo it," he said. "Undo it now!"

"But you doan believe," she said. Her hand went to her cheek. "An' you hit me!"

He'd never hit her in anger before. Always before, if there was roughness it was during sex, playfully administered, necessary to both their needs. She held her hand to her face where he had hit her and walked backwards as he came at her.

Her scent was hot in his nostrils. Somehow it made him madder. "No, not this time, you don't," he said harshly. "You need to learn it is I who am the captain and you are the one who serves. I want her to be safe, do you understand? Undo the hex!"

Edward grabbed her by the hair at the back of her head and walked her violently backwards until they were at the wall next to the pallet on the floor where she slept. He pushed her violently against the wall, pinning her with his body. She tried to push him away, but he pressed her harder, until she cried out. He picked her up from the floor and held her there, so they were face to face, her feet dangling inches from the ground.

"Tell me the truth," he said harshly. He put his hands around her throat and closed off her air. "What kind of hex did you put on Linda? I swear to God, if you make her die, I will wring your neck!" His breath hot in her face had sour anger and sweet peaty scotch on it.

"Bad Voodoo, Cap'n," she confessed when he let her take a breath of air. "Not to die. Bad juju, but de girl do white powder her own self. She like white-white and many men on her I tink. Hibiscus not good 'bout dis. Hibiscus did bad ting. You fix me, I fix her. Hurt me, then I take it part off de girl. Hibiscus been bad, sure. Doan be mad at me, I ax you."

"You sure she'll be all right?" he said. "Tell me she'll be all right and that you'll never do this again. I mean it!"

She nodded. "No more bad. I gib you dat. Do de ting to me I doan like, she be fine soon. Her smell still on you, yet you hard for me, my Cap'n. Let me taste her on you, den do me da mean way. She not die from de hex, but she hurt some. Dat all I kin do, sure. Hibiscus be your servant again. I supposed to be dat – forever."

In spite of his anger, and the scotch he'd had too much of, her scent made him hard. Indeed, he seldom went to her room without becoming aroused almost immediately. He released his grip on her, then backed away so there was perhaps a foot between them. Her back was still against the wall.

Slowly she sank to her haunches and unbuckled his belt. As she pulled his trousers loose, he grabbed the belt and withdrew it from the loops. With his other hand he took a handful of her hair and pulled her to him so she would have to taste Linda who he'd been with only eight hours earlier.

TWENTY-SEVEN
GOOD STUFF, HUH?

"Sorry Miss, we aren't open yet," said the prep chef as Linda came into the employees' entrance. "Oh, hi Linda. I didn't recognize you. If you want to see Valmay, be quick. The boss has been on our case lately about him selling while at work."

"Hi, Tiny," she answered. "I'll be just a minute. There he is." She had puffy eyes and poor posture. She walked to where Valmay was working.

"So, I got your text," she said to Valmay. "But after tonight, it's better if you don't text me or call me anymore. I'm not sure, but I think I'm being stalked or something. If I need anything, I'll call you. He wants me to move closer to where he is. Says he's going to divorce his wife, but I hope he doesn't. One way or the other, I need a change in my life. I'm probably going to be leaving town for a while. So, what's up about a party?"

"Cain't talk now. Boss bein' a mothafuckah. Got some good white shit. Short little party going down after work. Sumpin new, but you gonna like. Be where my car at. You in?"

"I shouldn't. But, okay. I guess. Why not? Good stuff, huh?" she said.

CHAPTER TWENTY-EIGHT
LOSERS, WEEPERS

"No offense, Miss, but we'd like Hibiscus to be our waitress," said Roger.

The waitress was cute. No doubt about that. And to Roger it didn't look like she'd taken offense. Her smile was genuine enough. "Sir, Hibiscus is the floor manager on weekends. She's behind the bar. If you want her to fix your drinks personally, or if you have some specific requests, you need to go see her there."

"Sure," said Roger. "No problem." He smiled at Dewey, slid out of the booth and went to the bar.

He had to wait for a minute or two, until one of the three barmaids working the bar found Hibiscus. To Roger, she looked different. He wasn't sure what it was. No hibiscus flower behind her ear, but still, she looked different, contrite or something. Her face was slightly puffy on the left side.

It was nearly eleven o'clock. When she got close enough, he said her name, then "Scotch. Johnny Walker Black. Neat please."

She gave him a warm smile, although it was not as quick and not as genuine as it had been in the past. He added, "And an iced tea for my girlfriend. She's driving. Let her have as many as she wants. Cut me off at four, please. It's all I need."

"Runnin' a tab for ya, mon," said Hibiscus. "I keep it here when you wan' de total. Cap'n Teach upstairs taking a nap. He be down shortly. You need 'im?"

"No ma'am," said Roger. "It's our night out. Don't need to bother the boss. We got a babysitter tonight. Gonna dance barefoot and drink scotch. That okay with you?"

"Blackbeard doan mine' Mr. Teach doan mine' I doan mine' neither. Jess you be polite and no problem," said Hibiscus. She put his scotch and a tall glass of iced tea with a slice of lemon stuck on the rim in front of Roger. She gave him another smile. This smile was warmer. Whatever had bothered her before seemed to have passed. Her smile made his heart skip a beat.

"I tink ah need to brink you some ah de house spe-cial," she said. "Man lak you wan some special cabbage lak nobody else make but de Cap'ns cook. Maybe some dat hot-hot cooked meat wit spices you git lass time. Got some Jamaican curried goat if you wan'"

"Sure, bring us some Cole slaw and curried goat. Sourdough bread too please." He paused, then added, "Ma'am, I'm not trying to be fresh with the boss's lady, but you smell awful good. Can I ask what perfume you use, so I can buy some for Dewey?"

Hibiscus leaned forward on the bar so her breasts showed cocoa cleavage. Roger leaned forward to hear what she was going to say.

"Doan use no perfume mon' Doan use no soap. It steals de soul. I wash it wit crush vanilla bean and de bakin' soda and rinse it wit pure rainwater, mon. Dat de truth. Been doin' it lak dat for tree hundret years and drivin' de men crazy wit mah kitty scent dat long too."

Hibiscus leaned back depriving Roger of her cleavage and her scent, laughed an earthy laugh and turned away. Whatever was bothering her before, she was definitely fine now.

When Roger turned to take his scotch and Dewey's iced tea to their booth, he noticed two working men in plaid shirts, dirty jeans, and muddy boots leaning over her - trying to chat her up. They had two-day beards, slicked back hair and were clearly just over the minimum drinking age.

Their intrusive posture and body language suggested too much testosterone, a drink or two before they'd gotten there – and trouble. Dewey wore an insincere smile and was trying to scoot to the back corner of the booth. One of the men was sprawled across the booth from her, the other had a single knee on her cushion and an arm draped over the back of the booth next to her shoulder.

Roger was smiling as he walked up with the drink. "Need to find another place to park your ambitions, guys. The lady is with me."

"Loser's weepers. Finder's keepers," said the guy who was kneeling on Dewey's cushion. He barely took notice of Roger.

"Sometimes," said Roger. "Sometimes, but not tonight. She's with me and we're here to dance barefoot and drink." He stood over the guy who was kneeling next to Dewey, placed the iced tea in front of her, took a sip of scotch, then put it down.

"So, I know you're gonna find somebody else to hit on. Right now."

The guy looked up at Roger. Roger was still smiling his most engaging smile.

"Sure, no problem", said the guy. He stood.

There was barely a millimeter between his nose and Roger's forehead. The man was two or three inches taller than Roger. "Dude, you're gonna have to get out of my fucking face, so I can leave you and your bitch to dance."

Roger didn't blink. He continued to smile. "Say please," he said. "And you can go. But if you say another disrespectful thing to her, or about her – ever again, I will hurt you."

"Please," said the man. He took a moment to do it.

Roger moved aside just enough to let the man brush by him.

The man sitting across from Dewey got out, sniggered, then said to his rude friend, "Guess who just came in?"

Roger watched as clones of the plaid-shirt pair walked across the floor to meet up. They punched one other on the shoulder, raised their hands with fingers spread in some kind of recognition he didn't understand, and moved to the booth behind his. Ignoring them, he pulled Dewey to her feet to where an old-fashioned jukebox was playing reggae music. "Come on hon," he said. "let's dance."

Roger and Dewey danced. Their dancing attracted admiration from the others on the dance floor, although the bar crowd was a true Friday night blend, many loud laughs and a few shrieks came from the various booths. The place was nearly full. Not many of the patrons were interested in dancing, but those that did, had fun. After thirty minutes on the floor, Roger led Dewey back to their booth.

The men who had been trying to chat up Dewey were still in the booth behind them, talking loudly – using the gutter talk of working men who had been drinking.

Hibiscus approached Roger and Dewey's table with a fresh scotch and iced tea. She noticed Roger had barely touched the hot spicy pork and Cole slaw. He'd eaten half the curried goat before he started dancing. Rather than pick up their empty glasses, she smiled, put her fingers to her lips as if she had a secret and turned to the table with the four men.

"You gentle-mons will please come to de bar and pay your tally," she said in her musical lilting voice. "And den you will go home. I call da taxi if you wan'"

"In a minute, Missy," said the man who had been kneeling next to Dewey earlier. "We ain't done drinking yet."

"I will convey dis to Mr. Teach," said Hibiscus. "But he not a man to trifle wit. He ax me to be nice and git your tally."

"Look, you nigger bitch," said the man, "What the motherfucker does for a living don't mean shit to me. If he teaches babies how to crap cookies, I still don't give a shit. Just bring me and my homies another round, and we'll pay up and go – when we goddamn please."

His friends snickered and clapped their hands in slow unison. They were having a good time.

Roger and Dewey heard the exchange. The entire patronage of the bar heard the exchange.

Roger only thought for a second before he said to Dewey, "Be right back. Gotta see a man about some manners." He was smiling.

He was still smiling when he slid out of the booth barefooted, and did a one-eighty on his right heel to stand directly in front of the offensive speaker.

"Lady told you nicely to pay your bill and go," said Roger. "And you're being rude. Real rude."

He moved closer. The same millimeter's space between his nose and the nose of the rude man separated them as it had before. The smile remained on Roger's face. No *tell* in what action might take place next. The man was drunk and had a snarl coming from his mouth, "Look, you sawed off motherfu…"

He didn't finish the sentence. A fist the size of a small ham flattened his nose like a hammer smashing a grape on a hot sidewalk. He barely got an "ooof" out when the fist withdrew, took careful aim, launching again, this time landing between the

164

open mouth and nose of the man sitting across from the rude guy. Both men were done.

Their two friends attempted to stand up to wade into what would surely become an ugly bar fight, when a very tall, very bearded man with long hair and a diamond stud in his ear grabbed the man with the smashed flat nose – by the throat – and lifted. His long fingers circled the man's throat, like it was a bath sponge that needed to be squeezed dry. He lifted him out of the booth and held the nearly unconscious man to his tiptoes. He reached past him and grabbed the man who was sitting next to him, again by the neck, with his other hand. Surprise reigned.

Roger knew teamwork. He tried a sloppy imitation of the hand on the throat trick, but his fingers were too stubby and he lost his grip. He retrenched and opted for a fistful of shirtfront of his two, one in each hand.

Wordlessly Edward Teach and Roger goose-walked the four men backwards to the nearest door, an emergency side exit.

Just as they reached the exit and hit the panic bar, Hibiscus cut the alarm that would normally have sounded, allowing the four to exit quickly and soundlessly. The entire episode lasted less than thirty seconds. The door closed, leaving the sounds of the bar inside. The silence in the alley contrasted sharply with the noise inside the bar, creating a deep terrible moment for the younger men.

Edward dropped his two. They fell like bags of wet horse manure. Indeed, the man who had played the great insulter, lost sphincter control and fouled himself - compounding the image of dung in a sack.

Roger looked at Edward, who gestured for him to drop his payload. Roger let go and his pair sagged to the ground as well.

Only one of the four, the second man Roger dropped, was conscious. He was confused, drunk, and scared. Edward said to him in his booming deep voice, "You gentlemen are hereby excused from ever visiting my establishment again. Your tally for tonight's visit came to sixty dollars. Make it eighty including the tip. Would you like to gather that sum in the next few moments and give it to me willingly, or shall I take sterner measures?"

The sole conscious member of the foursome started nodding his head and didn't stop. He pulled himself to his knees, fumbled with the billfold attached to his belt by a chain. He found four twenties and finally found a lung-full of air. The shirt around his neck had choked him sufficiently to induce panic.

With the money in hand, Edward said, "Which of you is driving?"

"Him," said the man who'd just paid Edward. He pointed to the insulter. "And me," he added.

"Keys," demanded Edward.

The man dug into his jeans and got his truck keys, then handed them to Edward.

"His too," said Edward.

166

Taking a deep breath of exasperation, the man bent over, rolled his friend onto his side, then groped until he found a set of keys.

Edward took both sets, and said, "Keys will be locked inside your truck. His truck will be locked too. Send triple-A to come unlock the trucks tomorrow so you can drive them away – when you're sober enough to do so. Hibiscus has called a taxi by now, take it home. And like I said before, you aren't ever welcome back here again."

To Roger, Edward said, "I never, ever let a drunk get behind the wheel. Ever. Drunks don't drive away from here. I have an arrangement with tow trucks, with taxi cabs and with the local constabulary. Remember that." Then he led Roger to the front door.

As Roger and Edward got to the front door to go back inside, Roger said, "Boss, I didn't mean to cause you no trouble. I swear. These guys were being rude and Hibiscus deserves better than..."

"No trouble," boomed Edward. "Next time, let me get there before you start teaching manners to assholes. I get paid to keep problems down. You don't. You're the customer. Your hand is bleeding where you hit that guy's teeth. Get Hibiscus to clean and bandage it. I'll sit with your lady for a minute."

"Got it," replied Roger. His silly grin was back. Indeed, it never left.

CHAPTER TWENTY-NINE
AIM FOR DE TEETH?

"Dis gonna hurt some, mon. Gonna do it de Cap'n's way, de way he tell me. Not mine," said Hibiscus.

Roger and Hibiscus were alone in Edward's office, next to the kitchen. He looked behind him only once, noticing a half dozen flat screen security monitors that displayed the bar, inside and out. Scarcely a portion of the establishment was unmonitored. He turned back to where Hibiscus was getting her kit ready so she could play nurse. He vaguely heard dishes clicking next to glasses, next to pots, and pans being washed or thrown aside as the lone grumpy cook and a helper kept up with orders taken from the one page laminated menu on the other side of the wall. While she tended to him, he stared at Hibiscus, feature by feature trying to decide what it was that excited him when he was near her.

Her touch seemed to anesthetize him as she held his hand firmly over a white enamel bowl like the one his grandmother had in her wood-framed house. He held his hand still as she poured sterilized water over the wound and probed with a sterile pick until every tooth mark bled freely. That done, she poured hydrogen peroxide over his wounds.

Roger didn't wince.

"You always aim for de teeth?" she asked.

"No ma'am. I usually try to hit a man on the nose as hard as I can. Sometimes I miss," he said. "I'm pretty quick, but my aim is off sometimes."

"You miss a lot, I tink," she said, noting there were many old scars on his knuckles. "You doin' dis a lot, I tink. You a funny man, sure."

"Huh?" said Roger. He was in a trance and felt very little pain.

"You hit dem two mons in de face really fast on account dey rude mons," she said. "I woulda fix dem sure, if you or de Cap'n ain't. Cap'n doan lak de way I fix mons 'bout bein' rude. Dey end up sick for days and days. Wait here, I tink doctor wanna put a needle an tread to dat spot dere. Got some bone on de knuckle pokin' out." She got up and straightened her long skirt.

"Nope. Emergency room is way busy on a Saturday night. It'll heal in about a week. I heal really fast. I swear. If it's bleeding really bad or gets infected tomorrow, I'll go to the emergency room. They're not as busy on Sunday morning. Sit back down for a minute," Roger said, then added, "Please."

"Wasn't talking 'bout no 'mergency room, mon," she said as she sat down. "He sew it. Cap'n Teach know more medicines and stuff dan all dem hospital doctors together. Got learnin', he do. I got magic. He know about doctoring'. I could get him to fix you. Or I could use some Voudu magic, if you be hush about it."

169

"I can keep a secret," said Roger. "What you got?"

Hibiscus smiled, released his hand and walked out of the office, all hips and sway and female smells. A moment later she came back. She had a small tin with a screw top that could have been used as a peppershaker once upon a time. Holding his hand palm down, knuckles up, she looked into his eyes and raised her eyebrows.

He nodded. She held the tin over his hand with her thumb and three fingers, then tapped it with her index finger until a brownish power fell onto his knuckles. Then she put the shaker away and began to wrap his hand with gauze.

"Be all fine dis time tomorrow, mon," she said.

As Roger returned to the table, he found Dewey telling Edward what a sweet, but very precious and precocious little girl Clarissa was. His hand felt remarkably fine.

CHAPTER THIRTY
DIS (IS) HOLY WATER NOW

"Your cell phone," said Roger, "it's buzzing. Just thought you ought to know."

Edward yawned, then patted his pants pocket. He didn't retrieve the phone. "Yeah, a friend in Miami who's still mad at me, thinks I'm still down there. Been sending me text messages. I'll look at them tomorrow. It's been a long day and my head hurts. I'd still be asleep if Hibiscus hadn't signaled me those boys were getting unruly."

"Me too," said Roger. Turning to Dewey, he said, "Hon, you're driving. I only had two scotches, but it's time to go. That okay with you?"

She nodded, then gave her biggest, brightest smile to Edward before scooting out of the booth to join Roger.

"Want me to settle up yet?" Roger asked Edward.

"Not yet. Still running a tab. Catch you later. Thanks for helping out. Remember, next time wait for backup," said Edward.

As he waited the wait all men must endure while dates or wives, or the lady of the day collects herself, Roger cast a glance at Blackbeard, who appeared to be asleep. Tempting fate, for Blackbeard had not spoken for two full days, Roger said to him, "Bird, this must be a fun place to own. Lots to see."

Blackbeard opened one eye.

171

As Roger and Dewey headed to the door, Blackbird said, *"To be sure of hitting the target, swing first. Then call whatever you hit – the target."*

It was late, nearly time to close up, and Edward was exhausted. The short nap he'd had after having sex with Hibiscus had given him a brief reprieve, but a day that started nicely with Linda, then turned sour with Linda, followed by too much scotch with Chip, a confrontation with Hibiscus and the aftermath, as nice as it was – had done him in. And too, the rude rednecks had been the final leg in a long endurance race. He was tired to the bottom of his soul.

As he looked for where Hibiscus was, his phone buzzed again. He opened it, didn't look at the screen and then turned it off.

Hibiscus was behind the bar, closing the register. When she finished, she whispered something to the girl helping her. The girl smiled and nodded. Hibiscus patted her on the shoulder and went through the beaded curtain. Edward followed. He went into his office to sit. She walked with an exaggerated hip movement to the stairs leading up to her apartment above the bar. Evidently, she presumed all was good now she'd accepted a ritualistic sex punishment.

Twenty minutes later, Edward had brooded enough. He walked to the stairs and mounted the first step loudly. It creaked the same creak it always did. As he got to the top step, he grabbed the doorknob and turned it without knocking. When he opened the door, he saw her bathing herself next to the kitchenette.

"I'm going to Miami to see a drug dealer," said Edward.

Hibiscus was standing nude in a large washtub washing herself with a pitcher of clear water. The water ran off of her in rivulets, splashing into the washtub loudly like rain on a tin roof.

"Fine Cap'n. I finish my bath and mind de bizz-in-ness while you gone. Dat what you wan'?"

"Please do," said Edward. "I'll be gone for two or three days. I would appreciate it if you stayed close by. Do the drum circle if you want, but no more trips to Ybor City, no more spells, no more magic or incantations. Okay? You promised me. And you lifted your spell or whatever about Linda. No harm will come to her, right?"

"Da girl not choke. Her neck be fine. She gonna live long, sure. Maybe sore some, but she gone be fine by and by," said Hibiscus.

"What are you saying? She's all right, isn't she? You promised."

Hibiscus stepped out of the washtub, picked up a towel, and began patting herself dry. "I promise, Cap'n. Some spell get started, not stop by and by. But she not die, for sure. Maybe you bring her to see Hibiscus, and I say I grief for what ah done. I do dis for you only, my Cap'n. Odder girl for play some maybe? "

"Probably will bring her back here. But first the drug dealer," he said. Changing subjects, he asked, "I know how you feel about letting your bathwater go to waste, but why you take such pains to save it? It seems like an extreme to me."

"Potty water best go where de sun not shine," she said. "Dis water is holy now. It belong on de flowers dat grow fine in de back where I make my potions and say mah prayers."

"Cap'n?" she said.

He watched as she patted herself dry. "Yes," he said, and yawned.

"Be a good ting if you go down dere all 'appy an fresh. Maybe you lie wit me for a while and go dere in de morning. You eyes need to close for a while."

"I think," he said, "that's a very good idea."

CHAPTER THIRTY-ONE
SOME LATE VISITOR
ENTREATING ENTRANCE AT
MY CHAMBER DOOR

Not long after two a.m., Edward sat up, not quite awake, with an ugly start. A very unhappy dream clung to the cobwebs in the corners of his darker brain. Even as he sat up and tried to remember what the dream was about, he couldn't piece it together. Stella, the ghost of his wife was in it, but why? Chief was there, and the memories of whales' bones that littered the beach off of a remote whaling station on an island near the Falklands haunted him. All else was darkness and bad.

Hibiscus lay on her side facing him. As he moved to a sitting position on her pallet, she whispered, "Bad Juju been visit you, my Cap'n. You stir and dance asleep. My bad. De ghosts say to go fine de girl you breed odder day and fix tings."

"Some late visitor entreating entrance at my chamber door," he mumbled. He was not yet awake. He added, "This it is, and nothing more."

Hibiscus watched him dress in the dark. As he pulled his boots on, she sat up, legs folded underneath her, expectantly. "Cap'n," she said. "Dat you juss say. It from a poem. You wake now?"

He didn't answer her. He walked to the door, slipped out of *The Eloquent Parrot* and drove in the still of night to his condo, a bit more than a mile away. He was the only traveler on the beach road.

CHAPTER THIRTY-TWO
THE LADY IN DE CAR,
SHE DEAD.

He cleared his head by taking a long hot shower followed by a long cold one. Taking his time, he packed an overnight bag. He thought about his black box, the illegal one, and decided he didn't need it. Not yet anyway.

He drank a cup of cold coffee, left over from days before and grimaced. Then, to make sure he'd stay fully awake, he downed a five-hour energy drink.

He headed to the door, then stopped. Quickly bringing up his cell phone, he checked to make sure it was charged.

This was a pickup truck trip, not a Mercedes trip. Perhaps she'd need to move some stuff out of her apartment.

He didn't bother to read Linda's text messages or listen to her voicemails. He'd seen the first text message from her. It reminded him of a seventh-grade girl who was pissed at one of her parents. Most likely the others would be echoes of the first. She was probably still pissed when she sent them.

She should be cooled off by the time he got to Miami. And with Hibiscus's hex removed – real or not real – there was really nothing for him to worry about.   After all, he'd been with Linda in the sailboat just twenty-four hours ago. A very long twenty-four hours, but still, she couldn't come to any harm in the short time she'd jumped ship and run off into a parking lot in a snit.

He drove until he was looking directly east and into the sun on Alligator alley. When his eyes burned so badly they started involuntarily closing, he promised himself he'd stop for a break and a cup of coffee at the first opportunity. If he got there in time, he could join her for a morning run and work things out.

But when he got to Miami and Linda's neighborhood, she wasn't anywhere on the path where she did her early morning run. Edward checked twice. She'd told him her morning run was a ritual, one she never, ever departed from. Start at six, run until seven-thirty. They'd run together three days ago. It had been good to run with her. It showed him she was capable of self-discipline. It wasn't seven-thirty yet. She should have been on the running path.

He would have preferred to surprise her, talk it all over as adults in person, but since she wasn't doing her run, a phone call wouldn't hurt.

He pulled her number from the contact list in his cell phone. Evidently her phone was turned off, because it went immediately to voice mail. He remembered from conversation with her, Linda didn't listen to voice mails, so he didn't leave a message.

Just slightly concerned, he went to her apartment.

Her SUV, an older black Ford Expedition with cracked leather seats and faded hood paint wasn't in her designated parking place. The running path she used was close enough to her apartment to walk to. So the SUV should have been there. Returning to the running path, he followed the entire path one more time. Still no Linda.

Puzzled and more worried than before, he returned his attention to his cell phone. It was time to read all the text messages she'd sent and he'd ignored, and not read.

The first one was one he'd already read. *"Your mean. I don't ever want to see you again."*

She'd sent the second one, three hours later. *"I'm sorry. I lost it. You deserve better. Call me, k?"*

The third one said, *"Are you still in town? I need a friend to talk me out of doing something stupid"*

The fourth was sent while he and Roger were teaching manners to some young rednecks. *"I think I'm in over my head. Call me, come get me. Can't drive."*

The last text message was sent at three in the morning. It simply said, *"help...please..in trouble..."*

After a few moments thought, he realized she must have presumed he was still in Miami, instead of six hours away.

He drove his pickup truck back to her apartment. At her front door, he saw her mail had been opened and then sloppily stuffed back into the mailbox. The front door was unlocked, yet she wasn't home. If she'd gone for a run, her car should be there, yet it wasn't. He walked through her apartment. Apparently, she'd started packing but had stopped halfway through. His heart rate increased another notch.

Opening his phone, he brought up the same app – a software program application – that used the GPS unit in her phone he'd used when he was watching her at the sailboat basin to locate her cell phone. As long as the battery was in the phone, the app would find the location of her phone, even if it was turned off.

It took him thirty minutes to locate the phone – and the Expedition.

Her car was in a rundown section of town, parked under a sad looking oak tree a block from the projects. There were five or six teenage kids, some black, some Hispanic, standing on their toes, trying to look into the Expedition through the side windows.

All but one, a black kid about thirteen years old, took off like they'd been doing something bad and didn't want to get caught. They ran off as Edward got out of his truck.

"You a cop?" the kid asked.

"No," said Edward. He was trying to stay in slow and calm mode. Yet his heart was racing – afraid of what he might find. He continued his trek to the Expedition, still in deliberate slow mode in spite of his heart rate.

"Then you might wanna call the cops," the kid said. "The lady in de car. She dead. Dead, or fucked up bad."

Edward approached the Expedition, and peered in the back window the young men had been looking in. At first he didn't register what he was seeing. Then it came to him. It was Linda. She was in a most unnatural position. She was on her back – tied spread-eagled in the back of the SUV. The back seat had been folded down. Her head flopped back unnaturally, falling under the console next to the driver's seat. Her legs were open, fixed so her knees were bent and pulled towards her shoulders. Her feet were tied at the ankles. The rope at her ankles looped up inside the cargo area across a ring for hanging clothes, then joined to pantyhose tied around her thighs above her knees. In this position, as many men who wanted, could use her like the proverbial chicken in a basket. Clearly, many men had. Her sex was exposed. Her arms were tied with rope to the inside grip on the front doors. She'd been wearing a short pullover dress of some sort, but it was pulled up over her face and head. She was naked from her breasts down, save a pair of sneakers. There were scattered patches of blood on the soft material of the pullover dress.

"Go on home," said Edward to the youngster. "You don't need to see this."

The youngster took off as if he was in a track meet.

Edward returned to his truck, opened a first aid kit, put on latex gloves as he walked back to the Expedition. He pulled at the door handles. All four doors were locked. Linda's keys were in the ignition.

From his side pocket, he pulled out a heavy knife on a clip. Like the knife Valmay carried, the knife had a spring-actuated blade and could be used for a variety of things. However he didn't open the blade. Instead he used the butt end of the knife where there was a very short, hardened steel point. Covering his eyes, he punched against the safety glass of the driver's side rear door. He had to hit it three times before the safety glass crumbled into thousands of tiny bits.

He reached inside, unlocked the door and crouched over Linda. Several tiny packets of white powder, presumably cocaine, lay scattered on the floor behind the passenger's seat. He reached under the console touched her neck, feeling for her carotid pulse.

CHAPTER THIRTY-THREE
FORGIVE, TIMES TWO

"Eloquent Parrot Bar and Grill. Jasmine speakin'. What can I do for ya' mon."

Edward whispered into his cell phone, "Jasmine, get Hibiscus on the phone. Now."

"Yes, Cap'n. You all right? You sound trouble."

"Now, Jasmine," said Edward.

It was a full minute before Hibiscus picked up the phone. "Cap'n?"

"Get Cookie to take you to the bus station, Hibiscus," he said curtly. "Right away. Bring enough clothes for two or three days. She's beat up pretty bad. For once, I think I believe you really did put a hex on someone. This – I blame you for – and you're going to have to help me fix it."

"Yes, my Cap'n. I do et now. We short on hands now, what you wan'…"

"I'll pick you up at the bus station in Coral Gables," he said. He closed his cell phone with a click, ending the call.

The click he made with the phone startled Linda.

She lay on her bed curled in the fetal position opened one eye, and moaned lightly. She opened her other eye, saw Edward and closed them both again. Edward sat in a chair three feet away.

He'd planned to make peace with her, find the man who had been supporting her – if that was what

183

it was called – and extricate her from his grasp. Now he had different priorities.

"I'm awake. Sort of," she said without opening her eyes. "Where are we?"

"Glad to see you decided to come back to life," he said. "You had quite a night. You're in your own bed for the moment. After you return to the land of the fully living, and I'm sure you're all right, we're going up to Siesta Key for a while. Then we'll see."

"What time is it?" she asked.

"It's a few minutes before three," he said. "In the afternoon. You've been in and out of consciousness since I found you."

"Don't hate me," she said. "I fucked up. Bad. Really bad."

"Figure of speech," he said. "But yes, I know. You got seriously fucked. You had help though."

"If I didn't hurt so bad, I'd laugh. You have a way with answers, you know." Her voice croaked harshly and he had to lean forward to hear her.

"I know," he said. "Sometimes."

"I'm sorry," she said.

"Me too." He poured a glass of water, held her head gently as she sipped, then put it down.

"How'd this happen?" she said. "Okay, stupid question, but why would Valmay...? He's my friend, sort of..."

"He never was your friend. Ever. Valmay got you, got me – got us – by surprise. I should have known. My fault too."

"Just tell me you don't hate me," she said. A single tear waited at the corner of her eye.

"I don't hate you," he said.

"Don't bother with the long answer, then," she said. The tear took that as an excuse to make its escape and ran down her cheek.

"Take your time," he said. "Don't get weird or panicky. Wake up, then sit up. You need to finish waking up before anything else."

"I'm still sleepy. Fuzzy headed. Tell me you didn't call the law," she said.

"I did not call the law."

"Should I see a doctor or something?" she said.

"You have," he said. "After I found you, I brought you back here, examined you and cleaned you up. Nothing major hurt. You have a few small cuts. I put some antibiotics on them. You'll heal up in a few days. Not too much doubt about how the cuts and bruises got there. A few bruises around your neck, arms and legs too. Your knees and ankles in particular are going to be hurting for a day or so. Your vagina is also going to be sore for a while, but nothing is torn or damaged. You really ought to tone it down on the kinky roleplay, though."

"Shit," she said. "Not funny. You know way too much then."

"I can guess," he said. "You couldn't resist one last line of coke. Made you want to party. Valmay planned this, you know. Maybe he figured if I found you all messed up like this, I wouldn't want you after he'd had his fun. He was wrong.

"He knows I'm going to be pissed, and he's probably waiting for me to come find him expecting to take revenge. No doubt, he'll have some friends with him to put me away, because that's the way he thinks – ghetto warfare and all."

"He'd do that. He thinks he's tough," she said. "But he doesn't know anything about you. So he doesn't know who to look for or, where to look. This was all my fault. I was mad at you, or Roger, or maybe just mad at life. I was mixed up. So, I partied with Valmay one last time. Just a line or two. Then it got out of hand. Whatever it was he gave me was way stronger than usual."

"He knows who I am now, which is fine by me. Valmay is dirty. He's gonna pay," he said. "You know what a roofie is?"

"You said he thought you wouldn't want me," she said. "Why'd you say that?"

"Because just before we went out on the boat, I went to his house. I told him to leave you alone," he said.

"Oh shit," she said. "Men always fighting over me. Supposed to be a good thing. But I don't think so anymore. Sorry, that isn't funny. I'm still fuzzy. Yeah, he has his illusions about owning white girls, me in particular. He's not the only one, either. Men seem to want to own me."

186

"Somebody you haven't met seems to have helped out in other ways. She's gonna pay too, but not like Valmay."

"My head hurts. Tell me about that part you just said – some other time, okay?"

"Some other time," he said. "My bad too. I guess I could have found a better way to try to talk to you on the boat. Not to dwell on this, but how much of the rape do you remember?"

"Wasn't rape. Not to begin with. But he and his homies kept egging me on, and that coke he gave me was really hot. As it got more intense, I was aware, but couldn't stop it. I hollered I'd had enough and…. Oh wait! I remember. He made me take one more drink when I said I was done - to stop. Said something like *All fruits be ripe. Yo Cat tanks mi laddah.* His friends laughed at him for trying to talk like a Jamaican, but I wasn't sure what it meant.

"Wait! A roofie? He gave me a roofie? That's mean. But he's like that. Sleazy when he's in a mood. I'm so stupid. I can't believe I…."

"We can talk about it later," he said. "Or not. I'm going to get you situated, then I have something I need to do. Here's a bottle of Gatorade. You need to sit up and stretch anyway. Work the kinks out, so to speak."

"Very funny. Thanks for taking care of me. A girl could get seriously attached to you, you know," she said. "I'm not going to ask how you found me or why you're taking care of me. I'm just grateful.

So, if you're working for Roger, why did you come get me?"

He ignored her last statement. "Take your time. Drink the Gatorade. Drink it slowly. You need to re-hydrate. I have to go to the bus station in a while. I'll bring back something to eat. Just be sure you're here when I get back."

"Not to worry about that, my friend. I'm not going anywhere, but where's my Expedition? I think I need to take a nap again."

"Your keys were in the ignition. You were locked in there. Somebody was going to have to break the window or call a locksmith to get you out. So, I broke in. You were tied up pretty seriously. You might have died. There were several small bags of coke on the floor. Just enough, I'd guess, to rate a felony charge for possession if a cop wanted to overlook you being tied up and raped like that."

"Tied up?"

"Tied up," he said. "He wanted to make sure... whoever found you...knew what happened to you. Wasn't any doubt about it, the way you were tied up. Sport fuck to begin. Rape to prove a point, at the end."

"I wasn't tied up when he gave me that last drink," she said.

"I won't keep on about it, but with your heritage, alcohol is not your friend, and never will be. Easy to hide a roofie in a drink. "

"Okay, I got it. Just don't rub it in today. I'm hungover and fuzzy still. So, what about my Expedition? Where is it? It's old but..."

"It's fine. I put a garbage bag over the window I had to break, to keep rain from getting in. Put it in pretty good with duct tape. A friend of mind is storing it for you."

"Thanks. You really *are* taking care of me, aren't you?"

Before Edward could answer, she'd gone back to sleep.

He checked his watch. The bus would be in soon. He left a note for Linda on her dresser. Then he drove his pickup truck to the bus station.

**

It was dark and the streetwalkers were working.

She didn't have a hibiscus behind her ear. But she was standing at the taxi curb at the bus station with a carpetbag by her feet waiting for Edward to pick her up. She wore blue jeans, a seldom-made concession to the twenty-first century. Yet, as a holdover to her beliefs of who she was and her image, she wore a homemade coarse cotton peasant shirt – dyed yellow, braless, wearing sandals she'd made herself.

He pulled his truck, passenger side to the curb and unlocked the door. She got in. Neither of them spoke.

He drove to a motel three blocks away that had a boring plain sign that said *Comfort Inn*. The motel rented rooms by the day, or week – probably by the hour if requested.

Neither Edward or Hibiscus had spoken.

"Sit here," he said. "I'll get a room for you."

He got out of the truck, turned the ignition off and removed the keys. He'd never before left her in any vehicle without leaving the engine running and the air conditioner on.

Fifteen minutes later, he returned. "Come with me," he said.

Hibiscus got out of the truck and followed him to room number seven. The room had jalousie louvered panes on the door, and a cheap window air conditioning unit that hummed loudly and had green mold around the casing.

Edward opened the door with a key that had a plastic fob with a return address and instructions to drop it in a mailbox if found. There was a single bed in the middle of the room, terrazzo floors, a yellow tiled bathroom with a dripping showerhead. A small television sat on an unfinished plywood stand bolted to the wall. The room didn't appear to have been remodeled for fifty years.

"I doan lak dis place," she said softly.

"Well then, it appears we have things to talk about then," he said. "Things we like and don't like. I don't like what you had those men do to Linda," he said. "When we discussed this yesterday, you promised you'd undo any hex you put on her. Obviously, you didn't."

"You been sayin' you doan believe," she said. "So what I do, doan matter."

"I'm a man of science. A true man of science knows when to admit there are things beyond his understanding. So, don't try to play word games with me about what I believe or don't believe, or what happened, or who made it happen. We both know you wanted to hurt her and you did. Do I have to describe to you how she was tied up and the things those men did to her before I found her? Shall I tell you what happened? It looked to me exactly like the dead chicken trussed up inside a fish-crate somebody hid in the bottom of the garbage dumpster. Shall I describe the details, Hibiscus?"

"No Cap'n," she said. "I start de fire. De light a day make me see et fine. I know dey done bad tings wit her. I know what de ashes smell lak."

"Hibiscus, I have no room in my life for a jealous woman."

"You throw me out?" she said, "forever?"

"I'm considering it," he said.

"I do good ting some de time. Be a good slave girl for ya'. Lemme try more time. I fix your friend hand where he hit dem bad boy in de teet lass night. It better today. You ax him. Hibiscus got good spell too. Please Cap'n, doan throw me out." She stood ramrod straight, arms at her sides. Small involuntary hiccups made her shake. She didn't try to approach him, nor did she cry out, yet twin streams of water ran down her face.

"We can't go on forever," he said, "pretending to be something we aren't."

"We been Cap'n an slave tree hundret year," she said. "You doan believe. An I know it true. You said jess now, some ting you doan understan'. You save me from de slaver. Den you save me from bein' da whore for de crew. You let me serve you fine and free. When dey cut de head off dat man what dey thought Blackbeard, I save you den. You been shot five time and you still live, 'cause I fix you lak I fix your frien' lass night. I save you den. I hide you in de small-boat. Maybe you doan remember, maybe you do. Tink on it Cap'n. You promise me den to keep me forever. We still in dat time – forever."

Edward sat down on the bed. He bent forward, put his elbows on his knees and rested his face in his hands, face cast down.

"Hibiscus," he said through his hands. "Dear Lord, what am I going to do with you?"

"Possible?" she asked, "Dat a man who know what you know, know it without know how much he know?"

"No word games," he said.

"Cap'n," she said. "I an old, old woman. A witch. Jess for you. You born and die over and over, but always you my massah. Just gimme dis. One time. Look at mah back." She stood and untied the homemade twine that held her peasant blouse together. She began to lift the blouse over her head.

"Hibiscus," he said. "I've seen you naked many times before. Now isn't the time to seduce me with your body and your scents...."

"Dat so," she said. "You evah see dees whip marks befo'?"

She turned and stood with her back to him.

There, where for three years there had only been flawless smooth black skin, he saw raised scars crisscrossing her back like erratic tiger strips – where a whip had cut her cruelly once upon a time.

"Jesus, Joseph and Mary," he exclaimed. He stood up abruptly, then sat down again.

"Possible?" she asked, "dat tings not always what you tink dey are?"

"Yes," he said very slowly, "it's possible."

"Cap'n," she said. "Tell dis ole witch what you wan'. Den tell me I kin still be de grateful slave of Cap'n Teach. Dat all I wan'."

"Put your blouse back on," he said.

She walked to him, still holding her blouse in her hands. "Any-ting you want, my Cap'n. Any-ting. Forever in dis life and lass life and next life. Any – ting."

Her breasts were level with his face. They were the breasts of a young woman, not the breasts of a three-hundred-year-old witch. Her scent circled him like steamy fog covering a boat cast adrift on a windless ocean.

"Perhaps, you're right," he said. "Some things are beyond my understanding or comprehension. It seems I might need to forgive two women for transgressions today."

His fingers sought the knotted string that held her hand-sewn jeans closed. But somehow it had come undone on its own. All she had to do to be completely naked was to step out of the jeans that lay in a puddle at her ankles.

CHAPTER THIRTY-FOUR
A ROOM NOT FIT,
AND FORTY DOLLARS

"You're going to help me do something that needs to be done."

"Yes, my Cap'n."

"The men who hurt Linda," he said. "You know how to find them?"

"I tink so," she said.

"All of them?" he asked.

"I tink so," she said. "Dey many men. More den Hibiscus ax for in my spell. I done bad, Cap'n. Tie me to de mast and whip mah back and I bleed good. Dat be all right wit me."

"The punishment should fit the crime, Hibiscus. I will never hit you again, I promise. I'm not going to tell Linda what you did. Maybe one day you will do that. In the meantime, you find the men who violated her like this. No woman deserves to be used like that, not even if she thinks she wants to be hurt. So, you find them and you punish them. All of them, except Valmay. He belongs to me. Understand?"

"Yes, my Cap'n. I kill dem if you lak. Make it hurt too."

"No. They didn't kill her. The punishment should fit the crime for them as well as for you. Humiliation, emasculation, and a great deal of discomfort is a fair payback. You find a way. Just leave Valmay to me."

195

"Yes, my Cap'n"

Edward walked out of the room. Halfway towards his truck, he turned back and removed his billfold.

"Here's forty dollars," he said as he returned to her. "I passed an open air Cuban outdoor market a mile away. They sell fruits, herbs, vegetables, and the kind of roots you like. Maybe that'll help you some. I'll get back with you the day after tomorrow."

"Yes, my Cap'n" said Hibiscus.

CHAPTER THIRTY-FIVE
SNIPS AND SNAILS,
FISH IN AN AQUARIUM

Ah fixes dem bad-boway, Hibiscus thought when she woke the following morning. *Dat what de Cap'n wan. Dat what ah do.*

She'd slept on the floor of the cheap motel room, sans blankets or pillows. Unless her Captain was in it, she wouldn't sleep on a modern mattress. And since he'd left her to tend to his whore, she retreated to a dark inner primitive piety she'd learned from the ancients as a child. Bedbugs - *bad-bug* to her – dwelt in common beds. Particularly so in cheap motel rooms. Hibiscus had no intention of feeding bad-bugs.

So, when Edward left, she meticulously washed and rewashed a casket shaped spot on the terrazzo floor, then dried it with the worn single bath towel the motel provided until it was a tattered grey rag. Then, with the baking soda she kept in her carpet bag, she washed it again. Finally satisfied the floor was clean enough, she used her carpet bag as a pillow and laid down to sleep soundly and dream of a punishment suitable for *bad-boways*.

Edward had given her forty dollars. Hibiscus never asked him for money. Indeed, she kept only a portion of the tips the patrons of *The Eloquent Parrot* gave her. She was unique, friendly, and efficient in her job. And she was popular with the patrons who tipped her generously. She shared her tips with the cook, the bus boy, and the other waitresses on a purely subjective basis and had a substantial excess afterward. But her needs were almost nil, so once a week, she took a bundle of one and five dollar bills to the local bank to exchange for crisp new fifty and hundred-dollar bills. Money was dirty – yet necessary. When she woke, she divined she'd need some of what was tucked tightly into a compartment at the bottom of her carpet bag to do this spell. In her sleep, she'd formulated a plan.

Common schistosomiasis is a parasitic worm hosted by a snail and found in fresh waters, typically in Africa, Asia, and less so in South America. Hibiscus knew of a variant of the parasite unique to South America - known there as *verga-inu'til* , or *the useless cock.* That particular parasite is found only in the roe of a rare multicolored small freshwater fish found in feeder streams leading to the Amazon. Because of the rarity of affliction, very few incidences of *verga inutil* are reported to the World Health Organization. So, containment, diagnosis, and treatment are virtually unheard of. Importation of the host fish is permitted into the United States, so it is sometimes found as featured fish in the upscale restaurants and hotels along Miami Beach in large freshwater aquariums. Indeed, under normal circumstances, the fish is not a health threat.

She'd seen and noted the fish twice in Sarasota, but had never commented on it to anyone, not even

Edward Teach. As a child in Haiti, she'd been taught how to harvest, the *useless-cock* larvae and how to infect men who raped young girls. She'd watched in awe as a black Voodoo priestess harvested the tiny larvae, so small it took a clean drinking glass with a thick bottom held just-so in the light to act as a magnifier. Then afterwards, she'd seen the man who raped her sister suffer. Hibiscus, like Edward, had a phenomenal memory. She knew what to do.

The parasite, when ingested in larvae form, follows a curious course. The larvae, if dormant, waken in a human colon. Burrowing through the protective lining of the colon until they pass through, they enter the bloodstream, until eventually they find the source of a man's eternal demise – testosterone-rich semen. Rapidly growing in the elixir of a man's motivational fluids, they settle down in the vicinity of erectile tissue and a man's prostate. They gnaw, burrow, consume, grow and form a protective shell-like cocoon in the entire genital region - much to the host's discomfort. In three days to two weeks, an untreated man invariably becomes permanently impotent – hence the name *useless cock.* Coincident symptoms mimic kidney stones, and gonorrhea. A malodorous purulent discharge coupled with extreme difficulty in urination tortures the victim for months. Treatments for these conditions do not help.

Hibiscus began her search with pet stores specializing in exotic fish and aquariums. Few carried the fish Hibiscus sought. Even so, Hibiscus didn't want a live specimen, for healthy fish might not have the parasite worm inside it. She wanted fish that had died recently, or were nearly dead. At the second store she visited, a young female manager recommended Toot.

"Miss," said the girl at the store, "I think the guy you want to talk to is Toot. He buys replacement fish like the one you're looking for from us whenever we have a new shipment come in. He's the best around when it comes to freshwater aquariums and the fish. Doesn't work for anybody, instead, he contracts directly with the hotels and a few of the restaurants that have really exotic aquariums. I can call him for you if you like."

Hibiscus nodded and smiled largely. The girl called Toot from her cell phone and after telling Toot a tall sexy black girl was doing a study on the brightly colored fish, and needed his help, Toot asked her a question or two. Obviously Toot was intrigued. The girl caught Hibiscus' eye, nodded her head and ended with, "Ya, she'll wait. Fifteen minutes?" Then the girl nodded again and ended the call.

While they waited, the girl at the store explained he was called Toot, because he had a single oversize tooth that overhung so drastically it was constantly in sight. He had a slight lisp, and when his friends called him *Tooth,* it eventually got shortened to *Toot.* "But Toot knows fish," she added, "like a

French chef knows spices. This guy is like the fish-nerd of aquariums."

Fifteen minutes later exactly, a white van pulled into the parking lot in front of the store. The manager had described Toot perfectly, so Hibiscus picked her carpet bag off the floor, exited the store and greeted Toot with a smile and a curtsy. And as all men do, Toot fell under Hibiscus' spell immediately. Minutes later, Hibiscus was riding in the passenger's seat of Toot's truck, listening to him talk about aquariums and fish, what they ate and died of, which of his customers paid their bills promptly, who didn't, and about more fish. Hibiscus reminded him of the special fish she sought, and he agreed to get her a few *near death* specimens. He even knew to warn Hibiscus about coming in contact with the fish's roe and intestines.

Before the sun set that evening, Toot had *exchanged* six healthy fish for six not-so-healthy ones in various hotel lobbies in Miami. Then, with just a single hint from Hibiscus it would be nice of him to help her just a little bit more, he happily drove her to the Cuban open-air market where he waited while Hibiscus finished the rest of her shopping needs. Toot would have taken Hibiscus anywhere she wanted without a second thought, yet when she'd shopped and found what she needed, she asked him to take her back to the cheap motel where Edward had installed and left her.

"I won't ever see you again," said Toots, "will I?" He had hope, but he knew the answer.

201

Hibiscus reached across the van and took his right hand. Examining it, then turning it over, then looking at the palm of his hand for a long time where there was an angry festering wound, she pulled it to her mouth where she gently but firmly took the meat of the palm in her mouth and bit it until she left marks.

Toot closed his eyes, as she bit him, but did not cry out in pain.

"Beware," she said, "de scorpion, de lion fish, and de spider dat sleep under you bed. Dis spot here where I bite you now be clean for a long time, but after dat, ah can-not promise." Yet even as she opened the door to leave his van, she continued to hold his hand. Immediately a sense of well-being and happiness filled him.

Inside the motel room, using the barber's straight razor she kept tucked into her home-sewn skirt, she prayed for the fish, gutted them and carefully gleaned a thimble-full of the worm's tiny larvae. Spreading the larvae on a piece of waxed paper, she dusted, and separated, and dusted again with fine-ground cornstarch until each spec was covered to her satisfaction. Into a freshly empty Copenhagen snuff tin, she combined ground peppermint leaves, cloves, cocaine powder and heroin tar she'd bought from a drug dealer at the back of the open-air market. Finally, she stirred in her sleeping larvae. For wrapped snuggly in cornstarch, they wouldn't awake until they found warmth and happiness inside a human digestive system.

CHAPTER THIRTY-SIX
SISTAHS AND BROTHAS

"So, how you feeling 'bout Valmay now?" Taz asked.

"Same-same," said Ishak, "Why you ax me dat?"

"All about him," said Taz. "Jess him. Since that par-tay with the white bitch he say blong to him, he be jumpy. Always want ta git his back covered. No weed, no white fo his homies. Jus about him. I could use a good jolt of sumthin', ya know? Mothafuckah say he out, like I don't know. He lyin'."

"Ya, I'm 'bout ready to mellow out too, but why we talkin' bout it here? And now? Bus station a fine place to pick up strange, but too many fuckin' cops round here tonight. Don't even see no white pussy dat run away from dey momma up north. Dis place be bad for a dude. I got a feelin'."

"You ain't lookin'," said Taz. "at what I'm looking at. Check out the sistah. She's holdin'."

Ishak looked furtively across the terminal. There, he saw where Hibiscus sat, slumped low on a seat set apart from all other travelers, head down, one knee cocked inward.

"Shit, ya'" said Ishak. "She's noddin'. Doan mean she's holdin' though."

"She holdin'. I can tell. So maybe I walks ovah and takes a look. See if she a friendly sistah."

As she said it, he got up to cross the terminal.

"Yo Momma," said Taz as he sauntered over to, then sat down beside Hibiscus. "You sittin' here all by your fine-self, lookin' lonesome. Care if a brotha share this bench?"

Hibiscus slowly lifted her gaze and gave him an unfamiliar smile, apparently trying to be just friendly enough not to cause a commotion. "Free at lass'" she said. "Ah you go. Ah you stay. No difference. Jus' doan ax me for no jookin'. Blood clot soon."

"Oh, I get it. You're an island girl. Look to me lak you medicated your fine-self to ward off the chills," continued Taz. "Maybe you got some left. Help a brotha out, maybe I can help you out. Need a place to hang?"

"Ah doan tink so, my black brotha. I gots no-ting dat be good for you. Ah be ah-rite. Me tanks you jus de same."

"Don't' be that way, Momma. I can tell. You holdin' something me an' my homies want. No point to argue. I could go ovah to the heat standing with his nightstick and his attitude and I could say, pardon me mister office-ah. But that sister over there, she's holdin a lot of smack. Tried to sell me some, she did. But my sistah, dat's not my style. So, what you say? Let's all go fo a ride, par-tay a bit, come back here feeling good. Just a taste of what you got. Dat all we wan."

Hibiscus took on a heighted alertness. The mention of being busted for holding drugs seemed to wake her.

"What ah got, you doan want. It ain' smack. Ah no lie 'bout dat," she said. As she said it, she smoothed her dress in an apparent attempt to cover the three inch round tin in her kangaroo pocket.

"Den give a po' brotha' a taste, and I be on my way." Said Taz.

"One taste," said Hibiscus feigning sleepiness. "Den you go on about your busin-ess? You promise me dat?"

"For real, my black sistah," said Taz. "Promise you."

Hibiscus put a hand into the Kangaroo pocket of her home-sewn skirt. Moments later it emerged with a black pea-shaped ball. She looked around furtively, then dropped it into Taz's hand. "Tuck dis 'tween yo cheek and yo teet. By and by it get warm, den melt. Make you feel fine all day, it will. But jess one. Work fine for de ladies when dey bleedin' but de mon's doan need. Now go way. I gettin' ready to ride de bus be gawn, sure."

Taz tucked it in his mouth like a redneck looking for the buzz off of snuff. Within seconds he got a silly grin and began to relax. Instead of leaving Hibiscus alone as he said he would, he slouched next to her and let his hand fall in her lap.

Sleepily, Hibiscus picked his hand out of her lap and let it fall between them. She let her head fall to his shoulder as if she was nodding off.

Taz slowly slid his hand into the open kangaroo pocket of her dress and grasped the snuff tin.

Looking across the terminal he caught the eye of his friends and smiled.

"Momma," he said, "Gotta leave you for a minute. Thanks for the taste."

He extracted himself from contact with Hibiscus, stood, then sauntered across the terminal where his friends waited.

He didn't notice as Hibiscus stirred and wiped her hands with a folded handkerchief soaked in rum to clean them.

By the time he had crossed the terminal lobby, Taz had a silly grin on his face. Derrek, Dwane, Ahmod, and Ishak took on grins too as they read his newly relaxed body language.

"Won't need that mothafuckah Valmay an' the high-priced shit he say he ain't got none of fo' a while," said Taz. "This is some fine shit, my brothas."

Twenty minutes later a bus pulled out of the terminal on schedule. Hibiscus was on it. She didn't have a snuff tin in her skirt. She did, however, have a smile and a carpetbag to accompany her.

CHAPTER THIRTY-SEVEN
ILLUSIONS

Edward and Linda were sitting side by side on a loveseat in her apartment. She had her legs curled up underneath and was leaning against him. His arm was draped around her, holding her lightly.

"We can talk now," he said to Linda. "About issues. If you want to, that is."

"Thanks," she said, "for not pointing out this loveseat needs to be thrown into a dumpster. I got it cheap at a garage sale."

"I'll overlook the coil spring trying to poke a hole in my gluteus," he said.

She smiled and curled closer to him.

"My brain is still kind of mushy," she said. "I mean, I'll talk, if you want to. Tell you stuff. But I'd really like to create some kind of illusion you can buy into. One that doesn't paint me as a dirty whore."

"An illusion?" he said. "Okay. I suppose. Today seems to be a day of illusions. What can we talk about that lets you keep the illusion you want? You're not a whore," he said. "But even if the term fit, there's such a thing as a whore with a heart of gold. Misunderstood, under-appreciated. That kind of woman. So what do you want to talk about?"

"Tell me how a sailboat works," she said. She nuzzled closer to him.

"Good question," he began. "There's a lot of energy in the wind. The wind...."

He stopped talking. She was asleep, snoring lightly.

CHAPTER THIRTY-EIGHT
HIBISCUS IN THE WIND

"The lady in room seven," he said to the desk clerk at the Comfort Inn, "isn't in her room."

"Happens all the time, mister," said the clerk. "They come. They go. Happens more often than.... Wait! You said room seven. She checked out first thing this morning. Said to give you this."

He handed Edward a piece of a brown paper bag that had been cut, then folded into a rectangle approximately the size of a standard envelope. The corners were folded to the center and closed with melted candle wax. On the outside was the letter *E.*

She'd written him a note, but it didn't make sense to him, and her handwriting was atrocious.

All fruits ripe Capn.

Mi a go a door now.

Dat bad bwoy and di man dem beg fa jooks.

Dem craven choke puppy, sure.

Fuckery fix soon time come.

Hibiscus gaan now, sure.

"Thanks," said Edward head down as he tried to decipher the note. He looked up then turned away, dismissing the desk clerk. He walked to his truck, head down, staring at the piece of brown paper sack with Hibiscus's scrawl on it. *Damn that woman. Am I really supposed to understand this scribbling?*

CHAPTER THIRTY-NINE
JAMAICAN SLANG,
WHAT DAT MEAN, MON?

Edward was moody during the entire trip back to Siesta Key. Linda seemed to sense something was wrong, and left him alone.

He considered himself a worldly man, able to understand many English dialects. He spoke Spanish, a little French, and some Portugese, but Jamaican slang often defeated him.

He glanced at the brown paper off and on as he drove. Twice Linda scolded him for wandering out of his driving lane as he concentrated on Hibiscus's scrawled message.

All fruits ripe Capn. That had to mean everything was good. But how so?

Mi a go a door now. Whenever he'd heard it said before, it meant "I go through the door now." As in, I'm leaving. He hadn't thrown her out. He was just punishing her.

Dat bad bwoy and di man dem beg fa jooks. Perhaps she meant "The bad boy, or the gangster and his friends beg for sex."

Dem craven choke puppy, sure. He'd heard the phrase. It meant someone wants everything but, when they get it, they can't handle it. Surely it meant Valmay and friends.

Fuckery fix soon time come. Fuckery didn't mean what it implied. It meant an injustice of some kind. So, what Hibiscus had written had to imply soon the injustice done to Linda would be fixed.

Hibiscus gaan now, sure. He didn't want to think too hard about that line.

CHAPTER FORTY
PART WHORE, PART VICTIM

"Presuming some things I don't want to explain just now, I have a friend I would like you to meet one day soon," said Edward.

They were in his condo, near *The Eloquent Parrot* in Siesta Key. She'd slept in his bed, he'd slept on the sofa. In the middle of the night, she'd left the bed and come to him. She had cried like a baby, then begged him to hold her, do nothing more until she could feel safe. They'd slept like that for a few hours.

Still on the sofa, Linda curled tighter towards him, reach up and stroked his beard. He usually hated it when women did that, but somehow when she did it, it felt right.

"The last time a man said that to me, I was supposed to have sex with the friend," she said.

He looked at her, lifted her chin and looked at her face for a long time.

"You recover quickly," he said. "You just made a joke. I had to see your eyes to be sure."

"There you go with the one-liners," she said. "So, you hate me for what I am? For what I did?"

"What you are," he said, "is a very attractive, Nebraska woman-girl, surrounded by sharks. You like sex. You're very good at it. You use it to get your way – sometimes when you shouldn't. You have an impulsive and addictive personality. You need to understand that about yourself. You can't handle booze or drugs. As for what you did, I'm coming to the conclusion while it was in your power to stop it from happening before it started, Valmay and somebody else pushed very hard to make it happen."

"Am I forgiven, then?" she said, then added. "What do you mean somebody besides Valmay?"

"About forgiveness, I think *you* need to decide what's bad and good for you. Not me. Certainly not me. I'll take you just as you are," he said. "About somebody else being to blame, I'll get to that some other time."

"Oh, I get it," she said. "I need to forgive myself. Hey, did you mean it about taking me the way I am?"

"Pretty much. You haven't got a mean bone in you. You're a pretty terrific woman. Only exception I see about being mean, is being mean to Roger. You said some really mean things to him."

"Guilty as charged," she said. "All this talk is making my head spin. But you're right. I do need to make peace with him and I need to stop the drinking and…you know. The other stuff."

"The whoring," he said.

"Ouch," she said. "But you're not judgmental, right?"

"Nope. Not me. I'm a corrupter of fine young women with undiscovered propensities. I'm not really a sweetheart of a guy. In another life, I could have been a man to take advantage of your talents. Instead, maybe I was a pirate or something.

"What I'm thinking is, there might be a limit on how many times you can forgive yourself for being weak. That includes the drugs and booze as well as men who want to corrupt you. As I recall you were pretty spry without any of the aforementioned sex aids when we were on the sailboat."

"Okay, so, tell me," she said. "Are you still working for Roger?"

"I am," he said.

"Did he ask you to come to Miami to get me?" she said.

"Nope, I thought that one up on my own," he said.

"So, does he know....?"

"Nope. Me coming to move you out of Miami was sort of a conflict of professional interest. But I think I told you, on the day we met, I'm sort of a non-conforming guy. I came to check up on you just becau....just because.... Well, I want to see you get out of whatever bad cycles you're in."

"Oh, that's sweet. You said you wanted me to meet a friend," she said.

"I did," he said.

"Ummm," she replied. "So, what kind of friend am I going to meet?"

She said it jokingly, yet in a way and with a tone that implied that whatever his answer was, was probably acceptable.

She was still sleepy, probably wouldn't remember the conversation later on, so he said, "Forget it for now. I have some work to do. I'll be

214

back in a while. Before I go, I want to ask you again. Who do you have your arrangement with?"

"Not gonna say," she said.

"Because why?"

"Because. Because, it's all I have left. If I tell you who it is, you'll end it for me."

"I will," he said.

"I can't let myself be vulnerable right now. I'll end it. But on my terms, when it's time," she said.

He left her alone, went to do some work on his computer at *The Parrot*, and settled back into his reclusive mode.

With a few tips Chip had provided, he researched all of Judge Beans' decisions – and found nothing amiss.

His computer confirmed R. Simon Shuster of Miami had never tried a case in front of Judge Bean in Bradenton, but that didn't necessarily mean they didn't know each other. From what Linda had told him, it was obvious The Judge knew R. Shuster Simon. But Edward couldn't find the link.

It seemed most of The Judge's past court decisions were or slightly skewed to the man in divorce proceedings. Certainly nothing he read indicated a standing bias or previous relationship. Nothing indicated a relationship with underworld connections. Not even remotely.

At three the following morning, he got a clue. It didn't come from his computer. Instead, it came from Linda's cell phone. When he picked her up in Miami, it was on the floor of the driver's side of her

SUV. He'd slipped it into his pants pocket before taking her back to her apartment to examine her for potential life threatening injuries. He hadn't given it back to her yet.

A warning beep from the phone reminded him he still had it. When he opened it, the battery on the phone was dangerously near dead. He plugged it into the charger next to his computer.

The battery was slow to charge her phone, maddeningly so. It became functional in twenty minutes. Ten minutes more, and he figured out her password to open the phone to look at what she'd been up to.

His first thought was to charge it up, and give it back to her without snooping. That would be the right thing to do. Let her keep her privacy and dignity. Surely her dignity had taken a big enough hit. But still, her smartphone could tell him a lot. Perhaps it could give him the identity of her special friend whose name he still didn't have.

He gave into temptation.

He began with her contact directory. Evidently, she stayed in touch with all her high school friends, but hadn't made many friends here in Florida since moving here from Nebraska. Quickly sorting the list, he coaxed the phone to show him all her Florida Contacts. Valmay was there. He touched a few buttons, then found a list of her text messages and emails to and from Valmay.

It made him feel dirty. He was poking into her personal life, where he had no business poking.

Still he did it. Everything she'd told him was born out. She hadn't lied.

She hadn't lied, but she hadn't told him the extent to which Valmay and her friend had gone to, to set her up with dates with other men. They'd been pimping her out. No mention was made of money for her, still the inferences were unmistakable. She owed Valmay. She owed Valmay's other friend. No other way to say it. Reading the texts, it didn't exactly look to him like she hated it. She hadn't hated it at the beginning, but for the last six months, she'd tried to say no.

She'd said no to Valmay. She's said no – until Edward has pushed her over the edge with his questions while they were on the sailboat. Then she'd given in to a night of cocaine, Valmay, and his friends.

Shit, if I'd left it alone about Valmay, she would have been done with him - maybe. But Valmay now had a debt to pay – to me, if not to Linda. But who in the hell is her special friend?

Only one email from owendalholmes at yahoo stood out. Owendalholmes wasn't a highschool friend. Wasn't somebody she worked with either. Could that be her special friend? He or she wasn't in Linda's contact list. The message was brief and could have been spam. It said, *"payday soon. Come up, I've got a nice place nearby. All forgiven."*

Perhaps that fit in with the unidentified incoming phone calls she'd received. Clearly her special friend had coached her on secrecy.

So much for ethics about snooping. He closed the phone.

Ten minutes later it came to him. One of the early supreme court justices was Oliver Wendell Holmes. A judge. *A JUDGE*

Perhaps the theory about The Judge being Linda's sugardaddy wasn't out of bounds after all.

So, how could he check it out? He had to think a bit on that problem. However, he had a plan about how to take care of Valmay, first.

CHAPTER FORTY-ONE
AN ILLEGAL BOX

Edward pulled the tattered leather black briefcase from underneath his desk. He stroked up with his thumb on the five number combination on the lock on the right side, then he turned the dials of the combination lock on the left side. He opened the briefcase.

He removed a smaller, military grade, rectangular black box from inside a fitted cavity. Attaching the black box to his laptop computer with an umbilical cord, he began opening programs.

A dialog screen prompted him to enter a phone number. He entered Valmay's cell phone number. Then he entered the approximate latitude and longitude of three places where he was certain the cell phone had been in the last week. When he hit the *enter* button on his laptop, the screen went blank for a moment, then showed a message, *Target acquired.*

A full minute later, the words *CLONE created* appeared on the screen. Under that, the message *Use of this program without a valid warrant signed by a sitting Federal Judge constitutes a third degree felony punishable by up to ten years in Federal Prison.*

Below, the screen read, *Press Enter to continue, Escape to terminate.*

Edward tapped the Enter key.

The box he was using had been *lost* while being used by a Federal Agent three months before. Edward had used it twice since acquiring it. It worked splendidly. However, it wasn't a tool to use too often or use carelessly.

Next, Edward programmed the box to record every conversation Valmay had, every text he sent, and every text he received.

CHAPTER FORTY-TWO
THE ENEMY CREW

"Taz," said Valmay into his cell phone.

"Sup' dog?" said Taz. "Got anothah par-tee planned?" He laughed.

"Yo, time to show me you for real, Taz. You been sayin' you kin cut a man bad. I got a dude needs it bad," said Valmay.

"Got yo back muthafuckah," said Taz. "Dude we gonna cut. He a brotha, or a honkie?" said Taz.

"Honkie muthafuckah. Big 'enuff to play ball. Got attitude. Gotta full 'fro and a beard like a badass preacher. Got a beef wit me 'bout the wet-wet we party on."

"I thought you own her ass, not some cracker," laughed Taz. "Cut his throat juss da same. Yo, he carry uh gat?"

"Dunno, but he big. Bring a brotha with a sawed off," said Valmay.

"Dude, you had lak six mo homies do her besides me. They got yo back too?"

"They ain't that kind of playas. Talk shit, bang a girl when it's fun, hit on her maybe, but this is fo real. You a real gangstah, or I got to...?" said Valmay.

"Yo, I'm cool. Know a guy. He down. How long we hangin' fo'?" said Taz

"Dunno. He won't try nuthin' while I'm workin'. Mothafuckha try for me after I git off late.

Or maybe when I come outta mah crib. Ah got a place to hang while we wait."

Edward's black box caught it all. He added Taz's number to the phone list. A few hours later, he added JT's phone number. JT was a recent friend of Taz, and a new enemy of Edward.

CHAPTER FORTY-THREE
WAITING, DEDUCING

From the moment he'd found Linda and put the scene together in his head, he knew what he was going to do about it. Valmay would pay, but Linda's needs were immediate. Valmay's punishment could wait – for a while. Whatever Valmay and his friends were planning for Edward, wasn't going to happen. Ever. Edward intended to be the one to set the pace.

Besides, Hibiscus had been missing for three days now. Edward began to worry.

Edward couldn't call what had happened to Linda rape in his mind. Although she hadn't told him all the details yet, he knew from the tiny cuts on her inner thighs, and around her nipples and on her throat, what Valmay had done.

He knew what she had done too. From the size of the bruises on the inside of her thighs, and ankles and arms, he could guess how many men Valmay had invited to the party. That's when it quit being a party and started being a rape scene.

From the seemingly careless placement of cocaine at the scene, he deduced the neighborhood kids would eventually call 911, law enforcement would find her in the same condition he had, and would presume it had all been consensual. No real effort into an investigation would be made, even if Linda told the cops about Valmay.

Hibiscus was missing, and yet *The Eloquent Parrot* needed managing. So Edward managed the bar, poured drinks, kept order, waited, and worried.

It took three more days for the pieces to fall the way he wanted.

CHAPTER FORTY-FOUR
RING MY BELL

They giggled and bumped hips provocatively as they came into *The Eloquent Parrot*. There were two of them, college girls from their looks. Every man inside looked up. Every man noticed their dark tans, their sunglasses pushed up on their heads, their polished, painted fingernails and their carefree surfer attitude. The women inside the bar hated them, as women do. Men gave up in the two-second appraisal, and went back to drinking, conversation, watching a baseball game or throwing darts. The girls were teases, nothing more. Every man knew he didn't stand a chance.

Both girls were blondes, the taller one had long sun streaked hair, or possibly custom cut, layered so it look like she really didn't tend to her hair. The shorter girl had a pixie cut.

Both girls wore flowered, wrap-around cover-ups, tied loosely over very tiny bikini swimsuits. Both wore sandals.

Still giggling and jostling one another, they walked in, sat as closely to Blackbeard as they could, and started to talk him up.

Blackbeard ignored them.

Jasmine was serving. She came up to them. "Cool drinks – you two ladies?"

"Sure," said the taller blonde. "Give me a Heini in a bottle? Her too, I guess."

"Sure ting," said Jasmine. "Gotta see ID first."

The girls giggled. Giggling was their shared call-sign and trade mark. Each made a show of patting herself to see where her identification might be hiding. Tall Girl found hers in a laminated protector in the bra of her bikini. Short Girl found hers tied to a waterproof pouch on a string in her bikini bottoms. They laid them on the counter for Jasmine to examine. They giggled again and leaned over to let Blackbeard see their charms.

Jasmine looked closely at the IDs, then said as if to Blackbeard, "Dey old enough. Barely, but old enough."

She returned a few minutes later with two bottles of beer. She didn't bring a mug. "Dat be six dollar," she said.

"Run a tab for me, willya, sweetie?" said Tall Girl. "I've been here before. Captain Teach is around today, I hope."

"Oh, he around," said Jasmine. "He always someplace."

"Thanks, sweetie," said Tall Girl. Then, ignoring Jasmine, she began to talk baby talk, dirty baby talk to Blackbeard.

"Hey big boy. You remember me? Mommie needs to hear you tell me what a dirty little boy does when the lights go off. You like my ta-ta's, don't you sweetie?"

Blackbeard cocked his head and looked intently at Tall Girl, then at Short Girl. They giggled. Blackbeard did nothing.

"Come on, big guy. You bought Annie a drink last time I was here. Talk to me. Say something sweet and I get to ring the bell. I'm all wet right now, just for you and your captain. Want some of what I have for you, big guy?"

Blackbeard hopped from one foot to the other, but didn't speak.

Short Girl took a firm hold of the brass foot-rail with her toes, propped her elbows on the bar and bent over so Blackbeard had a delicious view of her breasts – almost showing her nipples in the process. Her wrap-around barely covered her butt. She looked around, then lifted the Heinekens beer to her lips and drank seductively. She had to arch her neck to do it.

Blackbeard hopped back from the up foot to the down foot. He turned and looked long and hard at Short Girl. Still he said nothing.

"You really think the pirate guy will come out if we ring the bell?" she asked Tall Girl.

"Definitely," said Tall Girl.

"So, let's just ring it then. What if we cheat? Would he know if we ring the bell and the parrot didn't say anything?" said Short Girl.

"Probably. Give it a minute. Let me drink my beer. We're hot today. Every guy in here would love to bang us. Are you sure you have the guts to bang him if he asks?" said Tall Girl. "I did it. Jesus, that guy started slow and kept working on me. Turned me into a pretzel and inside out. I came like ten times."

"Ten times?"

"Maybe fifteen," said Tall Girl. "I was pretty tipsy. Better than prom night, for sure."

"You never went to the prom," said Short Girl. "You went straight to the party after and got totally blitzed. You bypassed the prom. I was there, remember?"

"It was prom night. I never said I went to the prom," said Tall Girl. She lowered her bra just a little more and encroached on the *do not cross* line.

Blackbeard noticed but didn't comment.

Both girls finished their beers, then signaled for another.

"Nice pair to draw to," said Blackbeard. *"Looks like a full house in the making. King on Queens."*

Short Girl shrieked in surprise, then giggled. Tall girl giggled then reached over and grabbed the lanyard attached to the brass bell and rang it hard.

Everybody in the bar looked over. A few men smiled. Women rolled their eyes. Jasmine rolled hers too before putting the beers down to remove the caps. She waited.

The girls waited. Moments later, Edward Teach came through the wooden beads.

"Good afternoon, ladies," he boomed. "I take it Blackbeard found your charms irresistible."

"Oh," said Short Girl. "Hi." She had apparently become at a loss for words. She stared at Edward Teach in awe. "Jesus, he's big," she muttered.

Tall Girl had no such loss, "Hi, Captain. Remember me?"

"I do believe I do," he said. "Fondly, in fact. You do know the rules about the bell, don't you?"

"What rules?" said Short Girl.

"If a beautiful girl gets Blackbeard to speak – and both of you qualify – he is obliged to pay her bar bill. But as with so many of life's boundless gifts, there is a limit to his generosity. A beautiful girl is allowed to drink from the fountain of youth just once at Blackbeard's expense."

Pausing for a moment, he looked at Tall Girl and her charms, then added, "As I said, the memory is a fond one, but Blackbeard's rules are his rules."

"Oh, well, it was her he was talking to," said Tall Girl. "I just pulled the rope for her, she's the one he wanted to play with. I mean....I'm just here for the ride, but of course if you want both of us...."

"Mmmm, I'm sorely tempted. But a task once started must be done properly. My time is limited this day."

"Oh," said Tall Girl sadly. "You mean...."

"Not today, girls," said Edward. "Although my sword truly is tempted, as I said."

"Maybe..." said Tall Girl.

"No," said Edward. To Jasmine he said, "Only one of them is paying for her beer today. The other drinks for free – on Blackbeard." Without looking back at the girls, he turned and went back through the beads.

"Does that mean...?" asked Short Girl.

"Shit," said Tall Girl. "What's up with him? I would have bet anything we'd end up letting him take turns on us. I can't freaking believe it. Shit. The bastard turned us down."

"Does that mean….?" asked Short Girl.

CHAPTER FORTY-FIVE
PATIENCE VS LOYALTY

Edward returned to his office. He'd been posting deposits and paying bills when the girls rang the bell. He was multi-tasking. As he worked with QuickBooks, he finished making the last online payment to his vegetable vendor. He had an ear bud plugged in, listening to a recording of Valmay and his friends talk to one another two days before.

Taz said, "Yo, Valmay. Been lak six muthafucking days now. Where he at?"

Valmay replied, "Soon. Be cool. I know this mothafuckah. He gonna come for me. I dissed his wannabe. He gotta be pissed. He gonna come real soon, maybe tonight."

"Look, I gotta get some fresh," said Taz. "JT cover for ya for a day. I got a sure thing on something fresh off tha boat. Black momma in heat for me. I be back if ya holla."

"Don't be that way," said Valmay. "Stay cool."

"Lak ah said," Taz said, "Something get going, you holla. I'll be there."

"Whatevah, mothafuckah. Something get going, it be ovah. Don't come round begging for no more favors." Valmay hung up.

Edward smiled, then moved on to the next conversation. Evidently, JT, Taz's replacement didn't have much in the way of dedication either. Both men were antsy to get on to something urgent, and most probably female.

That's when Hibiscus poked her head in the door. "All fruit's ripe, my Cap'n"

Edward jumped up and walked to the doorway. He held his arms out and Hibiscus came to him. She put her head on his chest.

"Where you been, girl?" he said softly.

"Lak ah said. All fruit's ripe. Every-ting took care of. Bad boways gwine be soft lak uncook bread long time, sure."

Edward laughed out loud. "Hibiscus, some things I just don't really want to know. Like exactly what you did about them. Just as long as you don't qualify as a fresh momma just off the boat from Jamaica. I'm glad to see you back."

"See? De slave girl not to throw away so fast," she said.

Then they laughed together.

"Hibiscus, it's time for me to pay a visit to Miami again – by myself. I'm going to finish this business with Valmay. Can you mind *The Parrot* while I'm gone?"

"Sure ting, My Cap'n."

Edward packed his bag and headed to Miami late in the afternoon.

CHAPTER FORTY-SIX
A GELDING? NO, NOT THAT!

"Don't bother to scream," said Edward. "There isn't anybody around here for miles. If you scream it might hurt my ears. And if you don't shut up with your ghetto shit talk, I will shut your mouth in a very uncomfortable way. You really aren't much of a man when it all boils down. You got no ethics, just balls. Had to have one last poke at her, didn't you?"

Valmay was secured with nylon cable ties to a fish-cleaning table next to a rundown launching ramp for canoes in a state park in the Everglades. He was spread-eagle, naked except for his sneakers, and he was in pain. His throat hurt from where Edward's huge hand had wrapped around his neck and pinched his carotid artery until he passed out. His face had rub burns from the tarp he'd been wrapped up in the back of Edward's pickup truck. He reeked loudly of drug-sweat, for the pickup truck had a waterproof cover over the bed and it was steamy hot inside. He'd been hogtied for a while. And the buzz of mosquitoes and unidentifiable biting insects was intolerable.

The park was closed for the night. No park rangers on site. They'd open the boat ramps and fishing docks in another two hours. That's when the rednecks with airboats and the yuppies with kayaks would arrive.

233

Mosquitoes, croaking frogs, darting bats and bugs Valmay' d never heard of filled the night. All Valmay could see was the penetrating bright light of a sodium vapor lamp three feet above his head. The light attracted moths and flying night bugs.

He was groggy. A really bad headache was coming on. All he knew was when he left work, he had an uneasy feeling. That was just before midnight. It was still dark, so it must be before dawn.

"So, what I'm going to do is this," said Edward. "I'm going to help you out so you never, ever make the same mistake like you did with Linda. A man's nuts are the source of much of his motivation in life. Unfortunately, they motivate a man to do things he sometimes shouldn't. You follow me, dude?"

"Whut's fuckin' happenin'? Where am I? You the big asshole that came to my house, aintcha? I'm going to gut you, mothafuckah. Me an Taz…."

"I am. I did. And no you won't. Taz won't either. I have it on good authority his cock is going to be useless for a long time. As a matter of fact, the entire team you put on Linda won't be having much fun of any kind, for a long, long time. They have you to thank for that, and I'm sure they'll figure it out pretty soon. You wouldn't listen. You're still selling coke and weed to anybody and everybody. And you hurt Linda. I don't care much about weed, one way or the other. Now, coke, crack and meth are something else. And I do care about Linda. Had to get one last poke of her wet-wet in trade for some coke. Your words, not mine. And you did it *after* I told you not to. So, what I'm going to do is fix things for everybody," said Edward.

"Lemme fucking go, asshole," spat Valmay. "What kind a law are you?"

"I will do that. I will definitely let you go. I am the law of common sense and I will definitely let you go. In a few minutes. You want gas before I operate?"

"Doan know what you mean. Lemme go," said Valmay. He was pleading. "I be good man. No shit. Stop all the bad stuff. Lemme go home. Untie me."

"Good idea. See? After I fix you up, you got one last chance. If you don't stop dealing drugs, I'm going to come visit you again and make sure you get five years hard time in Starke. A pretty dude like you will make a nice bitch in prison. Those pretty dreadlocks and all. Nice tight buns. The brotha's up there will like you good. Your voice will get higher and higher as time goes on. You'll get kind of pudgy and your pecks will turn to breasts with nipples. No male hormones on their program for a man like you. No nuts and a two-inch cock will make you a nice bitch. But they'll let you cook for them before they bend you over. Obviously you like to organize trains. So the guys run a train on you up there after you cook their grits. So, this is your very, very last warning. Don't sell any more drugs. Oh…and get your wife and kids off welfare. Work a second job. Got it?"

"Whutyoutalkinbout? I ain't nobody's bitch. Got a nice long cock for the bitches. Linda like it fine. Ax her. Ax all of them. They all say so. Lemme go dude."

"Tomorrow morning, your cock and your balls will be in a fish's belly. I'm going to leave you two inches to piss with. But don't worry. I'm a trained professional. I know how to do this. You won't bleed to death. Not this time. Okay?

"Breathe deep. When you wake up, you should be in a hospital if you're lucky. If not, then don't look between your legs. You might die from shock."

Valmay tossed his head and thrashed as hard as he could when Edward put the mask over him. Edward took the mask away. "Your choice, dude. Nitrous oxide or nothing. All your oxy pills are in your car parked illegally in front of the Coral Gables Police station. Oxy might dull the pain, but no oxy for you today. So what's it gonna be. Nitrous or nothing. Nothing might hurt a lot."

"Gas me, motherfuchah."

"Glad to. First, I have one or two tiny questions to ask you. It's about a judge you introduced Linda to...."

When Edward was satisfied he'd heard all he needed to hear and then some, he touched a scalpel to Valmay's scrotum.

"Gimme dat gas shit.... You promised. Please, please please oh mommy, mommy. Oh motherfucka..oh oh oh,"

236

CHAPTER FORTY-SEVEN
SO, TAKE ME, NOT HIM

"Okay Linda," said Edward. "Can we talk now?"

They were at Edward's apartment, in his bed, although they hadn't had sex. Linda was cuddled close to him as if they had. Nine days had passed since her ordeal.

"You mean talk – like you wanted to talk – when we were on sailboat headed back to Miami and I threw a fit?"

"That kind of talk. Yes."

"I'm sorry I was a bitch. I just hate it my life is so screwed up and I didn't want to talk about it. You bringing it up got me all weird."

"Let's let that part go for a bit," he said. "I want to talk about the arrangement you have. I'm sure I know who it is, but I'm not exactly sure about some of the details about stuff. To say something I've said before, I'm not judgmental. Really."

"It's complicated," she said.

"Of course it's complicated. Talk to me like I was a sorority sister or something. Somebody you trust totally."

She laughed. "Actually, Edward, I do trust you. Way more than some backstabbing sorority sister. I flunked out of college twice already. I want to finish this time. And as silly as it sounds I would like you to pin me down and make love to me, or have sex with me. Very soon. Really, I'm not sore anymore."

"And you want to take classes and finish college." He said, ignoring her come-on. "So, talk to me. Tell me about him and how it got started."

"Let's see," she said. "Okay. Valmay had been after me to play with him. I told you, and I told you how he got to me. I'm not proud of it. But in a sick way, I'd had these fantasies, you know."

"I can guess," he said. "We all have a list of fantasies. So where does The Judge come into this?

Linda got quiet and tried to get out of the bed. Edward restrained her, wrapped his arms tight around her and wouldn't let her go. Neither of them spoke for a while.

"So, you *do* know about The Judge," she said. "How's you find out? He's gonna cut me off. Please don't bother him. He's all I have left. My ace in the hole, so to speak"

"I know some. Too much. Not enough," he said. "Look, I really want to finish fixing this thing. I need to know. No wrong answers I promise. Tell me."

"He's married," she said.

"I know."

"Says he wants to leave her and be full time with me," she said.

"How do you feel about that?" he said.

"Sick. Creeped out. I couldn't handle it if he really did leave her for me. But I'm sure he's lying, just trying to tell me so I'll move into a condo he owns. It overlooks the water. Not far from here."

"And you're tempted?"

"Why not?" she said. "Lots of girls do it. I know it wouldn't be forever. I don't make enough money working the crappy jobs I get. This could be a way to get ahead. Finish school. Move on. You got a better offer?"

"Yes, as a matter of fact, I do," he said.

"So lay it on me, Edward," she said.

"Work hard. Two jobs if you have to. Go to school nights. Apply for Pell grants. Borrow the least amount you can for student loans. Let me deal with the lawyers you owe. If you let The Judge go, then the lawsuit with Roger will be over. You'll be legally free. Finish school..."

She laughed. "You're an idealist. I thought you were going to make a counter offer, to beat The Judge's offer."

"Actually, I could afford to do that," he said. "but it wouldn't work, and we both know why."

"So, when are you going to throw me out on the street?" she said. "I'm staying here rent free. Or is it truly rent free? See why I need The Judge?"

"No charge. But you can't stay here forever," he said.

"So, you're not going to take care of me?"

"Not my job. You can take care of yourself, just fine. I'm not quite twice your age. That makes everything between us problematic. I'll help you get a start and help you get away from The Judge. We can date, hang out and stuff. Maybe more. I like you, but you need to be your own boss. You don't need a pimp or a daddy, you need your life. Life is like that. Ultimately we're all responsible for ourselves," he said.

She started to cry.

He extracted himself from her hug and got off the bed.

"Where are you going?" she said.

"I'm going to a place where I don't have to hear you crying. When you get done crying, maybe we'll talk. When a woman cries, she's cheating. She's using unfair emotional leverage over a man who doesn't like to see an unhappy woman. Sometimes the hard thing to do is the right thing to do."

"Asshole," she said. She turned on her side to face the wall.

Edward left. He didn't look back over his shoulder.

CHAPTER FORTY-EIGHT
SHREWS TOGETHER

"De tame of de shrew," said Hibiscus. "How it go now?"

They were prepping the bar for the evening. They expected a larger than normal crowd, especially after the drum circle broke up.

"You're not supposed to know anything about Shakespeare," said Edward. "If that's what you were referring to."

"Why so, my Cap'n? Juss 'cause he dead a hundret year before dey cut de head off dat poor mon, and I save you, sure? I live long time now. I heard 'bout 'im. Scribbled many fine stories. So, tell me my Cap'n, de shrew not bein' nice? I could fix dat."

"I thought we had an agreement, Hibiscus. No good spells – or bad spells. I'm really sorry I slapped you, but if you want to continue to live with me like we do, you can't be doing Voodoo anymore. That's not negotiable."

"You say – Hibiscus lissen, my Cap'n. I doan poison no more drink for rude mens, 'sides, true slave girl lak me crave de hand dat hurt some."

She smiled her warmest smile for him, then turned to busy herself with a chore that suddenly needed to be done at the other end of the bar.

Although he was sure she'd tuned him out, he said, "I wasn't talking about rude men. I was talking about all your magic. All of it."

Two hours before sunset, Edward Teach entered *The Eloquent Parrot* with Linda in tow. Hibiscus was at the bar.

Edward had Linda by her hand. If he'd pulled any harder, it would have appeared like she was a child being taken to her room to be spanked.

He pulled her to the bar and motioned for Hibiscus to come.

When Hibiscus was within talking range, he said, "Linda this is Hibiscus. Hibiscus this is Linda. Say hello to one another."

Neither woman spoke.

In the tone of a father speaking to a child, he said, "Hibiscus!"

"I see," said Hibiscus. "She quite pretty. She drain all de juices outta you, my lover?"

Edward didn't smile. "I recharge quickly Hibiscus. Be nice. She's someone I want you to get to know and to get along with." He turned to Linda and said, "It's not my style to put people in awkward situations. But unfortunately, this may be awkward for both of you.

"Hibiscus is a very unusual and very talented woman. We sleep together. You had your itches, I have Hibiscus. I'm not giving her up. I haven't told you anything about her, nor have I told her anything about you. But Hibiscus thinks she knows you. She thinks she has special powers. Just ignore her if she starts in with it."

He turned back to Hibiscus. "Like I said, talk nice. Be nice. I'm going to see a man about some justice. When I get back, I expect to see the two of you getting along. Understand? If I don't like what I see when I get back, you both will have hell to pay. Believe it."

Hibiscus glared at him.

Linda glared at him.

CHAPTER FORTY-NINE
CIRCLE OF DRUMS

Seconds after Edward was out of earshot Hibiscus said to Linda, "You clean de toilets up. Den maybe I show you sum tings." Hands on hips, she waited for Linda to bow up at her like a snake poked with a stick. Instead, Linda smiled, did a little curtsy and said, "Show me where."

At five o'clock, Linda left the bathrooms and found Hibiscus. "Come see," she said. "They're clean."

Hibiscus gave the tiniest hint of a smile, then said, "Dey clean. I read it dat way. Less do sumpin fun before de sun hit de water, sure."

She didn't wait for Linda to answer. Turning to one of the other girls at the bar she said, "Jasmine, c'mere girl. Ah we go to da circle. Be bock soon."

She grabbed a bright yellow shawl from underneath the bar, adjusted the Hibiscus flower behind her ear and took Linda by the hand.

Clinging tightly, she led her across the parking lot to the access road, then to Gulf Boulevard, and finally to a hot asphalt parking lot that gave way to sea oats, which in turn gave way to a wide sandy beach. The white sand gave way to the soft relentless swooshing of light surf. And far, far to the west a flaming red ball began to descend into the water.

A weekly pagan ritual began as the sun set.

They crossed the parking lot full of cars, where people were spilling out of every imaginable kind of vehicle – eagerly, like salmon swimming home.

On the other side of the sea-oat-covered dune, a loose unorganized throng of people circled around a scattered assemblage of drummers – each with a unique drum of his or her own. Some were just beginning to warm up, others were already in the groove. Still more were trying to find the rat-tat-tat that matched the boom boom boom. An occasional high pitty pitty pitty pat of bongos augmented the deep thumps.

"What's this?" said Linda.

"De drum circle, girl. Let your feet feel de sand, let your insides feel de soul of de drums. Bring de devil out. Bring de woman to heat. Bring de heartbeat back from de dead. Good magic, sure. De drum kiss de sun goodbye one more time." She paused, then added, "And de drums set right what was wrong between us, sure."

Virtually everything and anything that could be called a drum was present. Steel, bongo, kettle, African, snare, base drums, and some Linda was positive were homemade. Twenty drummers thumped already, and more streamed in. For every drummer, there were four onlookers. The rhythm was awkward at moments, then as different members found the rhythm, it became a heartbeat that picked up in tempo and took on a life.

Linda held tight onto Hibiscus's hand. She began to skip like a first grader. Hibiscus skipped too. The closer they got, the higher their energy became.

Without saying a word, the two skipped directly into the middle of the drum circle. By then, Hibiscus was all hips and waist and sway. Her arms flowed like waves. She twirled like a wild merry-go-round, circling little girls and fat librarians alike.

"Aaah, look," someone said. "Hibiscus is here. Hibiscus is here." Others took up the chant and smiled, clapping their hands to the beat of the drums.

People continued to flow to the circle, until a crowd of hundreds stood, sat on blankets, or collapsible chairs, or their heels – all facing the center of the circle. All facing Hibiscus who danced with controlled frenzy in a twenty-foot circle like a pagan goddess. Others danced too, but for the moment all eyes were on Hibiscus.

The drum rhythm became stronger, like the heartbeat of a newborn lioness. No dissonance now, all drums were in rhythm.

Everyone made room for Hibiscus.

Hibiscus ran with the shawl, dancing, lighting the circle with her femininity, then came back to where Linda stood.

Linda began to dance too. Her arms rose up, her hips swayed, her feet went heel and toe. The circle was now for Linda and Hibiscus. All the others were decorations only. They alone owned the soul of the circle.

The drums got louder.

"Girl," shouted Hibiscus, "Where you come from, make you dance lak dat?'

Linda didn't understand. She shrugged her shoulders.

"You dance lak you black," said Hibiscus. She laughed – a warm deep laugh.

"Oh," shouted Linda over the drums. "My father was Native American. Maybe that's it!" They were standing inches apart, laughing and trying to shout into the ear of the other to be heard.

The drums were so loud her words were drowned. But it made no difference. She and Hibiscus were now two pagan goddesses with one soul – the soul of rhythm.

For one full hour the circle took on a life, as worshipers danced and pounded on drums, sticks, tambourines, and anything that could make noise. Little girls, nurse's aides, octogenarians, and high school girls alike joined in. One man, with a felt derby, bare arms and skin browned by years of sunshine and dressed with gay Indian garb joined in, but most of the dancers were women.

And of course, Hibiscus and Linda danced. They were the circle this night. They did not stop, not even for a moment.

Then the sun extinguished in the Gulf of Mexico, an infinitely distant dream away. The rhythm continued but subdued and dying in vigor and ferocity.

As the sun disappeared into the horizon, Hibiscus again grabbed Linda by the hand. This time she pulled her away from the drums and people to return her to *The Eloquent Parrot*. The two women ignored the cries of the crowd to return. They fled like a pair of Cinderellas leaving the ball just at the stroke of midnight.

They got to *The Parrot* just in time. The bar was beginning to fill with beachgoers who'd danced, laughed, and let their hearts and inhibitions go. Sandy-shoed patrons with sunburned faces bellied up to the bar, ordered tropical drinks and healthy but unusual recipes Edward brought in from exotic places were displayed on a colorful laminated card, or occasionally simply beer or wine so they could hold onto the mood for as long as possible.

Without being asked, Linda pitched in. She poured beer or wine and served customers happily as she danced around Hibiscus carrying up to three mugs in each hand, never spilling a drop. She helped Jasmine, and the other barmaids, sometimes taking food orders for the grumpy short order cook in the back, sometimes just serving drinks.

By eleven, the drum circle crowd thinned, and the regulars were able to take back their places at booths, or favorite bar stools.

That's when Roger and Dewey came into the bar.

Linda saw them walk in, and froze. She had no idea of why they were there. If this was Edward's idea of some kind of resolution....

248

Blackbeard noticed them first. He hopped on one foot and seemed pleased to see Roger.

Hibiscus noticed them next. She handed Linda a pitcher of beer and pointed to a group of patrons sitting at a table near the back. Holding her arms out, she made walking motions with her fingers while trying to decide what to do next. Linda took the pitcher of beer to the customers Hibiscus pointed at. She looked over her shoulder only once to see what Hibiscus was up to.

Roger had evidently been having a good time that evening and was oblivious to everything but the music. Pulling Dewey to the dancing area near the jukebox, he bent his knees, shuffled his bare feet and put his arms above his head to Bob Marley singing 'Stir it up, Little Darlin'.

Linda completed the beer delivery and headed back to the bar, ashen faced.

Hibiscus resolved her flusteration, then headed toward Roger with stern intentions etched into her face.

Only Roger, head still down, feet trying for an Astaire inspiration knew what he was thinking at that moment. Yet he stopped dancing, put a single finger in the air for Dewey to see, suggesting he'd be back in one minute, then swung on his heal and headed to the bar. That's when he lifted his head and came eye to eye with Linda.

"Son of a bitch," he exclaimed without thinking.

Hibiscus completed her journey and stood in front of him, blocking any closer proximity to Linda.

Linda's eyes grew hot and she tried to bore a hole in him with her stare. "Yes," she said, "You are."

She turned and ran. She ran around the end of the bar, took three more running steps, and crashed headlong through the bead curtain not sure where she would end up.

"No dancin' for you tonight, mon," said Hibiscus. "Take de lady and come back soon, some odder night, mon."

"Son of a bitch," said Roger. "Where'd she come from?"

Dewey grabbed him by the hand and pulled hard. She pulled him to the front door. Clearly Roger was still in shock.

"Son of a bitch," said Roger one last time.

It was Blackbeard who got the last word though. Ever the mimic, he recited a line from a western song that had been playing on the jukebox earlier,

The last one to know
The last one to show
I was the last one
You thought you'd see there

CHAPTER FIFTY
SIR, THIS LADY THINKS
SHE'S MY WIFE

Edward had said he was going to see a man about some justice. But in reality, it was a judge he was going to visit.

Judge Jack Bean sat in a corner booth of the small lounge. The lounge on University Drive, just across from Sarasota International Airport wasn't a local watering hole. It was more like a place of refuge for hotel guests who had just checked in and wanted a drink before taking a shot at Sarasota's non-existent nightlife. A stretch limo disgorged guests newly arrived from the airport.

Edward strode over to him confidently and said, "My name is Paul Dooley. A friend told me you were a good man to talk to. The bartender told me you were drinking Crown Royal. I'm a single-malt scotch man, myself. I told him to bring us another. Tab is on me. Hope you don't mind."

Edward extended his hand. The Judge hesitated, but the man who said his name was Paul was big, and he was smiling. Prudence suggested acceptance of a handshake.

He replied, "Well, thanks. But you probably have me confused with somebody else. I uhhh, don't live around here. I'm just getting a drink while I...."

"You're a judge. Judge Jack Bean. You decide family law cases if I'm correct. Twelfth Circuit

Court. That would include Manatee County," said Edward.

"Who was it who gave you my name?" asked The Judge.

"A guy who neither one of us would invite to our home if we wanted to impress our family. Friendly when it suits him. Met him a bit more than a month ago. His family hails all the way back to Africa, in fact," said Edward. "Like I said, the man has a lifestyle and does things we don't want to talk about, but it helps to know people like that sometimes. But that's not why I'm here. He said you'd be a good guy to ask some advice of."

The Judge colored red, then looked at his watch. "Well, okay. I'm not saying I have any idea at all about who you're referring to, but what advice are you in need of?"

"Short version — I'm a traveling man. Work the boats. Got good licenses and a good income. Some of the places I go to, I have meaningful relationships with women who live there. Some of the women find it more convenient to consider they're better off if they begin their name with the title of Mrs. As in Mrs. Paul Dooley."

The barmaid brought a tray with two drinks on it. Both men sat quietly as she placed the drinks in front of them. Edward pulled a fifty-dollar bill off a roll and tossed it on the tray. "Pot's right," he said, suggesting no change was necessary. "My friend seems to have an appointment."

The Judge smiled. "Actually, I have a few minutes to spare. I just now got a text message on my phone from the lady I'd expected to meet with tonight. She's being a typical woman – playing hard to get. We had a fuss. But she'll come around soon. Women are always late, but they make up for it in other ways. So, tell me again. What I can do for you?"

"Well, all I really want to know is, as long as I never bought a marriage license anyplace, and as long as I never told a woman who was a citizen of this country she was my wife, am I free to…you know?"

The Judge laughed. "Is that all? That's pretty easy. Anybody who says they're married to you has to have proof of some sort. No paper, no proof. Any attorney could tell you that. I can't vouch for what other countries you go to. They have their laws, we have ours. But unless you're here in the US with papers from some legal entity saying you're married, you aren't married. Just be careful at your end to never represent yourself as being married to a woman in a state that has common law statutes. Florida doesn't. Of course there's exceptions. I'd have to have my clerk check it out, if it was really important. But even if you are married, there are ways to make sure you aren't. You have any other problems I can help you with?"

Edward smiled and took a drink of scotch. "That was about it. Well, unless you happen to know an attractive woman who likes to play house for a day or two while I'm in port. I'm the kind of guy who doesn't like to mess with hookers. Maybe a girl who's looking for a part-time sugar-daddy. Something like that."

The Judge smiled and took a sip of his drink. Then he took another sip and looked at his watch. "No promises, Paul. But it just so happens this lady I was stood-up by, and who will undoubtedly return, can be coaxed into becoming available. She's very sexual. Very. She's sweet, Midwestern sweet. Like I said, no promises. But if you give me your card...."

No doubt remained in Edward Teach's mind. He had his man.

CHAPTER FIFTY-ONE
A RELIABLE SOURCE

Rosemary called Edward. "Ten days, Edward. That's all we've got. And then Chip and Roger have to be in front of Judge Bean. Today is Friday. We have to be in court one week from Tuesday morning. We're only allowed thirty minutes, but Chip gets to speak first. Whatever you're going to give Chip, have it ready soon."

Edward closed his cell phone and looked at the woman across the table from him.

"Here he comes now," said Jackie D. "It's his weekend to play. He's so predictable."

Edward's coffee cup was halfway to his lips. He held it in check, turned to his right just slightly, to see Judge Jack Bean walk across the airport terminal, heading toward gate sixteen.

Edward and Jackie were sitting in an almost deserted café where people read paperbacks, chatted on cell phones, or pecked at laptops to pass the time as they waited for a plane to arrive, or depart from Sarasota International Airport. Whatever they came for, it wasn't for the cuisine.

"Sort of an all-in-one event," said Edward. "Having breakfast with you and seeing the object of our conversation. Wouldn't you say?"

It hadn't taken a great deal of persuasion to get Jackie to agree to meet him. She really didn't care for The Judge. She let that be known straight away as they spoke on the phone the day before, but then most former mistresses tend to harbor ill feeling once the affair ends.

Armed with what little information he had about The Judge's past history, Edward took a long shot. He called Jackie – the court reporter who had filed a complaint against Judge Jack Bean three years earlier and then withdrawn it three weeks after she filed it.

Edward cold-called Jackie D., and she succumbed to his telephone charms, a rare event. Usually he had to be in the presence of a woman to charm her.

"All this is off the record," she said as they watched The Judge wait with his back to them at the check-in counter. "Right? No court testimony or anything, right?"

"Absolutely," said Edward. He finished noting details of how The Judge was dressed, what size bag he carried and his body language, then returned his attention to the attractive thirty-something woman in front of him. "Not particularly impressive from a distance. Obviously, I'm missing something."

"Not much to miss," she said. "He's just a typical lawyer turned State's Attorney, who kissed the right asses, and got an endorsement and the go-ahead to run for a judgeship. It's an elected position, but party politics, and campaign money determines who runs, who gets the nod and who gets elected. The election itself is just a formality."

"Politically connected then?" said Edward.

"Not high enough to get into real politics," she said. "Just high enough to have appellate aspirations. He's still serving time for banging me and getting caught."

"Serving time?"

"He wanted a seat on criminal court, then a shot at appellate. He's almost bright enough to sit on appellate. We ended in an ugly way. I got a lawyer and filed suit for harassment. He wanted it to go away, I settled, and he got a reprimand and transferred to family law. In about another year, he can get a shot at it. Until then, he hears domestic cases and stays in the doghouse. Ironic, kind of," she said.

"Ironic. Care to tell me about the affair?" he asked.

"Not really. I agreed to keep quiet. Part of the settlement. But then again, I suppose I did agree to meet you. I'm glad I did. You're somebody I'd like to know better. You could be fun. You're not a reporter, that's obvious. Private Investigator? What's in this for you? He set up another court reporter with a condo and have it go bad?"

"Something like that. I fix things."

"A private detective?" she said.

"I have a license letting me call myself that, but I refrain from the term. Sounds too ordinary. Too theatrical."

"So," she said. "Good-looking guy like you, what do you call yourself then?"

"Thanks for the compliment," he said. "You're an attractive woman. I could enjoy talking to you. I might even enjoy getting to know you better."

"So what do you call yourself if you don't call yourself a private dick?"

"You can call me anything you like. Here's my number." He handed her his card. "I think of myself as a fixer. Just a fixer. So, Jackie. How is he?"

"The Judge? Oh, I thought you knew. You're representing a court reporter and all who he's setting up in a condo. He's a pervert."

"I didn't say my client was a court reporter. Something less exotic, actually. Yes, I got it about the pervert part, but it would be very helpful if I can distinguish between current perversities and past perversities," he said.

"Clever choice of words," she said. "and smart. Just how interested are you in his particular perversities?"

"Very interested. Suppose you clue me in a little."

"Interested enough to take me on vacation for a week to Vegas or someplace? Have your way with me? Ply me with liquor? Tie me up and torture me until I tell all?"

"Probably not," he said.

"Okay," she said. "Just checking. Had to ask. See the departure gate he's going to? That gate boards a plane that goes to Costa Rica. Another plane leaves in eight, then another in twenty-four hours."

"I take it wicked things happen in Costa Rica," he said. "And you would know because The Judge has taken you to Costa Rica and you were part and parcel of those wicked things."

"Oh my," she laughed. "You're quite insightful."

"His wicked games in Costa Rica, is he good at them?"

She laughed a hearty earthy laugh. "Are you kidding? Look at him. He's fifty pounds overweight. He'll be sixty years old before he gets another shot at an appellate court appointment and he won't make it. He lives in Florida and I swear his skin is as white as a Klansman's' sheet. More like a pasty pink. He has no body hair and it's not because he shaves it off. Gross. I like a man who has hair and smells like man. You'd think he could take at least one walk a year on the beach. His willy is short and his record time for lovemaking, if that's what you call it, is not quite one minute. I think he averages about twenty seconds. But you knew all this, I suppose."

"He's more cerebral," said Edward. "In his proclivities, I take it."

"He arranges orgies is more like it. He likes to watch the girl of the year take on darker skinned sorts. Especially if she's reluctant and has to be tied up first. Then afterwards, he beats the woman of the year for liking it. He gets off on power. Power is his aphrodisiac. What a girl doesn't or shouldn't want, he wants."

"And you got tired of that?" said Edward. "Putting on private porno shows for him. With men of color?"

"Careful, Ahab. You're hitting close to home. I like my men built more like you, when the choice is entirely mine. Let's just say if I want a man who is tall, and athletic, then I like to make my own arrangements. Say, how tall are you anyway?"

"We can talk about me later," he said.

"Maybe we could talk about us. Are you married?"

"Informally – many times over. Once formally," he said. "They don't last."

"You fool around?" she said.

"Often. I have no scruples, and few moral tenants. We can discuss mutual carnal desires when the sun has cast a shadow over the yardarm. It's still early. Until then, tell me just a little bit more about our mutual friend."

"You won't catch him with his pants down, if that's what you mean," she said. "He's very careful. Very. He does what I said he does. But, like I said, he's careful about where he does what with whom. His wife doesn't know or doesn't care. She's very rich, was born rich and holds tight to her money. He told me he'd divorce her, and I'm betting he's told the current one he's getting a divorce. But he won't. It's not politically or financially prudent. He takes one mistress at a time and he pushes, pushes, pushes until she pushes back, or refuses, or throws herself off a bridge without leaving a note. If she pushes back, he throws her into the street."

"That ever happen? A girl throwing herself off a bridge because of him, I mean," he said.

"Check it out. I can't prove it. But a few years back. Seven years, I think," she said. "A third year staffer did a swan dive off the Sunshine Skyway Bridge. Was in the same firm he worked at."

"He a generous lover?" he said.

"Paid my car off. But then I was his playtoy for more than two years. He likes to space things out. He didn't do it in one installment, you can be sure of that. Paid my student loans off. Gave me a gas card and a Victoria's Secret card. He paid my rent until I got tired of the trips to Costa Rica. Truth is, I'd been tired of him long before I refused another trip to Costa Rica," she said.

"Drugs much?"

"Me yes, him no. I quit after him. It made it bearable, the drugs. But they made me feel dirty afterwards. He likes to watch. The drugs loosen a girl up to the things he wants to see. He got me started with weed, then a bit of coke, other stuff too. I'd done them before. Schoolgirl thing. Most everybody does. He had connections."

"Black guy named Valmay?" he said.

"That's him. Kind of ghetto. Slim and athletic. Valmay wanted to take over managing me. Everybody wanted to pimp me out. I was supposed

261

to be a high class hooker, but always available to them, and keep my day job too. It was a game between me, him and The Judge. Three people, all vying for control. I think this guy Valmay and The Judge trade names of likely girls from time to time."

"How so?" said Edward.

"The Judge gave me his number. After I'd bought his stuff a few times, The Judge suggested I trade favors for drugs. He got off on it. Valmay didn't mind, but he wanted more favors than he offered in drugs. The Judge knew about every time I played with Valmay. Wanted a one hour description of what I did with him for every thirty minutes I spend on my back or on my knees, you know, bent over."

"This didn't happen in Costa Rica, I'd guess," he said.

"No. Thing is, The Judge had a thing about not being present when I did it with Valmay or anybody else here. He got off, just knowing, and having me tell him what dirty things I did. I think he had a way to secretly videotape stuff. Not sure. But in Costa Rica. That's where the gloves came off. You ever been to Costa Rica?"

"I have," he said "Good place to fish. Low cost of living. Women are plentiful."

"You like women?" she asked.

"I love women," he said.

"More than one at a time?" she said.

"Whenever I can," he said.

"You like watching – like The Judge does?" she said.

"You mean one woman many men?"

"Yes," she said.

"Not particularly. I'm not opposed to it. I just like women better."

"You like the other thing The Judge likes?" she said in a lower voice.

"I thought I just answered that," he said.

"No, you implied you preferred multiple women to one woman many men. The Judge likes other species too. You into that?"

"I told you I have no scruples and few moral tenants. But that would be one of my limits. To answer your question, no I'm not into that. Not into underage either."

"See there? You and The Judge are different then. Would you like to go to Costa Rica? I could show you around."

"The sun hasn't gone over the yardarm yet. Are you typically this forward?"

"I'm never, ever this forward. I'm on vacation for two weeks, starting yesterday. You called an hour after my plans for a deliciously wicked vacation went all to shit and I'm crazy in the mood to be wicked. Talking about The Judge has brought back some old memories. I probably wouldn't go with you to Costa Rica if you asked me to."

"But the sun hasn't crossed the yardarm yet and we haven't had a rum runner or a Pina colada yet.

And a great deal of wickedness can be had right here in Sarasota."

"You teasing me?"

"I am. But like I said, the day is young. I have plenty of time to investigate. You're on vacation, I have no scruples and few morals. From the tone of our conversation, I don't think you do either. That makes a basis for extended conversation. I will, however tell you I prefer to be the aggressor."

"Sorry, I was being a slut wasn't I?" she said. "I happen to like aggressive men. Tell me more."

"A woman who is easily compromised is not necessarily a bad thing. Notice I did not use the word slut. Sounds too common. I like uncommon. I might even surprise you. But the sun ...."

"Hasn't been over the yardarm yet," she finished for him. "Boy that sun is slow today."

"True, but I have it on excellent authority it will eventually make that journey. Now, tell me about the breakup. Off the record. I really need to know. And when you've told me what I need to know, perhaps we can have an early lunch."

"I just had coffee and breakfast," Jackie said.

"Mimosa's are part of lunch," said Edward.

"And Margarita's too, sometimes," said Jackie.

"Exactly."

CHAPTER FIFTY-TWO
MARGARITAS FOR JACKIE

Jackie wanted to go to Costa Rica. After she'd ordered three Margaritas, she was more than ready. Two for the price of one. That made six Margaritas, but she wasn't counting.

"Thass my place," she said as Edward drove her to an understated apartment two blocks from the sailor-kissing-a-nurse statue in Sarasota. "Come on in. Be just a sec. Woan take long to pack. How long we going for?"

"Not long," said Edward.

"Wanna see my bed. Room?" she asked, then giggled. "Didn't make my bed thisss morning."

"Sure," said Edward.

He followed her into the bedroom.

"Oopsie," she said, falling flat on her back on the bed. "We might have to take advantage of me and take a lil nap before we get high, hee hee hee."

She closed her eyes just for a moment.

When she woke, she had a headache and it was dark outside. A note was on the sink in her bathroom, but she didn't notice it until she rinsed her mouth out.

The note was brief. *A gentleman does NOT take advantage of a lady who is under the influence.*

Edward had gone to Costa Rica without her.

CHAPTER FIFTY-THREE
THE CLEAR SOUND
OF HELL-NO

"Why do I get the feeling you are following me?" asked Judge Bean.

Judge Jack Bean looked quite at home at the Sportsman's Lodge in San Jose, Costa Rica. He was checked in as O Wendell Holmes, and the entire staff knew him from many visits. His friends called him Jack. That included everyone in San Jose.

Edward walked up to him amongst a cluster of balding middle-aged men telling grandiose stories about the women he'd bedded. The subject of discussion that moment was a young woman, probably underage, who'd just left the table. Many of the men at the Sportsman's Lodge told tall tales. Most of the stories involved women and sex. Many were true. The crowd of listeners took a look at Edward, smelled trouble and found seats elsewhere.

"Not following you anymore, Judge," said Edward. "I'm joining you for a drink. Your underage girlfriend will be back in a few minutes. In the meantime, I'm trying to fix something before it gets broken so bad not even superglue will work. We need to talk."

"I'm not sure we do. Are you really who you said you were back in Sarasota, or is this some kind of game? A shakedown maybe? If so, it won't work," said The Judge.

"I'll be quick about it," said Edward. "I've been doing my homework. You're a dirty old man. I don't care, really. Except you're going to give it up with Linda. Recuse yourself from her divorce case. Any other course of action is far too expensive for you."

"Ahh, so that's why you're here", said The Judge. "My answer is no."

"No? You have to be kidding me," said Edward.

"How about *hell no*, then," said The Judge.

"Can you afford it?" asked Edward. "The consequences, I mean."

"Actually, I can," he said. "Lay your worst scenario on me. And after you've done that, I'll ruin your day, the purpose of your trip and I'll tell you hell no, again."

"I prove you've been having an affair with her. If I have to, I show the world other dirty little things that dirty fat old men like you don't want to get put into the local papers. You should never have allowed yourself to sit in judgment on her divorce. You shouldn't have found her an attorney who would trade sexual favors for services. You're going to get removed as The Judge of record, which is what I want anyway, so you're not ahead at that point. If I have to do it my way, your wife divorces you. You lose your judgeship. Linda still won't get much – if anything – from Roger. Is that motivation enough?"

"That the worst you got?"

"Not bad enough for you?" asked Edward.

"Look, it's like this. I've been poking pretty girls for a long time. I know the difference between a lazy slut and a woman who's God's gift to men. Linda is in the second category. She's not a hypocrite like most girls. Not particularly vain. Doesn't give a crap for Louis Viton. Doesn't ask for much, almost nothing actually. But she's totally and completely grateful when I do little things for her. A grateful woman! How rare! My wife – well let's just say she's been driving me crazy since Nixon got nominated. After this weekend, it's all about me and Linda. This is my last fling with puberty. I have no intention of seeing my wife again, ever. EVER.

"It also just so happens I have got something slow growing in a part of me that insures an unhappy ending. So, I totally and completely don't give two shits about much of anything anymore except the next few weeks or months. I could be happy for a while with Linda. If it gets in the papers – so what? You want to know something?"

"Shoot," said Edward.

"Linda has a few flaws. But she's loyal as hell. When you and Roger's lawyer do your worst to me, she'll see me make this sacrifice for her – my marriage, my judgeship – which by the way is not a fun job, and which would not have ended up with an appellant appointment, and Linda will definitely stand by me until my light burns out. You ever meet her? Or are you just a bully who works as a private dick for her redneck husband?"

"I know her," said Edward. "Quite well in fact."

"Really?" said Judge Bean.

"Really," said Edward.

"So, there's probably not a lot left to debate. You know my motivations and you know I'm right, don't you?"

"Actually, she's probably that loyal," said Edward. "But she deserves better. She couldn't stand being with you for long."

"I don't have long. I'll take what I can get. Besides, she and I have some adventures to enjoy together. Adventures she hasn't tried yet. Adventures I need to enjoy one more time. Or more."

"She tells me you're pretty below average in the bedroom," said Edward. "That bother you?"

"She's probably right. Nope. Doesn't bother me much at all. I get off when I'm with her. That's the goal, isn't it? I put other men on her. She tell you that?"

"I understand it's your thing," said Edward. "Watching – playing God."

"We all have our buttons," said The Judge. "Don't tell me you don't have any."

"I do. Different buttons, though," said Edward.

"Care for another scotch?" offered The Judge. "Maybe you can tell me what your buttons are. If you're really as hot for Linda as you suggest, maybe we can come to some sort of compromise. Get our buttons lined up, so to speak."

The Judge raised his hand, got the attention of the barmaid who had served them their drink, and pointed at Edward, indicating she should bring him another drink.

Edward sat expressionless until the barmaid came around with his drink.

"I have a better than average working knowledge of modern medicine," said Edward. "Perhaps you'll be so kind as to tell the name of your ailment."

"I doubt you've heard of it," said The Judge. "I had to endure a great deal of discomfort from three different clinics before going to Johns Hopkins. They confirmed."

The Judge named the cancer. He used the formal Latin name.

Edward looked into The Judge's eyes. He wasn't lying.

"You were informed correctly. The ending will be extremely difficult. Painful. Since you say you're willing to endure public exposure, to suffer humiliations of the highest kind, I would presume you're not a particularly religious man."

"You're entirely right about that," said The Judge. The smile on his face suggested he'd played poker once or twice without giving up a clue as to what he was holding in his hand.

"So, when the time comes, you'll overdose on something that will give you a painless, perhaps even a euphoric exit," said Edward. "Without qualms of any kind."

"Again, you're entirely correct. Somebody else can deal with the aftermath. I won't be around and when the pain outweighs the pleasures Linda will give me, I can be gone. So, as I suggested a moment ago, perhaps a compromise of sorts? You have yet to tell me what your buttons are."

"A compromise is indeed in order," said Edward. "I agree. You recuse yourself from Linda's case. You retire from the bench. You give her an endowment of one thousand dollars a month for ten years, and I'll get your divorce for you. She won't be named though. Nobody has to be hurt more than minimally, not even your wife. There are lots of girls who would love to accompany you on your journey. Just not Linda. You'll never see Linda or speak to her again. And…"

"I don't think you understand," interrupted The Judge, "I'm keeping her. One way or the other, she'll stay with me. She has to. She needs the security and comforts and guidance I can offer her. I intend to give her a great deal more than a measly thousand dollars a month. If you start a bidding war, she'll hate you for it. I was there for her long before you. She'll be loyal to me."

"And," said Edward, "By doing this my way, when you die by whatever means you die, you will have all your body parts attached. All of them. And just so you understand what I mean when I say that, I suggest you check the current status of Valmay's reproductive organs. He's recovering now, but he is a very, very unhappy former pimp."

"Oh, so you're going to be mean to me. Is that what you're threatening me with? Really, Paul. It is Paul isn't it? Oh my, maybe you have another name too? No matter. So, you hurt me, I get Linda hurt. I happen to know a lot of people. And if Valmay is out of commission, that's his problem," said The Judge.

"I wasn't threatening you judge. I was telling you what will happen if you don't recuse. My offer is good. Think about it. It could be a lot worse. And in case you'd forgotten something, Judge." Edward paused. "I shouldn't need to remind you. If you're in prison, even if you're maimed, you can be put on suicide watch. And on suicide watch, no oxy pills. Not even from Valmay. The end would *not* be as you planned."

Edward got up from the table, turned to walk away, and placed his drink on the edge of the tablecloth directly in front of The Judge. He began to walk away from him, and in the process, bumped The Judge's wrist. The Judge was holding tight to the tablecloth with both hands. The slight movement of the tablecloth tipped the glass of scotch into his lap.

Edward smiled as The Judge jumped, then said, "You asked me what my button was. I'll show you…some other time."

CHAPTER FIFTY-FOUR
RECUSE A CONDEMNED GAVEL

"Is the doctor in?" said Edward.

Rosemary laughed as his silhouette filled the doorway, then walked into the reception area in front of Chip's office. As usual, he wore a black turtleneck, black jeans and suede boots – also black. "No, you're stuck with me for the moment. He's still taking a deposition downtown. Another malpractice thing. But he should be back pretty soon."

"Okay," said Edward. "I'll wait on the sofa in his office while I ruminate on my failings in life, if that's okay with you. Might even go to sleep. It's a comfortable sofa."

"Or," she said, "You could sit out here and tell me all your dirty private inner thoughts. I'm just as good a shrink as he is. Almost anyway."

"Rosemary, you're flirting with me again," said Edward. "And it won't get either one of us anywhere but in trouble."

"That's why I'm doing it," she said. "A girl can have fantasies, even if she knows that nothing will come of it. You're safe to flirt with. Nothing will come of it, right?"

"I promised Chip," he smiled. "You and Cindy are off limits."

"Cindy definitely. The boss's wife is definitely off limits. She thinks you might be a bad influence on him," she said. "I'm an aging widow woman with needs, you know. But any promises you made to Chip about me were made under unfair duress. I'm just sayin'…"

"What promises?" Chip said as he entered the front door, ignoring Edward for the moment. He handed Rosemary a file folder and said, "Court reporter will have it all transcribed and in our hands by Thursday. No need to do anything with my notes at this point. This thing is going to settle out cheap and quick. Doctor McCarthy's insurance company won't get hurt on this one. Fees only."

He looked at Edward and repeated, "What promises?"

Rosemary blushed and answered for Edward. "I was flirting with him, just like always, boss. He was being a perfect gentleman. Just like always. He has that look on his face today. You know the one."

"No, Rosemary, I don't," said Chip. "He hides wrinkles, scars, and facial expressions behind that beard of his. Part of his charm I guess. I figured a long time ago I don't want to play poker with someone whose face is covered with a beard like that."

"Boss, it's beer-thirty," said Rosemary. "Even I can see he has a *I want to talk things over* look on his face."

Chip shrugged his shoulders in resignation, loosened his tie, and headed to his office. Over his shoulder, he said, "I have a cold beer or two in my refrigerator. Evidently Edward and I have some guy talk to take care of. I'm done being a lawyer for today. Good night, Rosemary."

"I'm not invited?" she asked.

The door closed behind Edward. Neither man answered.

"So, it's official," said Edward. "You're my attorney when I need one. You get me clients when I don't need any. And now you're my shrink too. Rosemary finally figured it out. Same hourly rates for therapy as for lawyering?"

"Therapy costs double. I don't have a license to practice that. So it costs double," said Chip. "Not like I'd know how to bill for that kind of thing."

"But client patient confidentially rules still apply, I hope," said Edward.

"It does, but I don't do therapy cheap. It might require excessive thinking or I might have to go back to school, or read papers on the subject of your peculiarities if we do therapy, which would give me a headache. Counseling, is free though. My lawyering bill is Rosemary's job to compute, figure out, and then send out in the mail. The total cost for therapy today depends on what my bar tab is at *The Parrot.*"

"Your bar tab is an ongoing thing. One day we might settle up," said Edward. "Or not."

"As your underpaid shrink, I now get to say – so, how do you feel about that?" said Chip as he handed Edward a bottle of beer.

Edward made it to the long leather covered sofa first.   Chip had to settle for his overstuffed executive chair to sprawl in.

"I think I messed up," said Edward.   "I gotta change my methods when dealing with people. Maybe find a new approach to convincing people to do things the easy way.   Latest mess-up is The Judge."

"I thought it was going to go smoothly," said Chip.   "Him being a pansy-looking dirty old man and all."

"New circumstances, new rules," said Edward. "Bastard wants to keep her, and he has a potentially workable, very devious plan I haven't figured a way to overturn.   Evidently his stones are harder than tort laws in Boston."

"Don't start with the legal terms.   That's my job. Me-lawyer, you-pirate or something like that.   We have the goods on him.   He can't possibly hear this case.   He'll get…"

"Says he's got terminal brain cancer.   I believe him.   His citations and diagnostics   are right on. Unless he's the world's best liar and forger, and I don't think he is, then he's right.   He's got six months to a year," said Edward.

"Shit, so he gets to play God and drive us crazy until he loses his seat on the bench or dies?   I have to go the long arduous route?   Man, that's going to be a pain."

"He plans on losing it. If he hasn't already moved out on his wife, it'll be just a day or so. It's almost like he's happy to be a short termer."

"So, how are we going to deal with a man who has a death sentence and a gavel?" said Chip.

"Beats me," said Edward. "He wants to finish his bucket list of things to do before he dies – with Linda stuffed into the bucket – so to speak. From what I hear about his proclivities, he'd ruin her. Drag her so deep down in the sewer she'd never get out."

"And you couldn't tolerate that," said Chip. "Even though she isn't your client, and Roger is. Even though she's a grown woman who ought to be able figure his devious plan out without any help?"

"Nope. And nope again. I could not tolerate it. I even suggested I'd give him the same surgery Valmay got and get his ass thrown into prison. He didn't blink. He's calling my bluff."

"So, he's turned from a cowardly, sneaky, egg-sucking weasel, into a rogue mustang stallion protecting the last mare in the herd? Where did that come from?"

"You're the shrink, I'm a just a primal pirate, remember?" said Edward.

"Before we get too deep in the shrink stuff, let me ask you. Are you in love with her?"

"Unfair question. Let's just say for once, something should in the best interest of the lady in question, and if I happen to be part of the equation, then so be it," said Edward.

"It's getting past my pay grade as an already underpaid shrink, but let me take a guess. This guy, he's into domination, right?" said Chip.

"Heavy into it."

"Sadism too?" said Chip.

"Over the top," said Edward. "Been a closet henchman with a gavel for a long time."

"Guys like that, they sometimes like the taste of both ends of the whip," said Chip.

"Actually, I think that might explain a lot," said Edward. "Yeah, it fits right in with some things he said to me. I'm sure he's setting us up to get his picture in the newspapers and whatever TV or other media we can out him with. That's him getting kicked around, which gives him something to grovel in."

"And he doesn't really care, because plans of getting an appellant court seat are impossible if he's dying anyway. Got no kids and he's an avowed atheist, isn't he?"

"Avowed. In practice, more like an antichrist," said Edward.

Chip laughed. "So he doesn't care about divine judgment. He's stayed married because his wife owns the money-tree. He plans on us flogging him publicly, which makes us the villain. What else? His wife divorces him. Linda sees the sacrifices."

"Money," said Edward. "Best I can figure from the snooping I've done, he has more than half a mil tucked away in places his wife's lawyers won't look. It's sure enough money to let him live the life of debauchery for six months or so."

"And Linda, who you seem to be so hell-bent to protect, will see him as a victim who has been helping her monetarily for a while now. She'll feel guilty because all the crap that's hitting him is because of her. So, she'll hang with him and be his play-toy to the bitter end out of loyalty if nothing else," said Chip.

"Not bad ciphering for an amateur shrink," said Edward.

"So, how are we going to play this? I mean we have to get him off the case, one way or the other," said Chip. "Remember, Roger is the client."

"Got it. Protect Roger. That's a done deal one way or the other. I'll have to think about it. Linda and I have something going. No problem at all, except for The Judge. She's really a smart cookie in her own way. Maybe if I lay it out truthful and honest, she'll do the right thing," said Edward.

"Maybe. But don't count on it. No disrespect to her, but she's a complex woman, you said so yourself. We haven't got much time left before I go to court for Roger to do whatever we're going to do," said Chip. "Have you got enough info for me to take to the judicial review board to get him recused if we go that route?"

"It's ugly stuff, but I have it. It's legal enough to show, but not for minors to see. God, I hope I don't have to use it," said Edward. "Media circus would be unending."

"Okay. One thing more. How much will money play into Linda's decision?" said Chip. "I gotta tell you what people choose to do with their lives is their business, not mine or yours. Fact is, he's been keeping her as a mistress of sorts. How much does that play into her makeup?"

"It's heavy," said Edward. "I understand where she's coming from. She's been living a day-to-day existence. He's paying the rent, car insurance, lights, gas, everything. Gives her just enough spending money, but not enough to enroll in school. Makes demands enough to keep her from getting a job or a life. It's like giving a drowning victim just enough air to get one more breath, then pushing them under again."

"You're financially able to offer Linda a better deal, aren't you?" said Chip.

"I am," said Edward.

"But you're not going to, are you?"

"I am not," said Edward.

"Principle?"

"You changed to lawyer from therapist," said Edward. "Changing back again isn't allowed. That was a trick question."

"Counselor, not therapist. There's a difference," reminded Chip.

"Still a trick question," said Edward. "If I say no, you bring up Hibiscus. I say yes, then you still bring up Hibiscus. I can't have principles about keeping women because of Hibiscus, who is a kept woman – after a fashion."

"This counselor thing is working out pretty good," said Chip. "I might need to add something to my shingle outside. I got you anticipating my questions and answers. So, let me guess. You think you can save Linda?"

"She has everything she needs to move forward in her life, except confidence. She's smart enough, good-looking enough. Job skill short, but who isn't? I've checked her out from every angle. She does stupid stuff, but she's never, ever once done a mean thing to anybody – ever. She just needs a little self-induced nudge. So, if The Judge drops her, then I get to catch her and set her down gently, then she's like the bird you set free that ultimately comes back to perch on your finger. But I can't take care of her like The Judge has been. That would keep her caged. She needs to be *with me* because she want to."

"Not to get too metaphorical," said Chip, "but you have Blackbeard on a perch. That's one and he's a real bird. You have Hibiscus at your fingertips and she's batshit crazy and getting away with it only because you give her credence. That's two birds on one finger. What appendage do you really expect Linda to sit on?"

"They aren't caged, and you're trying to get me off the subject," said Edward. "Should I emasculate The Judge, or should I play it out and see if Linda really and truly will stay loyal to him just because she's a loyal type of girl – which will totally mess her up?"

"I guess I would be out of line pointing out one more time that Roger is your client. And mine too. Valmay's been taken care of. The Judge will get recused, voluntarily or not, sooner or later. Given any reasonable circumstance, everybody wins – with the possible exception of Linda – who you do not owe anything to."

"I suppose it would be fruitless to offer an explanation involving buttons and starfish," said Edward.

"Only after one more beer," said Chip. He got up and took the last two bottles of beer out of the mini refrigerator. He opened both, handed one to Edward and took a sip from the other. "You have ten minutes to tell me about buttons and starfish. After that, I'm going home, and Cindy is going to let me grill a steak in the backyard."

"Our illustrious and evil minded judge tried to negotiate with me about Linda. Implied we could share – pro tem. I told him no. He had something else in mind, wanted to know about what buttons I had that needed to be pushed. I told him I'd show him. Or something like that," said Edward.

"So you have buttons that do it for you, but you're holding those cards close to your vest. Got it. And the starfish? What about them?" asked Chip.

"Starfish, crabs, conchs, scallops, and hundreds of other sea creatures have their own method of navigating across the seafloor. People generally don't know that. They think of the creatures they

282

see in aquariums and fail to notice there's a certain requirement of mobility – or locomotion. Sometimes the tides move our creatures, sometimes they swim by opening and closing valves, or sometimes they crawl tediously across a rocky bottom to get to where they want to go. But they get where they need to be – most of the time."

"Sea creatures," said Chip. "Move in mysterious ways people fail to understand. I got it. Next lesson please."

"Occasionally they mess up. Singularly or in groups. They get their bearings wrong. Take, for instance, a lovely beach where a sudden falling tide has stranded thousands and thousands of starfish all at once. Imagine it in your mind," said Edward.

"Sea creatures failed to know about tide change. Got it," said Chip.

"This is an old parable, but imagine a little boy, who's at the beach and sees the crisis. Instead of standing as an observer to mass suicide while hundreds of these beautiful creatures die, he breaks rank from a group of gawking onlookers and rushes to pick one up and throw it back into the water. Everyone laughs at him. They tell him what he is doing won't make any difference. Thousands of starfish will die, regardless of his feeble efforts," said Edward. "But the little boy says to them, *It makes a difference to this one*, as he throws the starfish out to deeper water where it has a chance to survive."

"So that's your button. You want to save a starfish. Only the starfish is named Linda."

"Well, maybe Hibiscus too," said Edward. "That was always a given."

"I think, my friend, you missed your calling," said Chip. "You should have been a marine biologist."

"I wanted to," said Edward, "but at the urging of a messed up, bible thumping theologian who wanted to mess with peoples' souls, I went to medical school to work on brains and such. And look at where that got me."

"Trying to save starfish," said Chip.

Edward got up and stretched. "I believe you have a date with a pretty woman and an outdoor grill." He moved towards the door.

"One thing we haven't considered yet," said Chip. "Suppose Linda is smarter than we think she is. Suppose she leaves The Judge regardless of all his schemes and your honesty. Where does that leave us?"

"Everybody would be pleased," said Edward, "Except The Judge, who would probably put a gun into his mouth and pull the trigger. That's a pleasant picture."

CHAPTER FIFTY-FIVE
SHITTY EXCUSES

"Hey, guess what!" said Roger.

"Not much to guess at, Roger," said Edward without looking up. He and Chip were reviewing legal documents at the captain's table in *The Eloquent Parrot*. "You said you'd be by Chip's office before noon to sign an affidavit of residency. Rosemary was going to notarize it. You weren't there. Now we're in a time crunch – again."

"Jesus, Joseph and Mary," said Roger. "You sound so much like my boss I think you must be related. I got a good excuse. I swear."

Edward raised his eyes to look directly at Roger.

"Oh, come on," said Roger. "Don't tell me I can't say the name of Baby Jesus without getting in trouble. First, you tell me I can't say the *N* word. Then I got to be polite to Jews. I'm always polite to women on account of you never know which one might want to take you to home for an hour – so you gotta give me that one. Wetbacks gotta take whatever I say, 'cause I'm bigger and badder than the ones I've run into so far. Besides, most of 'em don't *hable' inglese* anyways. Except the ones I work with, they're trying to fit in. I'm nice to them. So what's with the raised eyebrows?"

"We do our part. You do your part," said Chip. "We're close to the end here and we don't need any stupid hiccups, like failing to file required documents on time."

"I told you I got a good excuse," said Roger. His smile suggested somebody should ask.

"So tell us," said Edward, "why are you five hours late?"

"I was in jail," said Roger.

That got Edward and Chip's attention.

"Just for a while," said Roger still beaming at his own secret joke. "Silly state trooper had no sense of humor."

"Tell me you didn't hit anybody," said Chip.

"No boss. I'm done hitting on cops. But I got a couple of outstanding speeding tickets I never got around to taking care of, and there's something called a bench warrant I didn't know about. But Dewey sprung me out after I called her. I gotta be in traffic court in thirty days. Think you can add it to my tab and represent me in court?" said Roger.

"A bench warrant? You have to be kidding me," said Chip. "What did you do that made a state trooper pull you over? No, don't tell me. Let me guess. You were speeding."

"So was he," said Roger. "It isn't right. Those assholes get to drive as fast as they want, whenever they want. Nobody ever pulls *them* over for speeding. Fair is fair. So this yellowjacket comes whizzing up the interstate like he owns the left lane and everybody gets out of his way – except me. If he wants me to make room for him on my road, he has to have those lights going first. So, I hung in the left lane for about a mile with him smelling my ass until finally he goes and whips around me like he was in a roller derby. Fair is fair, so I fell in right behind him. Had maybe a foot between us."

"And he obliged you by turning on the blue lights," said Edward.

"Sure did," said Roger.

"Your road?" said Chip.

"I'm a taxpayer," said Roger. "So it's my road. He's a public servant. I got the same rights as he does. Maybe more."

"You *have* to be kidding," said Edward. "On your way to sign an affidavit in a court case that will decide the rest your life. That will decide who your kids live with, and what else I can't begin to imagine, and you decide to test the ownership of public roadways at that particular moment?"

"Well, when you say it like that," said Roger, "maybe it wasn't the best of times to point out to a public servant who works for who. Or is it whom works for whom?"

"So, he wrote you a speeding ticket," said Chip.

"Not exactly," said Roger. "I told him if he wrote me one, he needed to write himself a ticket too, on account of he couldn't tell me why he was driving down my road in the left-hand lane like Dale Earnhardt Jr. in the first place. I'm not a lawyer like you, but I know he's not allowed to do what he done."

"So?" said Edward.

"I gave him my license and registration real nice-like when he asked for them. So, he was putting it all in his dashboard computer and after I finished telling him what he could and could not do to me, that's when he told me about the bench warrant thing. I never heard about one of them. Handcuffed me and everything. But like I said, Dewey sprung me out. But the thing is, he *did not* write me a ticket for speeding."

Edward shook his head and got up from the table. When he returned five minutes later, he had three beers.

He sat down before saying, "As I recall from a story you told me once upon a time, when a certain person does something really stupid and gets put in jail for it, the person they live with, is clearly justified in leaving that certain person in said jail for about a week, so that said certain person does not repeat said certain stupid acts again. Dewey should have left you're goofy Irish ass in jail, like you did to Linda."

Roger laughed. "There you go again. Trying to teach me something. I knew Dewey would come bail my Irish ass out. So, Chip, are you going to go with me to traffic court?"

"Not one chance in hell," said Chip. "Best advice I have is to pay the outstanding fines and fees at least a week before your court date. And for God's sake, if you have any sense whatsoever, do *not* try to argue law with The Judge in traffic court."

"Awww, where's the fun in that?" said Roger. "Oh, and guess what else?"

"Not today, Roger. Please," said Chip. "Oh, all right. I'll bite. What else?"

"Maybe one of the first things I'm going to do real soon is get a can of yellow paint and paint *SHIT SHIT SHIT* all over the side of my work truck."

"Why in the world would you do that?" said Chip. "I'm certain you'd get another citation and maybe some jail time for that cute act of defiance."

"The county does it. So can I," said Roger.

Neither Chip nor Edward said anything. Edward pushed his ivory and driftwood chair back a foot and slouched – feet spread. The two men waited.

Finally Roger stopped grinning long enough to say, "It's on busses all over the place. SCAT, SCAT, SCAT. Everybody knows scat is shit spelled another way. Even if they don't mean it, they shouldn't say it. Still four letters. Still stinks when you step in it."

"Roger," said Edward. "SCAT is the acronym for Sarasota County Area Transit. And the *everybody* you refer to - knows it. Including you."

"If you say so," said Roger glumly. "I know what acronym means, but they coulda thought of another name like *Broke Folks Everywhere* or something like that. Then people could take a bus to BFE. SCAT just sounds, well, shitty."

CHAPTER FIFTY-SIX
FLOWER DELIVERY

A day later, Roger strolled into *The Eloquent Parrot* found Hibiscus and said, "Dewey said you called the house. Said I was supposed to get over here to *The Parrot* as soon as possible. What's up?"

"Ah mi and de Cap'n ah go," she said, "He got a fine-plan for sumpin'. You and Jasmine keep *de Parrot* 'appy, sure."

"Whatever," said a puzzled Roger as he watched Hibiscus take the hibiscus from behind her ear and throw it into trash receptacle behind the bar.

She slipped though the beads behind the bar, turned right, skipped up the stairs to her room, removed a long black shawl from a neatly stacked section of clothing, walked down the stairs sedately to Edward's office, poked her head inside and said, "Ah mi ready my Cap'n"

Five minutes later, she and Edward left *The Eloquent Parrot* in Edward's pickup truck.

As they drove, neither spoke at first, then Edward carefully chose his words. He began, "I made a promise to Roger. I'd hoped I could influence Linda and The Judge with logic, but it hasn't happened yet. I can't risk it. I simply can't let The Judge make a ruling tomorrow. Regardless of what I've said to you in the past, I need some of your magic. Here's what I want you to make The Judge do…"

After he finished his instructions, Hibiscus dropped the sun visor down to access the vanity mirror took the black scarf and wrapped it about her head creating a hijab.

Edward waited until she'd finished primping and adjusting, then looked to his right, then did a double-take. "Very good, you look totally different. That's perfect. You look exactly like one of those Muslim women I see in Sam's Club when I go with Cookie to pick up supplies for *The Parrot*."

She ignored his comment. "You ax me dis ting. I make it so. You know how to find 'im?"

"I think I can," said Edward. There's only so many places he can be. Right now I know where he's not, so that gives us a list of where he might be."

"Gib me dis judge what being so painful," she said. "You fin 'im and let my eyes see. Den I do dis ting."

"About what we're about to do, we won't discuss this with anybody. Ever. Okay?" said Edward.

"Irie. I need to spy dis judge, wit my own eyes, sure, first maybe I can, and maybe not. We see."

Edward nodded, and set his jaw. Just when they reached US 41, he pulled over into the parking lot of a flower shop. "Be right back. We might need something."

Hibiscus raised her eyebrows but stayed quiet.

"Might need these," said Edward when he got back to the truck. Delivery guys for florists don't get questioned when they deliver them. Most often it's supposed to be a surprise. So, if we need 'em, we got 'em."

Hibiscus noted the flowers weren't roses. They were a mixture of Hibiscus and tulips.

"Fine wit me," she said. "Can you fine where he at now?"

Edward nodded, set his jaw and drove with a purpose.

He went first to the courthouse and drove slowly through the parking lot until he found the spot reserved for The Judge.

"Not here," he said. "I wish I'd used the locator transponder. But we'll find him."

Then he drove to an upscale residential section of town where perfect lawns with perfect landscapes were tended by brown-skinned Hispanics. The houses were all the exact same distance from the road and all the mailboxes were identical except for the numbers on them. Upscale conformity was the rule here.

"Not here either."

Finally he drove back to Siesta Key, then up to Longboat Key where tall condominiums looked out over the Gulf of Mexico. He found the condo entrance he was looking for.

He drove the truck right up to the guard gate.

The guard came out of a tiny house not much larger than a phone booth with a clipboard in his hand.

Edward didn't even wait for him to speak. "Got a delivery of flowers for Judge Bean. Somebody has the hots for him."

"No problem, you know what unit to deliver to?"

"Says C-201 on the card," said Edward.

He opened the gate and let Roger and Hibiscus through. "There it is," said Edward, pulling into a parking lot. "The black Mercedes. It's his license plate. You know what to do. I think he needs some special words from you. Let's find out."

"I be bok soon," she said.

He sat in the truck with the engine running. Hibiscus got out, wrapped the shawl around her head once more so only her eyes showed. Taking a single flower from the tissue-wrapped bunch, she held it by her side. With her other hand, she draped the corners over her shoulders and as Edward watched her walk to the front entrance of the condominium unit, her gait changed from an island woman to the gait of a demure Muslim woman. It was as if he was seeing a magic trick.

She disappeared from sight, found the stairways to the second floor and walked up. At unit C-201 she knocked on the door.

Judge Bean opened the door with a glass of bourbon in his hand. He was wearing a bathrobe. She smelled the alcohol on his breath. "Can I help you?" he said.

"Allah has sent me to lift your spirits," she said in an Arabic accent. "You are deserving of gifts from the sacred one."

"Sorry," he said. "You have the wrong unit. I'm a non-believer."

"The place is right. You are he that I seek. It will take but a moment to pluck the sickness from inside your head. I must only touch your hand and then I will be gone. By this, you will know your destiny." She extended a hibiscus bloom. He didn't take it immediately.

For a moment, his eyes showed alertness, as if he might back away, withdraw into the apartment, and be gone. But her eyes held his. She nodded once and slowly as if approaching a cat that didn't want to be touched, she took his left hand and held it gently as she placed the hibiscus bloom into it. She took his other hand, held it firmly and stroked it with her other hand. She lightly squeezed the web between his thumb and forefinger.

His eyelids drooped and his body relaxed at her touch.

"That is all," she said, "I needed to do for you."

With that, she withdrew and walked away, leaving a mildly euphoric, smiling, mystified man behind her. He'd let the flowers fall to his feet. As she turned, she noticed he was becoming aroused. He had nothing on underneath the bathrobe. He smiled.

She smiled too, before disappearing into the stairwell.

Edward watched her as she approached the truck moments later. As she got nearer to the truck, her gait again became the gait of a sensuous Jamaican woman. He blinked his eyes several times to make sure they weren't tricking him. Inside the truck, she removed the shawl and sat sideways on the seat, exposing her leg.

"Bizz-ness done for now, mon," she said. "I tink de judge not a problem. Blackbeard gwine be 'appy when I tell him 'bout dis."

CHAPTER FIFTY-SEVEN
GIVE ME ONE MORE NIGHT

Edward punched the button to take them to the fourth floor, where the Columbia Restaurant overlooked a panoramic view of Tampa Bay. They were in St. Petersburg on a pier that was once dubbed The Million Dollar Pier, but was now scheduled for demolition. The view was still breathtaking.

Linda wore a long, flowing evening dress. She'd obviously spent a lot of time putting her makeup on, and fixing her hair.

Edward's concession to convention was to put a black blazer over his turtleneck. And he'd made reservations.

"I'm impressed," she said. "This is better than any date I can remember. Guys my age just don't get it. Thank you, thank you."

"Maybe this would be a good time to call the valet service, retrieve our car, and go home then," said Edward. He smiled. "Seeing as how you're already impressed and we haven't yet ordered anything that has flames as part of the entree. Maybe I should quit while I'm ahead on points and you're still impressed. It makes for a better outcome to quit while ahead."

He got a punch on the arm for his comment. "Don't short change me, big man," she said. "I'm having a good time so far."

"Crap," he said. "I think I made one of my strategic mistakes again."

"Huh?" she said.

"The last time we were on this kind of roll, I started a conversation that made you jump off a sailboat. Wasn't a happy end to an otherwise great date."

"I thought I apologized for that already," she said. "Oh. I get it, you're going to go there again."

"Either now or after dessert. Take your pick," he said. "The hearing is tomorrow."

She smiled. "Hit me now. Take your best shot. But when you've said what you want to say, let's drop it and finish the meal and enjoy ourselves. Okay? Let's worry about tomorrow, tomorrow."

"Deal," he said.

She looked down at her glass of ice water and waited.

"I think you should fire your lawyer," he said. "Get a new one. I'm thinking somehow we can find a way to cover the legal fees. Tell the new lawyer you'll settle this thing with Roger easily. You'd get a divorce out of it, probably limited visitation if you want."

"Nothing I would like better," she said. "But it's more complicated than…."

"I'm not done," he said. "Whatever deal you have with The Judge, I think it's time to let him go. You're not in love with him."

"That's true," she said. "He knows it. Says he doesn't care. He just wants me to brighten his life while… While, well, it's complicated."

"He told you he's dying," said Edward. "He's telling the truth. Whatever other promises he's made to you – might or might not be the truth."

"He told me if I stick it out to the end, he'll give me three-hundred-thousand dollars," she said. "Do you think he's lying?"

"He's a true-blue bastard," said Edward. "He might, or might not be lying. Who knows? But that's not the thing. The money, if you actually got it, would ruin your life. You wouldn't like yourself. You'd become something awful. And you know it. It's not enough to live off of for as long as you think. You'd snort, drink, or use whatever you needed to dull your senses while you're with him doing the things that might have been fun once."

"But only once," she finished. "You're talking about my bucket list of sexual experiences I want to experience before I die."

"It wouldn't be your bucket list," he said. "It would be his. And he's done just about everything. And too, you might end up dying. Not a good thing.

"He will push you into a slime pit you can't climb out of. You know that, don't you? I do hope you know I can't let that happen. Won't let it happen. But I'd prefer it was your choice, not mine."

"Are you trying to talk me out of it, for my sake, or for your personal sense of chivalry?" she asked. "Or Edward, my sweet Edward. Is it that you want me for yourself?"

"Shit, you must have a lawyer in your family tree," he said. "That was a question that has many answers. First off, I would like you to be with me and not him."

"I've been afraid it was going to come to this," she said. "You're telling me if I don't leave The Judge, I can't see you."

"A hard thing to say, but yes," he said.

"But you care about me. You believe he'll be such a bad influence I will hate myself for the rest of my life," she said.

"Yes."

"I love you for that," she said. "Anything else you need to tell me?"

"I could give you details of what a dirty-rotten bastard The Judge is, but something tells me you'll figure it out quickly enough. So, I guess I'm done."

"What about me? Seriously. What about my rent next month? How am I going to go to school and work and…"

"It's been done before," he said. "Thousands and thousands of times. Tough for me to say, but you asked. The only right thing to do is to climb the ladder one rung at a time. I'm thinking with a little persuasion, we could get some kind of program going that gets rid of your past legal bills. Your current lawyer is paid in full."

"Got it," she said smiling. "All this sounds a lot like the offer you made me the other day. So, you offer me – you – who happens to be living part time with a Voodoo witch. I get to get a job and work really hard, but you won't give me any money. But I can go to school until I'm employable.

"On the other hand, there's this guy who I don't really like who is offering me everything, including bucket list sex like I want, and a butt full of money. Plus, I really do owe him my loyalty because he's done a lot for me. And you want me to choose you."

"Well, we could definitely create a sexual bucket list. I'm all for that. Although probably not as sordid as The Judge offers," he said. "But hard honest work will set you free."

"Fine," she said. "So, why don't we do this? We enjoy the finest meal we can. No booze, not a drop. Since Hibiscus and I danced on the beach, I haven't had a drop to drink, a hit of any kind of drug, and I don't crave any of them.

"Then, after dinner, you buy me a nice light dessert before you get your car from the valet. And you take me to your place and you ravish me like a pirate who hasn't had sex in three-hundred years or whatever. Make love to me, too. We'll do some bucket list things, or not. Then maybe tomorrow morning after breakfast, I might decide what to do. The hearing isn't until nine-thirty. You have loads of time to seduce and influence me."

"I can do that," he said.

CHAPTER FIFTY-EIGHT
COME OUT, COME OUT,
WHERVER YOU ARE

"Mmmm," said Edward, "When you finally decide to come out of the head, I would kill for a cup of coffee. It's almost seven in the morning. A decision should be made soon."

The bathroom door he was speaking to didn't answer. The shower had ceased hissing a full ten minutes before, and he was sure he'd heard the whine of the hairdryer before he drifted back to sleep.

"Hello in there," he said.

No response.

Swinging his legs over the side of the bed, he debated on whether or not to put something on before knocking on the bathroom door. Surely she was engrossed in some girl stuff, but his condo only had one bathroom, and he had needs. Considering the play they'd engaged in the night before, he decided modesty was not required.

He stood and knocked on the door.

No response.

Still knocking, he turned the door handle. The room was empty. There was a note on the vanity.

It was short and sweet. *I'm so sorry. Last night was perfect. God, how I wish it could go on forever. But it can't. Please forgive my weaknesses. I just have to take what I can – while I can.*

CHAPTER FIFTY-NINE
DEAD END, END-TO-END

The day of the hearing was chaotic for everyone, especially for the parking attendants. Eddie always enjoyed a little excitement, but not like this.

"What the fuck is this?" asked Judge Bean as he drove to the blocked entrance.

"I'm sorry, your Honor," said Eddie. He looked down into The Judge's black Mercedes. The Judge had a reputation for being bad tempered. Today was no exception. Eddie could smell bourbon on The Judge's breath. The Judge hadn't shaved for several days, and he smelled like he needed a bath.

"So, stop being sorry, and clear the way so I can park my fucking car," said The Judge. "I'm late for court."

"I can't, your Honor. Judge Sanders has that triple homicide case starting today. They have the place full of potential jurors. Every slot, including the one-reserved for judges, is filled. Brought them in from everywhere. Judge Sanders wants all the press and paparazzi and shit out. He commandeered the entire parking lot, both levels. But he has a shuttle running for the other courtrooms. If you'll..."

"Fuck that," said The Judge. "I haven't time for this shit. Here, get in my car."

"Your Honor, I can't," said Eddie.

"You want to keep your fucking job, you'll do what I tell you. Get in."

Eddie got in the passenger's side nervously.

"So, here's what I'm going to do," said The Judge. "I'm going to swing around the building to the drop off point where the shuttle bus picks everybody up. Then I'm going to follow the bus to where he drops them off. I'll get out and you drive my car to wherever the fuck you want. Then you bring me my keys. When I'm done with court today, I'll call down. You come up, get my keys, get my car and meet me at the drop off point. Just like a valet would do it. Got it?"

"Yes your Honor," said Eddie.

The Judge drove through the back lot furiously, until he found a lane where the shuttle had been running and broke through to it. Cutting in ahead of the shuttle, he giggled a girlish giggle as he squealed his tires and sped to the back entrance of the courthouse.

Just as they got there, Eddie smelled the scent of fresh cut flowers and vanilla. It didn't come from The Judge. Perhaps The Judge smelled it too, because he smiled a satisfied smile.

"There," he said, as he viciously pushed the gearshift into park. "Just remember to bring me my keys before noon." He opened the door carelessly, got out quickly but unsteadily and walked directly into the path of a speeding shuttle bus that had *SCAT, Sarasota Area Rapid Transit,* printed on it in large letters.

The bus made two loud thumps as it drove over him – end to end.

CHAPTER SIXTY
JUDGE'S CHAMBERS

Dewey sat on the hardwood bench in the waiting room just outside The Judge's chambers and glared harshly at Linda who sat on the other side of the room, very, very alone.

Roger sat between Chip and Dewey, and tapped his foot impatiently. He looked at his watch at three-minute intervals. For once, he wasn't wearing a smile. But he was wearing a tie with a stain on it, and a shirt that had no business being in the same room as a tie.

Judge Bean was late. Several times in the thirty minutes before then, his legal aide informed them several times The Judge would be there in just a few more minutes.

Linda stood, straightened her skirt with the palms of her hands, then tentatively approached Chip, all the while looking at Roger.

"Could I talk to you for just a minute?" she asked. "Over there." She gestured to the other side of the room. "I have something really important to tell you."

"I can't talk to you unless you have your attorney present," said Chip. "I really can't. Sorry."

"I told my attorney I no longer wanted him to represent me," said Linda. "Maybe Edward could..."

"He's not here to fix all your problems in life right now, it looks like," spat Dewey. "Maybe you should just go take a long walk off a short pier or something."

Roger let his grin find its rightful place on his face, then laughed – releasing all the tension he'd been holding in. "Shit, Linda. You and me shouldn't be fighting anymore."

Turning to Dewey he said, "Honey, you can sit here for a minute and be real quiet, or you can go get a drink of water. If Linda wants to say something to me and if Chip happens to be sitting next to me when she says it, no harm I guess."

"Fine by me," said Dewey. "I need to go to the ladies' room anyway." She got up and left.

"Roger, I'm sorry I hired that sleazebag lawyer. I fired him this morning. I sent him a text and said the deal was off. I don't want anything more from you than a divorce, so you can marry Dewey. I'm really sorry about David getting killed in Ft. Myers. Really, I know how close you two were."

"Nope, no more marriages," said Roger. "Been there, done that. But me and her are good together. Just so's you know, I actually got my nuts clipped. Clarissa and the twins are all the kids I need forever. Edward made me..."

The Judge's legal aide came back through the doors. Her eyes were red, her makeup was running. She had a handkerchief in her hands.

"I'm so, so sorry, everybody. Court is postponed today. There's been a horrible accident. The Judge can't see you today." Without further explanation, she turned and hurried through the large, hardwood doors back to The Judge's chambers.

CHAPTER SIXTY-ONE
MERMAIDS – ONLY TWO?

A twenty-minute drive distance from the courthouse, Edward sat on a cast concrete bench on the sandy white beach near the sea oats where Linda and Hibiscus had danced in the drum circle just days before. A breeze blew in from the Gulf exciting the surf to create a soothing melody. Children played, built sandcastles, flew kites, and chased each other in circles while their mothers lay on towels and baked themselves. As he watched them, he wondered deep thoughts.

He'd been sitting there for two hours, just staring at the Gulf. The outcome was certainly over by now. Would Linda figure it out, or not? If she figured it out, would she understand? Was Hibiscus as capable in her manipulations as he hoped?

Hibiscus came silently to him from behind where he was seated. She was barefoot. In one hand she carried a pair of sandals. In her other hand she carried Edward's cell phone.

Wordlessly, she sat next to him.

For several minutes, they sat silently next to one another. Then, putting her shoes down, she reached over and grabbed his hand in hers and held it.

"I never asked you," he said. "Have you ever had any children? Have you ever wanted any?"

"Not in dis life, my Cap'n," she said. "Before you, maybe so. Not since I saw you wit your fearsome beard a'flamin' dat first time so long ago. Not since - ever."

He didn't reply. He continued to look at the Gulf and watch the children.

"Cap'n?" she said.

"Yes, Hibiscus," he said.

"Dis phone be yours. It buzz, den ring much just after you come to de beach to watch de chirrins. Important maybe? I brung it to you. An' Blackbeard been sayin' tings 'bout dead mons."

"Not now, Hibiscus," he said. "I'm contemplating my failings in life."

"Dat girl Linda," said Hibiscus. "I could share you wit her, I tink. She lak me, not exactly a white girl. Her daddy ancient like de land. "

"Her father was a Native American," said Edward. "So what are you saying?"

"Me and dat girl Linda dance here on de beach. She got rhythm lak me. Nice hips dat move wit de soul."

"Did you now," said Edward. "So what exactly does that mean? Are you telling me you aren't going to put any more spells on her?"

" 'Course not. She be for you now, lak me. She good in de bed lak Hibiscus?" she asked.

"Very good. But different than you."

"Better dan de young tings wearing mostly nothing, dat come to play wit Blackbeard and end up on dey back for you?"

"Yes, she's better at sex than the college girls who I sometimes take to bed," he said. "Hibiscus, you know how I am. So why are you asking me these questions?"

"In de other life, before dis one," she said. "You had ten and four wives. Maybe you could be 'appy wit me and dat girl Linda? I tink since you change your name, maybe dat girl could change hers. *Mary Ormond* would fit dat girl fine, sure. Maybe Hibiscus service both of you. Dere be anoder room lak mine in *de Parrot*. We fix it up maybe. Or maybe she move her tings in wit you."

"You mean *only* two wives," he said, laughing for the first time since he'd read Linda's goodbye note. "What modern man could possibly be happy with just two? Sorry, I'm being peevish today. I think what I want or what you want isn't relevant. I think maybe I overplayed my hand on several matters. But I do love you for wanting to make me happy. And yes, Hibiscus, I know who *Mary Ormond* was. She was the one and only legal wife of Blackbeard. One day soon, we need to stop playing this game. You do know that, don't you?"

Hibiscus frowned, then let his hand go. She stood, waited for a moment, then when he did nothing more, she said, "One day, Cap'n, by and by, mebee you listen to dis old woman. I'm de servant of you, my Cap'n. Juss a servant lak I been for all dees year, sure. I serve de both of ya, I tink. We kin be 'appy, I tink."

She left her sandals and cell phone on the bench and walked back to *The Eloquent Parrot* barefooted.

A young boy ran nearby with a kite on a string in his left hand held aloft. In his right hand, he held something he'd picked up on the beach. He stopped to look at Edward.

"Mister," said the kid. "What's this called? He held his hand out. His right hand held a starfish that had washed up on the shore. It was dead, dried out, and very much in need of burial in the white sand. It smelled strongly. No doubt the little boy would need a great deal of soap and water to be rid of the scent of dead starfish when his mother reclaimed him.

"That could have been the love of my life," said Edward. "But I wasn't able to put her back into the water in time."

He stood, then picked up the cell phone and the sandals.

Opening the cell, he turned away from the confused little boy and headed back to *The Eloquent Parrot*. He flipped the phone open, and saw three text messages from Linda. They were time-stamped an hour before the hearing was to begin.

The first message said, *You're right of course.*

The second one said, *I'm firing my lawyer.*

The last message said, *Is your offer still open? I'll get two jobs and a place of my own. What's Roger's is Roger's. Edward, Can I call myself your girlfriend? For a just a little while, at least?*

Edward smiled, then began to laugh. He laughed so hard the little boy turned back around and looked at him. He laughed so hard the little boy returned, perhaps to see what the joke was. Edward sat down, then motioned for the little boy to come closer.

"Kid," he said. "What you have in your hand is a starfish. Once in a while, maybe never, but possibly one day you'll see one that's still alive that's just been washed up on the shore. There might even be a lot of them. If that happens, and they're still alive, then throw them back into the water. Okay?"

CHAPTER SIXTY-TWO
STIR THE CAULDRON,
DIVIDE THE LOOT

Roger, Edward, and Chip sat at the Captain's table in *The Eloquent Parrot*.

"Where's Hibiscus?" said Roger.

"She and Linda have taken Edward's pickup truck to a yard sale. Linda's moving upstairs in the spare room here in *The Parrot*. She has the room that used to be storage, next to Hibiscus," said Chip. "She's working two nights a week here at *The Parrot* in exchange for the rent, and she has a day job as a professional caregiver to cancer patients. She's going to school full time too."

Roger traded his smile for a scowl, but he didn't comment.

Edward looked at him. "You knew she and I were going to get intimate. She and Hibiscus and I...are..."

"Got it," said Roger. "We smiled on it. I got no beef about it."

"You wanted this thing taken care of financially," said Edward. "It's taken care of. All except Linda. So this is what we're going to do..."

"Boss," said Roger, "what's with the *we* shit? Pardon my French. You just told me about you and Linda. What else is there to know?"

"You get to play daddy to your kids without interference," said Chip. "She gets to play mommy from a distance. She's agreed to forego regular visitation except for two times a year, one week – each visit unsupervised. If you two agree to which week it's going to be, then no problems. If you don't agree, she gets the first week in June, and the first week in January," said Chip. "The *we* Edward referred to means he and I came up with a solution and you're going to live with it."

"Okay, don't get all huffy and stuff. It's me the customer who's asking," said Roger.

"Client," corrected Chip. "Now about the money...."

"Had to come up sooner or later," said Roger. "So, what's the bottom line for me and Dewey."

"I'm glad you said it that way," said Chip. "Your take-home is $134,000.00 in round numbers. It's all here on the papers I've drawn up. That's after my bill and Edward's fee. You aren't going to like the rest, but that's the way it has to be."

"$134,000 is fine, so what's not to like?" said Roger.

"Your three kids get $25,000.00 each to be used for additional schooling anytime after age 18 until they turn 30. I will administer the trust fund, make low risk investments and give you and Linda an accounting annually. My fees have already been paid, so there's no expenses coming out of the money," said Chip.

"Still got no problem," said Roger. "I'm not sure where you two get off on telling me how to take care of my kids, and what Linda has to do with the kid's college money, but you've been straight and got me what I wanted."

Edward and Chip looked at each other. Then Chip said slowly, "Actually it wasn't your money that's getting put up for the kids. It's part of the divorce settlement. Linda has agreed to it, so the money is her gift to them as a part of the divorce settlement. It's her money."

"Bullshit," said Roger. "No money for her. She didn't die to get anything. My brother did."

"Roger," said Edward, "we have a deal. We're *telling* you how this goes down. We're not asking. You're getting what you wanted. Valmay's nuts are in a fish's belly. He's working two jobs full time, and he and his family are off the dole. He's a tax paying citizen for the time being. Trust me, he'll never bother Linda or any other woman again, ever."

"That part is fair," said Roger.

"The Judge, God rest his soul, would be somebody's bitch in Federal prison if he hadn't stepped out in front of the SCAT bus," said Edward.

"That works too," said Roger.

Chip took a deep breath. "So, what you're going to sign for in the settlement to Linda is $100,000. The kids get $25,000 each – which I already explained. Linda's take is $25,000, most of which goes to help her get through college."

The corners of Roger's mouth twitched. In a clear deadpan voice he said, "One more time, $134,000? That's the amount for me, right?"

"It's the amount," said Chip.

"So, I can go buy a Ford just like state troopers drive?"

"I don't see why not," said Chip.

"And get it painted exactly the same colors, yellow and black, like they do?"

"Ummm, you could. But I wouldn't exactly recommend it," said Chip. "Why would you do that?"

"So long as I don't put lights or anything illegal on the car, nobody could accuse me of impersonating a cop," said Roger as if that answered all questions.

"And?" said Edward.

"Shit," said Roger. "You guys don't get it. You ever notice how cops – all cops everywhere drive like idiots. They speed all the time. They tailgate. People move over to get out of their way. They don't yield at yield signs. They're practically ticket proof. If I get a car that's legal and I don't pretend to be a cop, but I look like a cop, then even the cops will think I'm a cop and I won't ever get a ticket no matter what. You guys are really pretty slow upstairs. So, that's what I'm gonna do. I'm gonna buy me a car like that. That is, if I take the deal. I haven't made my mind up yet."

Roger sat for a moment, then looked across the room to where Blackbeard was ignoring two overweight sunburned women in their mid-forties as they tried their best to coax a word or two from him so they could get their bar tab paid. He got up, finished all but the last swallow of his beer, then walked over to where the women were flirting with Blackbeard.

"Excuse me, ladies," said Roger. "I have to ask the bird a question. Just one, then you two can try as hard as you want to get him to buy your drink. But I wouldn't count on it."

"Humph," said one of the women. "We were here first, but this damned bird has lockjaw. You're kind of cute in a rugged bad-boy way. Would you and one of your friends like to join us for a drink?"

"No ma'am," said Roger. "I'm engaged to a lovely woman. We got three kids together. And my friends – well, one of 'em is married for real and the other one has a witch that watches over him. So he's kind of married in an old fashioned way."

"I've heard that line before," said the woman. "Witches or bitches. We get called all kinds of things. A girl out on the prowl can't get an ounce of respect anymore."

Roger cocked his head to one side and said to Blackbeard, "So, bird. What do you think about the deal my lawyer and the pirate captain made. Should I take it?"

Blackbeard cocked his head, mimicking Roger's pose. But he didn't answer.

Roger waited.

The two women waited.

Edward and Chip waited and smiled.

Blackbeard said nothing.

Edward lifted his beer mug and tipped the last swallow into his mouth. Chip took that as a signal and did the same. But still, Blackbeard didn't speak.

Roger grimaced and said, "Shoulda guessed. Just when you need a friend to give you a word or two of advice, he gets stage fright." He turned on his heel, shrugged his shoulders and headed back to the captain's table.

Two steps before he got there, Blackbeard whistled once, then sang out.

"Some people claim,
there's a woman to blame,
but I know
it's your own damned fault."

Staring directly at Roger, Blackbeard added in a different voice,

"You're fresh out of brothers. Take the money. You can't say you know someone until you've shared an inheritance with them."

Edward spewed his beer.

Chip had his mouth full and choked on an un-swallowed lump of beer until his face turned red.

The women looked at one another with full-on astonishment. One of them, the one who did most of the talking, intruded on Blackbeard's space and laughed too loudly.

Blackbeard wasn't through. Jumping from one leg to the other, flapping his wings as if he wanted to launch himself at the woman, he squawked

"Double, double toil and trouble;
Fire burn, and caldron bubble.

Cool it with a baboon's blood,
Then the charm is firm and good."

Blackbeard stopped flapping his wings for a moment, then opened his beak wide menacingly as if he was going to bite the woman in front of him. Again he squawked,

"Liver of blaspheming Jew:
Gall of goat, the slips of yew
Slivere'd in the moon's eclipse;
Nose of Turk, two bitch's lips;
Double double, won't take much trouble".

The woman who'd invaded his space jerked back. She looked at her friend with fear and disbelief on her face. Wordlessly the two slid off their respective barstools in one fluid movement, picked up their purses and with careful deliberate steps walked out of the massive carved oak door in the front.

Nobody noticed, or if they did, nobody made mention of the fact the women failed to pay their tally. But then, Blackbeard had spoken, so they didn't really need to pay.

#END#

About the Author

Robin Knowles, a native and lifelong resident of Florida, lives happily overlooking a river that leads into Tampa Bay, and so has access to all the salty seas of the earth. He also authored *Death of Rapunzel*, a thriller, available through Amazon.Com and from the publisher, and *One to Nuthin'*, a compilation of short stories about fishing with his father. *The Parrot's Revenge* is a second book with the same characters.

He welcomes comments about this book. He's available at RHKnowles@aol.com

Made in the USA
Monee, IL
14 June 2022

98016078R10184